1 MONTH OF
FREE
READING

at
www.ForgottenBooks.com

By purchasing this book you are eligible for one month membership to ForgottenBooks.com, giving you unlimited access to our entire collection of over 1,000,000 titles via our web site and mobile apps.

To claim your free month visit:
www.forgottenbooks.com/free120079

ISBN 978-0-332-60916-4
PIBN 10120079

This book is a reproduction of an important historical work. Forgotten Books uses
state-of-the-art technology to digitally reconstruct the work, preserving the original format
whilst repairing imperfections present in the aged copy. In rare cases, an imperfection in
the original, such as a blemish or missing page, may be replicated in our edition. We do,
however, repair the vast majority of imperfections successfully; any imperfections that
remain are intentionally left to preserve the state of such historical works.

See p. 22

"I DON'T LIVE ANYWHERE," SHE SAID AT LAST

FROM THE LIFE

Imaginary Portraits of Some Distinguished Americans

BY

HARVEY O'HIGGINS

Author of
"ADVENTURES OF DETECTIVE BARNEY",
"THE SMOKE-EATERS" ETC.

HARPER & BROTHERS PUBLISHERS

NEW YORK AND LONDON

CONTENTS

FROM THE LIFE

Owen Carey

FROM THE LIFE

OWEN CAREY

CAREY, Owen, author; *b.* July 16, 1867; ed. pub. schools; *m.* Mary Fleming, August 23, 1903; newspaper work in New York City, 1897–1900. *Author:* Fair Anne Hathaway, 1900; The Queen's Quest, 1901; Sweet Rosalind, 1902; With Crash of Shield, 1903; In Cloth of Gold, 1903; The King's Enemies, 1904; The Forest of Arden, 1905; Men at Arms, 1905; Lady Jane Grey, 1906; The Swan's Inn, 1908; Friends at Court, 1909; Robin's Roundelay, 1911; The Gage of Battle, 1912; Miles Poyndexter, 1913; Millicent Lamar, 1914; The King's Evil, 1916; Mistress Page, 1917. *Address:* Authors' League, New York City.—*Who's Who.*

1

O F course you know Owen Carey. That is to say, you know his name. And you know his books. And you know the plays that have been made from his books, and the moving-picture films that have been made from the plays that have been made from his books. And you know the syndicate portrait of him that has been going the rounds of literary supplements and publishers' announcements for the last fifteen years. And if you have looked him up in *Who's Who* and the biographical dictionaries you know enough about him to be able to write the dates on his tombstone. But of the man himself it is safe to say that you know nothing.

Or suppose that you happened to know him in the flesh. Suppose that you had studied him in the days when he used to attend the meetings of the Executive Committee of the Authors' League at its weekly luncheon in the City Club. Well? You saw a ponderous bulk of male middle age, that looked like Thomas Edison somewhat, and somewhat like a Buddha, and a great deal like a human mushroom. You observed him listening, in massive silence, to arguments and motions, and you heard him grunt, "Aye." You noted the deftness with which he made a cigarette in his blunted, fat fingers, and you saw him light it gloomily, consume it in three or four puffs and an enormous final inhalation, wash the taste of it down with a gulp of whisky-and-water, and roll another cigarette with the melancholy air of an elephant that is being fed shelled peanuts one by one. Or you watched him signing his famous name to the circular letters of the League, with a silver-mounted fountain-pen as big as a bath-tap, and as fluent— bestowing his signature on the paper with a few large passes of his indifferent hand, like an archbishop bestowing a benediction, pontifically. And you could not help thinking of the stupendous

[4]

trade value of that name, of the fabulous stream of income that had flowed from that fountain-pen, of the magic of his puffy hand that could transmute a word into a dollar, at his current price, and add the dollar to the disorderly roll of bills in his bulging vest pocket. . . . But of the man himself, it is safe to say, you learned nothing.

What business of thought was being carried on under that thatch of gray hair? What was the mind that sat concealed behind those eyes—slow-lidded eyes, as impenetrable in their gaze as if they were clear glass frosted on the inner side? Why did he always wear shabby gray clothes? What did he do with his money? Why did he belong to no clubs and go nowhere?—not even to the annual banquet of the Authors' League. Why, with all this unceasing advertisement of his work, was there no advertisement whatever of his personality? Why was there not even any curiosity about him? Why did his books arouse none? Why were they, for all their circulation, so without significance to their day and age, so without concern about its problems, so without influence upon its struggle? Why was he, in short, what he *was?*—as personally inaccessible as O. Henry, as withdrawn from the modern world in all his works as Maurice Hewlett in his early novels, as shy as Barrie, as fat as Chesterton, as impersonal as if his busy manufactory of fiction were some sort of flour-mill over which he presided in his dusty miller's gray, mechanically grinding out a grist that meant nothing to him as an honest, artistic output, or as the intellectual food of millions, or even as the equivalent of comforts and social joys to himself.

2

It has been said often enough that there are moments in life when the shock of some trifling incident seems suddenly to precipitate and crystallize a man's character—to combine the elements of his past and set the form of his future—out of a clear solution of his hidden qualities of temperament and absorbed incidents of experience and wholly invisible fermentations of thought. Certainly there was such an incident in Carey's life—on a rainy October night in 1899—and I believe that Carey may be better explained by a laboratory study of him in the chemical processes of that crystallizing event than by any character analysis and empirical formula of him as he was afterward.

In October, 1899, then.

3

And even so short a time ago as that is Owen Carey was unknown; he was poor and he was thin—although these are now unbelievable facts, all of them. He was trying to break into the monthly magazines with short stories; and the short story was a form for which he never had any aptitude. Meantime, he was writing specials for the Saturday and Sunday papers—chiefly for *The Commercial Advertiser* and *The Sun*—and his literary life was made up of such considerations as this: if *The Commercial Advertiser* paid only four dollars a column and *The Sun* paid eight, but *The Sun* printed 2,200 words in a column and *The Commercial Advertiser* had a column of 1,100, which was the more profitable to write for?

He was earning, on an average, about six dollars a week.

On this particular night he had been up Fifth Avenue as far as the Park and down Broadway to Madison Square, looking for a descriptive article of any sort, in the windows of the new Waldorf-Astoria, in the hansom cabs, in the theater crowds, in whatever he could see of the night life of the Tenderloin without paying for admittance. And he was on his way home, brooding over an article that he hoped to hatch out in his room and mail to an editor if it came to life.

He never went to the editorial offices with his contributions any more. He had never been able to pass the office-boy. He was too obviously a threadbare and eccentric literary aspirant; and literary aspirants are the bane of the newspaper editor, who does not understand why a man interested only in news should be persecuted by people who are interested only in literature.

It was raining on Carey—a cold October rain that rattled on the roof of his straw hat and squashed

2 [7]

about in his broken summer shoes. And he was not merely indifferent to the rain—he felt affectionate toward it. The men and women whom he passed were protected against the wet with umbrellas and waterproofs, as if against an enemy. They were apparently as afraid of the rain as they were of poverty. And to Carey poverty was an old familiar, and the rain, as the poets say, caressed his face with a pleasant coolness. He was footsore, and the water in his shoes was even refreshing. He had fought against poverty once with a desperate fear of it, like a man drowning. And now he had sunk to the depths, he was one of "the submerged tenth," and it was as if he had touched bottom and found that he could live and breathe there, peacefully. Poverty!—what fools people were about it. And the rain!—the world had refused him a shelter from either, and neither had proved to be a hardship.

He had a room on the top floor of an old house on the south side of Washington Square. It was a house that had been sold to make way for a new building, and some hitch in finances had halted the project after all the tenants had been moved out and the gas-pipes had been disconnected. Carey had hung on, alone, with a kerosene-lamp and an oil-stove on which he did his cooking. He expected any day to come home and find the house-wreckers at work and his staircase gone. As he rounded the Washington Arch he looked up, mechanically, to see whether his roof was still whole.

It was. He heard a dog give a sort of shivering whine somewhere, and he stopped at once and stood looking about for it.

4

If I tell you this, you'll believe that Carey was not quite normal—morbid, a bit mad—but it is true that the sound of suffering from an animal went through him more piercingly than a human appeal. When he walked in the country his gait was erratic because he was always stepping aside to avoid treading on ants. In one of his early stories—so unanimously rejected by the magazines—his heroine went out strolling with her lover; she saw him pick up a stone and throw it at a bird which, by some miracle, he hit; she promptly turned home, in silence, and refused ever to speak to him again; and it was impossible for Carey to understand that this was not a "sufficient motive" for his plot. Most striking of all, perhaps: his mother, a religious zealot, had intended her son to be "a minister of the gospel"; she had planned to send him to a theological college and, being too poor to carry out the plan, she went to her pastor for aid and advice. He replied that the boy should first familiarize himself with the testaments, and Carey set to work to study them ambitiously— with an unexpected result! The cruelties of the Old Testament horrified him. Without any intention of blasphemy, in the most obvious sincerity, he appealed to his mother to explain the murders and massacres ordered by Jehovah and carried out by the Chosen People. She took him to the pastor. The pastor examined him and decided that he lacked the necessary firmness of faith. They prayed for him—all three on their knees in the pastor's study, Carey praying as fervently as the others—and when he rose he was surprised to find that he was "no better." Those terrible barbarisms of the early Hebrews still revolted him. He made a list of them, filled a note-book with them, and went back to the pastor. He and the reverend gentleman quarreled. Carey shook the pages of his indictment in the face of the horrified minister, and cried: "It wasn't a god! It was a devil!" He was put out on the pious door-step, sobbing, defiantly: "A devil! A devil!" The minister preached a sermon about him, in which no names were mentioned, but all his friends understood who was referred to, and they spread the secret. He was marked as an atheist. His home life became unbearable. He ran away, was brought back, ran away again, changed his name, and was not traced. He never returned. His mother developed religious hallucinations and went to an asylum for the insane. And that is why *Who's Who* gives no birthplace for him, and names no parents. The story that he was a foundling is not true.

As a matter of fact, his real name was John

Aloysius McGillicuddy, the son of Patrick McGillicuddy, the driver of a brewery wagon, Irish, and a
Catholic. His unfortunate mother was Annie Kirke,
a servant, Scotch, and a Presbyterian. After her
marriage she kept a boarding-house. The father
had his son christened in the Catholic faith; the
mother was determined that he should be a Presbyterian; and she had her way—after her husband
tired of quarrels and deserted her—until the son
followed in the father's footsteps. And young Jack
McGillicuddy, under an assumed name that became
"Owen Carey" finally, worked as an errand boy,
as a shoe clerk, in a printer's office, in a press-room
—in Toledo, in Chicago, in Boston—tramping,
beating his way on freight-trains, working at anything temporary, even begging when he had to—an
absurd, sensitive, eccentric young victim of his own
intenseness, whose one consistent impression of
mankind was its good-natured inhumanity.

That was why the whine of an animal affected
him more than a human appeal. He had a fellow-
feeling for the animal. So, to return to his October
night in 1899—

5

He looked around for the dog, but he did not
see any. He saw a woman sitting on one of the
wet benches of the Square, and the whine seemed
to come from her. He supposed that she had the
dog on her lap.

As he neared her he saw that it was her hat she was nursing. She had taken it off and covered it with a handkerchief to protect it from the rain, and her hair was soaked and glistening in the light of the electric lamp above her. He supposed that she was a woman of the streets.

At his approach she looked up, and he had just time to appreciate that she was young and rather pretty, when she shivered and whined up at him; and, opening her mouth, with her tongue protruding over her lower teeth, she panted at him, ingratiatingly, like a dog.

For a moment Carey thought he had gone crazy. Then, "It's hydrophobia!" he thought. "She's been bitten by a mad dog!"

He looked around for a policeman, frightened.

His future was determined by the fact that there was no policeman in sight and he had time to recollect that it was one of his many grievances against mankind that dogs with minor ailments were always being shot as mad when, as he was convinced, rabies was a disease as rare as leprosy.

He approached her much as he would have approached the dog in the same circumstances. He asked, "What's the matter?"

She did not answer.

He bent down to her, putting his hand on her shoulder. "What is it?"

She shivered under his touch.

"Aren't you well?"

[12]

- Her face suddenly changed and cleared. She stared at him blankly. An expression of frightened bewilderment came into her eyes, as if she had been wakened from a nightmare.

He sat down beside her. "What s the matter?" he asked. "You're soaked through. Why don't you go home?"

She did not reply.

He put his hand on her arm. "Tell me," he said. "Aren't you well? What's wrong? Can I help you?"

And she answered, in a breathy, hoarse gasp of exhaustion, "I'm hungry."

"Come along with me," he said. "Can you walk?" And, taking her by the elbow, he helped her to her feet. Her hat dropped to the sidewalk as she rose. He picked it up, put the handkerchief in his pocket, tucked the hat under his arm, and started across the Square with her.

She staggered as if her feet were numb.

It was apparent that he could not take her to a restaurant in that condition, even if there had been a cheap restaurant near. But he had no thought of going to a restaurant. He had not money enough to pay restaurant prices. He had food in his room, and he was taking her there, to give it to her.

He had already concluded that her doglike whining and panting had been an illusion; that he had seen something like it, but not *that!* And he was going over the contents of his larder in his mind as he helped her across the Square. He did not speak. And she was obviously too weak to speak.

6

There was a characteristic reason why he did not consider taking her to a restaurant.

He had made a study of foods and their prices—a study as careful as any that he made subsequently into the details of life and local color for his romances of Elizabethan and medieval times. And he understood how grossly the restaurants overcharged. He knew, for example, that rolled oats, in bulk, cost him two and one-half cents a pound; that there were six teacupfuls in a pound, and that half a teacupful made a portion for one meal. Cornmeal, at two cents a pound, gave only four cups to the pound; oatmeal, at two and a half cents a pound, ran five cups to the pound; and hominy, at five cents a pound, four cups to the pound. (These, of course, were the prices of 1899.) He paid 30 cents a pound for coffee; there were 96 teaspoonfuls in a pound; and he used a teaspoonful to a cup of coffee—stingily. He paid 50 cents for a pound of tea, of 128 teaspoonfuls. He had figured out that granulated sugar cost him one-eighth of a cent for a spoonful. There were, usually, 240 potatoes in a bushel, and a cent's worth made a portion. He had learned where to get meat enough for one meal for 10 cents—remnants, rather, but edible. He made a two-cent package of salt last him about three months, and he sprinkled 8 cents' worth of pepper over as long a period. On an average his meals cost him $2.03 a week. And, naturally, a restaurant looked like a robber's cave to him.

He had covered pages of his note-books with these calculations. It was not only impossible to overcharge him. It was equally impossible to give him underweight, because he knew the number of spoonfuls that ought to be in any pound of staple groceries, and he measured every pound when he got alone with it.

Having a mind of that quality, it *is* strange—isn't it?—that he ever became a romanticist.

7

He took the girl as far as his street door without much difficulty, but he had to support her up the steps, and it was plain that her legs were too weak to climb three flights of stairs. Her knees gave under her. He brought her to the first landing with an arm about her, practically carrying her, swaying and stumbling in the dark. There he dropped her hat in a corner and picked her up bodily. She made no sound. Although she was tall, she weighed little more than a toggle-jointed skeleton wrapped in soaked clothing. He judged that she had fainted.

He laid her on the floor of his landing until he

got his door open and his lamp lit. Then he carried her in and put her on his bed—a camp cot, without a mattress, for which he had paid fifty cents in a second-hand shop of the tenement quarter. It was covered with nothing but a pair of gray blankets, and he was not afraid of soiling them. Her head lay, dripping, on a pillow that had no pillow-case, and she looked as if she had been drowned. Her lips were white, but her face was a yellowish green. For a moment he was afraid that she had died in his arms. A faint breath reassured him. He hastened to light his oil-stove and warm up the remains of his day's coffee, which he had drawn off the grounds to save it.

While the coffee was heating he unbuttoned her worn shoes and drew them off. Her stockings were just as wet as her shoes, so he removed her stockings, too, tugging at them gingerly at the heels and ankles, and bringing off, with them, a pair of exhausted-looking round garters. Her feet were as chilled as if they had been on ice, and he had a queer idea that they had shrunken with the cold —they were so small. He rubbed them dry with his only towel, and bandaged the towel around them to get them warm.

When the coffee was ready he poured it into his tin cup and took it to her, clear. "Here," he said, raising her to a sitting posture, "this will brace you."

She whined, with her eyes closed.

He put the cup to her lips. "Try a mouthful."

She stuck out her tongue as if to lap it.

"No, no," he said. "Drink it. Open your mouth and drink it."

She laid her hand on his, pressed the cup away from her, and stared down at it. Then she sighed and drank a mouthful. It was a rank draught.

"It m-makes me sick," she faltered, nauseated, turning away from it.

"All right," he said. "I'll warm some milk."

She fell back on the pillow and closed her eyes again. But the coffee had evidently done something to revive her, for when he brought her the milk—with his last spoonful of whisky in it—she drank it greedily. He followed it with a hard-boiled egg, chopped fine, and a slice of scorched bread, flavored with kerosene, from the top of his oil-stove. He fed the egg to her in a spoon, encouraging her; and she ate the toast without his help. "Now," he said, "you'll have to take off some of these wet clothes. You can put on my overcoat."

It was his winter's coat, from a nail behind the door. She let him unbutton her dress down the back, get her arms and shoulders out of it, wrap her in the overcoat, and draw the dripping gown off over her feet. The thinness of her girlish arms, and the hollows in her neck and shoulders, were no more pathetic than the poverty of the Canton-flannel petticoat that she wore. He buttoned the coat on her; and she lay on her back, gazing at the sloping ceiling, in a weak stupor.

He hung up her dress—a faded blue-serge gown that had been darned on the elbows—and he placed the oil-stove under it, to dry it. He proceeded to make her a cup of tea, and to fry, in slices, some cornmeal mush that remained from breakfast. This he served with syrup. She ate it in hungry silence, with her bloodshot eyes fixed on nothing. He got the impression that speech and tears had both been exhausted for her.

When her plate was clean and her cup empty he took them from her, and she lay down again, on her side, and seemed to go to sleep. He stood a moment, considering her. She was, surely, not more than twenty years old; he was thirty-two; and there was nothing in his thought but fraternal pity for her. She was apparently a young street-walker, but he had lived on the streets himself for the greater part of fifteen years; and if she was an outcast—well, so was he. She looked desperately frail; the bones protruded in her cheeks and her temples; her eyes were sunken and dark in their sockets; her teeth showed between pinched lips. It was merely a girlish face, but suffering had marked it with ascetic lines of character and intelligence.

He decided that what she needed most was food. He counted the silver in his pocket, did a problem in mental arithmetic with his eyes on the calendar, and went out noiselessly to buy her something to eat. She was still sleeping when he returned—

with her hat, and a bottle of milk, and some slices of boiled ham from a delicatessen shop, and a loaf of bread, and a greasy paper bag of potato chips. He moved an empty box to the side of the bed and arranged the food on it, but he did not waken her. It would be better to let her rest.

He took off his wet coat, removed the cooking-dishes from his pine table to the floor, and sat down in his kitchen-chair to write.

8

You see, he was already a professional. No amateur would have been able to write under the circumstances. The girl in the room, her misery, her uncanny trick of whining—not to mention his own discomforts of damp shoulders and soaked feet—these things would have distracted any one for whom work had not become a professional habit, any one to whom writing was not the essential activity of his life and the justification of his existence, as necessary to him as food, as consoling as tobacco, his refuge from every worry—from the struggle with reality, the obstinacy of circumstance, the intractable enmity of events that always contradicted imagination and falsified hope—the refuge to which he went to escape all the impotences of mortality as the religious go to prayer.

He began to shape up his newspaper article, with his hand in his hair, tugging at it thoughtfully as he wrote. (And it was this continual scalp-massage, probably, that preserved for him the characteristic disorderly gray shock of his later years.) There was nothing particularly characteristic about his room. He had piled a number of empty soap-boxes on their sides to make book-shelves and a dresser. An old steamer-trunk held all his clothes. He had hung a blanket over his window, as a blind; and he left it over the window even in daytime, and lit his lamp, because he had become so accustomed to writing at night that the daylight seemed to blanch his inspiration. The lamp was shaded by a sheet of copy-paper, with a circular hole in the center of it, that slowly settled down on the chimney as the heat scorched it. A little bust of Shakespeare, from which the pedestal had been broken, hung above the table by a shoe-lace that had been noosed around the neck of the sainted dramatist. Carey had always been mad about Shakespeare. Whatever other books came and went, on his travels, his volume of Shakespeare persisted. He had read everything about Shakespeare that he could find—about his works, about his life, about his times. He was already, unconsciously, an Elizabethan expert, but the only fruits of his study, as yet, were several blank-verse tragedies that were useless imitations of the sound of Shakespeare with the sense omitted.

So, with his hand in his hair, frowning and biting his lips, he continued to scribble at his newspaper article, glancing over his shoulder at the girl, now and then, absent-mindedly. It was after midnight when he turned to give her such a glance and found her staring at him, wide awake.

9

He put down his pencil at once. "Would you like me to warm your milk?" he asked.

She rose on her elbow, evidently frightened, and looked down at the towel on her feet.

He said, to reassure her, "I'll see that you get back safely, as soon as you feel better."

She asked, hoarsely, "How did I get in *here?*"

"Don't you remember? You told me you were hungry," he said. "You couldn't walk to a restaurant, so I brought you here. I guess you fainted."

She blinked at him in a bewildered daze. She demanded, "Why did you tie my feet?"

"Your feet?" he asked. "Oh! They aren't tied. I took off your shoes and stockings because they were wet, and wrapped your feet in a towel to warm them. Try some of this ham. It's generally pretty good."

He poured her a cup of milk and made her a sandwich of the ham and two slices of bread while he talked. "Don't you remember drinking a cup of milk and eating something?"

She shook her head, watching his hands in silence, sitting up against the wall with her feet drawn up under the overcoat.

"Don't you remember me helping you out of your wet things?"

She did not answer.

He gave her the sandwich and she took it in trembling, numb-red fingers eagerly. He began to make her another.

She swallowed the food in gulps, half masticated, because she was either too weak or too hungry to chew it. "Where am I?" she asked, in a thick whisper.

He told her. "You're all right," he said. "Now don't worry. I'll see that you get back safely, as soon as you feel able to walk. Is it far to your —to where you live?"

She did not reply. He gave her the cup of milk, and she looked up at him briefly, but her eyes told him nothing. She drank the milk as if her mouth demanded it but her mind was not interested in the matter.

"I don't live anywhere," she said, at last.

He accepted that as an evasion. "Where do you —work?"

She took the second sandwich, raised it to her lips, and stopped with her head drooped. "I don't work. I can't get work." Her voice broke. "That's what's the matter." The sandwich fell to her lap. She fumbled at it blindly, trying to pick it up again. He saw that it was tears that had blinded her. She was crying.

"Oh," he said.

And, to tell the truth, he was suddenly impatient with her—as impatient as an old convict when the quiet of his cell is disturbed by the inevitable tragedy and useless despair of a new-comer. He had received her as a girl of the streets, a fellow life-timer in that underworld to which he had resigned himself, working and writing with no ambitiou to escape, but merely to obtain food and a bed. He had helped her, in the expectation that as soon as she had been fed and warmed she would go off to serve her own sentence without troubling him further. But this weeping helplessness!

He began to question her, sitting in his chair, his hands thrust into his trousers pockets, his legs stretched out before him, his eyes on his wet feet. Where had she come from? Why didn't she go back? What had she been working at? Hadn't she any relatives to help her?

And the girl, aware of his change of voice, began to defend herself, to explain her willingness to do anything—*anything*—and, finally, to uncover, abjectly, the whole lacerating story of her misfortunes, her struggles, the injustices that had been done her, the ignominy, the misery, the suffering, the shame. It was a common enough story. There was nothing new in it to Carey. He listened as wearily as a physician hearing of pain. And the girl kept sobbing, at the end of each successive chapter of her degradation: "It was worse than the life of a dog." And, "If I'd *been* a dog he'd have

3

treated me better!" And, "If I'd been a dog on the streets, some one—*some one* would have helped me—fed me—"

Life had taken her—young, pretty, proud, sensitive, ignorant—and it had betrayed her ignorance, sold her prettiness, cheated her youth, beaten down her pride, and stripped and tortured the raw nerves of her sensitiveness. She told him of it, as if it were being wrung out of her on a rack, in paroxysms of sobbing, in hoarse and shamed whispers, in dull, exhausted tones of desperation. He hunched forward in his chair, his elbows on his knees, his head in his hands. What was the use? He knew it. He knew it all. The world was full of it. It only sickened the heart to hear it. He couldn't live and think of these things.

She was silent at last. He heard her moving, as if she were preparing to go. "Well," he said, frowning at the floor, "I don't know what I can do." And then he heard her near him. She whined. And, dropping his hands, he saw that she was on all-fours at his side, panting up at him ingratiatingly, with her tongue out.

He sprang up. "Don't!" he cried. "Don't do that!" He tried to raise her to her feet. She licked his hand.

"Listen," he pleaded. "You'll be all right. I'll help you. I can make enough for two—until you get something. You'll be—"

Her eyes were the dumb, devoted, appealing

eyes of an eager and willing animal that could not understand a word he said.

He carried her back to the bed, but he could not make her lie on the pillow. She curled up on her side, her knees drawn up, her hands closed like paws, her head down, blinking at him, shivering, and whining gratefully when he touched her.

He began to walk up and down the room.

10

He was not ignorant enough to suppose that she had merely gone insane. He was sufficiently acquainted with the theories of morbid psychology to understand that in her hysterical state she had, so to speak, hypnotized herself with the recurring thought, "If I had been a dog!" until she imagined that she had become one. Or, to use the fashionable idiom of our Freudian day, in her need to escape from the killing worries of her shame and destitution she had taken refuge in a loss of identity and become a dog subconsciously.

All of that did not help Carey. What was he to do? He could call a policeman and send her on her way to the psychopathic ward in Bellevue and thence to the lunatic-asylum. But if she had really been a dog would he turn her out? He had let his mother die in an asylum. (Or so he put it to himself. He had not known of it till after she was dead.) And the thought had been, for years, a horror and a remorse to him. He could not do it again.

He sat down on the side of the bed and began to talk to her. He assured her that he would help her; that he would take care of her; that he would fix the room, some way, so that they might both live in it; or he would rent two rooms somewhere, and she could work for him, or pass as his sister, or whatever else she pleased.

She listened, watching his lips, smiling with that open-mouthed panting, and evidently hearing nothing. He gave it up at last and made her comfortable between the blankets, and went back to his seat at his table to think it over. He rolled a misered cigarette and lit it, but it did not help him. He allowed himself, in these days, ten cents a week for tobacco. He fell asleep, with his head on his arms, and when he awoke, hours later, he found her curled up on the floor at his feet.

He took her back to the bed and made a sort of sleeping-bag of the blankets by pinning them together with safety-pins; and he pinned her into this, and tied her down with the line on which he dried his washing. There was a bathroom opening from the hall, and he shut himself in there, with his pillow, intending to sleep on the floor, but she whined so—like a dog locked in alone—that he came back and lay on the floor above her bed, with his feet to the oil-heater.

His problem, as he saw it, was this: The girl's mind had divided against itself under the stress of revolting ill usage; if he sheltered her and protected her for a while she would probably return to a normal condition. What he needed was two or three rooms in which she could have privacy, and quiet, and housework to occupy her. It would not cost much. He could earn more if he worked harder. He had done it before.

He had done it when he first learned that his mother was dead. In a fit of repentance he had begun to work and save, so that he might be able to take her from whatever pauper's grave she had been buried in and put up some sort of tombstone for her in a decent cemetery. He had saved a hundred dollars, and then he had been balked by the difficulty of writing, as a stranger, or anonymously, to the asylum—or where else?—to have the thing done for him. And, being the sort of person whom practical difficulties appal, he had continued living with the intention of doing what he never made any attempt to do. The money was still in a Chicago bank, untouched, waiting. Well, he could make a vicarious reparation to his mother by using the hundred dollars to rescue this girl from his mother's fate. A hundred dollars, with what he could earn, would carry them for a year at least. He fell asleep, easy in his mind.

11

And he awoke, next morning, to the responsibilities and the way of life that made him and his novels what they are.

She seemed, at first, almost rational when she opened her eyes to find him cooking their breakfast of oatmeal and coffee; and she went, at his direction, to wash and dress herself in the bathroom, sanely enough. But her silence when he talked to her was not normal; and whenever he caught her eye it was frightened and wavering, as if she were always on the edge of her obsession; and once, when he touched her hand, in passing her a second cup of coffee, her lips trembled, her teeth chattered, and she began to pant. He pretended not to notice, and the attack passed; but that was the first indication of what afterward became sufficiently plain to him, namely, that her delusion was partly due to what the psychologists would call her "subconscious desire" to have her relations with him the relations of a dog to its master. It was not only the world that she feared; she feared him, too. And he was peculiar enough to be relieved, at last, to find it so. He did not want a woman on his hands. He would have much preferred a dog.

He told her what he was going to do, about renting a small flat; and he set about doing it. He got his money from Chicago without any difficulty, and he found two rooms in a house on One Hundred and Tenth Street (going as far up-town as possible in order to take her away from the scene of her sufferings), and he was able to rent the two rooms for fifteen dollars a month because they were almost uninhabitable. They were in the basement of a private house that had been converted into "studio apartments" by the owner, an eccentric woman of artistic tastes who proved, on nearer acquaintance, to be a "Peruna fiend." And the rooms were almost uninhabitable not only because they were damp, but because the landlady was a pest. The important thing about them was this: They had been made into a sort of Dutch cellar with a red-tiled floor, half-timbered walls, beamed ceilings, burnt-umber woodwork, an open fireplace, and semi-opaque windows of leaded panes, sunken below the street level. They had evidently been a basement dining-room and kitchen when the house was private. Carey took them for a reason of which he was, I think, unaware; they did not look like modern rooms in New York City, and they would be a complete change of background for the girl.

He moved his belongings himself, making a half-dozen trips on the Elevated railroad with his suitcase full, and abandoning his cot and his table because it would be cheaper to buy new ones than to pay cartage on the old. The rear room—the kitchen, with a gas-stove and a sink—he furnished for the girl, since it was heated by the house furnace, which intruded its warm back through the side wall. He bought second-hand furniture and helped install it himself; and he avoided the curiosity of the landlady by refusing to answer her when she knocked on his door.

He brought the girl up after midnight. They

settled down in comfortable secrecy, as remote as if they had been cloistered in a crypt. And thus began what was surely the oddest romance in the history of American letters.

12

She seemed quietly contented, cooking and washing and sweeping and sewing for him. She never ventured out; she bolted the door on the inside when he left, and she opened it to no voice but his. The landlady, baffled, waylaid him in the hall with questions. He replied: "We're peculiar. We write, you understand. As long as we pay our rent you'll kindly leave us alone. We're busy and we don't want to be disturbed. For the future, as far as you're concerned, we're deaf and dumb." And when she found that they *did* pay their rent, and did not complain of the rain that came in under the windows and gathered in pools on the tiled floor, she left them to their privacy undisturbed. She would not have cared if they had been a pair of outlaws in hiding; she was out of sympathy with the police and the city government; her life was an endless quarrel with the authorities about the fire laws, the building laws, the tenement-house laws, and the regulations of the Board of Health—, all of which her house violated.

For the first month Carey and the girl lived in an atmosphere of accepted silence. He talked to her no more than he might have talked to a servant in similar circumstances. He brought in food for her to cook. He bought her a dress, which she made over. He got her sewing materials when she asked for them, and she made herself underclothes and mended his. He did not ask her any questions about herself. He accepted her dumb and doglike fidelity without comment. She ate her food in the kitchen—which he never entered, although the door was never closed between them. She served him his meals on his work-table, and he took them absent-mindedly, reading or even writing between bites. He noticed a gradual improvement in her appearance, but he did not remark it.

One evening, as he worked, he heard her humming an air to herself, over her ironing, in the kitchen, and he listened, smiling, but he did not speak. He discovered that she was reading his books in his absence, and he began to buy novels for her—Scott and Dumas and historical fiction, chiefly, because he was afraid that modern literature might affect her adversely. He worked very late, one night, on a story that he had picked up from a derelict in the Mills House; and when he returned, next day, from an afternoon in the Astor Library he found that she had copied out his manuscript for him in a clear, girlish handwriting. He thanked her for it, as matter-of-fact as possible, but he was worried. The story was not cheerful; it was taken from the low life on which it was not good for her mind to dwell. He had not the heart to tell her not to touch his manuscripts, since she had copied this one to help him. So he undertook to write something that it should not depress her to read.

Hence *Fair Anne Hathaway*.

He began it as a short story, in the intervals of his newspaper work, but it grew into a novelette, and then into a "three-decker," designed to carry her, as its sole passenger, to "the Islands of the Blest." When she had copied out the first three chapters, bit by bit, as he wrote them, she asked him, timorously, "What happened then?" · And thereafter he talked it over with her in advance, inventing it for her, and making it meet her expectations when she voiced any.

It was, for her, a complete escape from reality. And that, no doubt, was the secret of its success with the public—the great public who read in order to get away from themselves and their lives. When Francis Hackett, in *The New Republic*, lately ridiculed *Fair Anne Hathaway* and its successors in an article on "The Literature of Escape" he hit the secret nail on the head, blindfold, and in the dark. And in pointing out the connection between the success of such books and Jung's theory of mankind's "escape into the dream" he was not only analyzing a tendency of the American public; he was psychoanalyzing the disorder of Carey's first reader.

Carey wrote for her with a simplicity of expression that was sweetly reasonable and altogether charming—a style that conveyed romance to the public taste, without effort, through a soda-fountain straw. He found that she had identified herself with his heroine; so he fed her up, curatively, in the person of that heroine, with the loyalty and devotion of adoring heroes; and never had the feminine reader found a happier appeal to her pride of sex. And yet the heroine was a Shakespearian woman—a true masculine ideal—brave, wise, witty, self-sacrificing, chaste, and proudly faithful to her lord; and love's young dreamers fairly drooled over her. The girl was interested in every detail of the Elizabethan life in Stratford-on-Avon, and Carey made it vivid, with the help of the Astor Library, if he did not try to make it real. It glowed with the light that never was. The whole story had the "uplift" that is the substance of things hoped for and the evidence of things unseen. It was a school-girl's dream. It came to the publishers in her handwriting, and started the first report that "Owen Carey" was a woman. And when Carey called at the publishers' office, in response to a letter of acceptance, they were as astonished as if Marie Corelli had turned out to be G. K. Chesterton.

He had grown plump on the girl's cooking. She kept his clothes pressed and brushed and mended. She had made him buy a new gray suit for the occasion. He asked, "Why gray?" She replied, furtively, "*He*—he always wore black." And Carey never wore anything but gray afterward.

He had the gruff manner with which so many men of diffidence protect themselves in strange approaches. He was much more keen for money in advance and steep royalties than was seemly in the author of *Fair Anne Hathaway*. He drove a good bargain, because the publishers were certain that they had found a best-seller. And they were right.

The book was an immediate success. Carey took thirty thousand dollars out of it in the first year, and he put the money by for her, in case anything should happen to him. They rented the apartment above their cellar and built an inner staircase to connect the two floors. It was not until after the popularity of *The Queen's Quest* that they bought the whole house to get rid of the landlady. He furnished the rooms in antiques and surrounded the girl with the interior setting of a Shakespearian comedy mounted by a stage realist. He named her "Rosalind," partly in play, but also in order to disconnect her from her past. Her real name he did not know. He had never asked it. He began to collect the library of Elizabethan and medieval literature upon which he drew so copiously for his later novels. She learned to use the typewriter; and she was, at once, his secretary, his housekeeper, his valet, and his cook.

Their relations remained what they had been in the beginning. Carey made the mistake of being demonstrative toward her only once—when he bought her an old amber necklace with his first check from *Fair Anne Hathaway*—and she recoiled from his attempted caress into a morbid seizure of half-idiotic animal abjectness. He could not reach the source of this morbidity. He did not know how. He had to wait. And he waited nearly two years before he found his solution.

13

Then, one summer night, when they were returning from a walk in Central Park—for by this time he had persuaded her to come out with him occasionally, for a little exercise, after dark—a furtive-looking man passed and stared at her, as they crossed Columbus Avenue on the way home; and she clutched at Carey's arm, making a noise in her throat as if she were strangling.

Carey caught her. "What's the matter? What is it?"

She gasped, "It's him!" and tried to run.

Carey held her back. "Wait a minute. Go slow. *Who* is it?"

But she could only whisper: "It's him! It's him!"

The man had stopped in the street and stood watching them.

"Good!" Carey said. "I've been hoping he'd turn up. Go slow. If it's *he*—he'll follow us."

He took her arm, and she stumbled along with him, trembling against him, breathing heavily. The man, as Carey had hoped, came sneaking after them at a distance.

Carey took her up their steps to the front door, and descended with her, inside, to the basement, switching on all the lights. He left her in the kitchen and went out noiselessly to the [basement door. The man was standing on the steps, looking up at the street number. Carey came quietly behind him. "She wants to see you," he said.

The man wheeled, startled. Carey was blocking his escape. "Who?" he asked, temporizing. "Mary?"

"Yes," Carey answered. "Mary. Go right in." (So her name was Mary!)

"Well," the fellow said, in a wheezy voice, "this 's a su'prise. I wasn't sure it was her."

"It's her," Carey waved him on. "She wants to see you—inside."

The man looked him over, hesitated, said, "Well, tha's all right, too," and entered, slouching.

Carey pointed him the way down to the basement, directed him to the Dutch dining-room, and followed in.

"Mary!" he called. "Come here."

She came from the kitchen. And standing in the doorway, supporting herself with one hand on the door-jamb, she looked across the room at the man with an insane and helpless horror.

"Is it?" Carey demanded. "Is it *he?*"

She made a fumbling gesture as if either pleadingly or defensively.

The man put back his rakish derby from his forehead. He had a prison hair-cut and a prison pallor. He bared his yellow teeth in an evil grin and said: "Sure, it's me. Eh, Mary? You're lookin' swell!"

Carey slammed the door and shot the bolt.

The man turned instantly, crouching, his hand at his hip pocket. Before he could draw his weapon, Carey had sprung at him, open-handed, from the door-step; and they fell, grappling.

Carey was no featherweight. He was still tough from the hardships of his youth. He was blind with hatred. And the touch of the struggling malevolent flesh under his hands put him into the sort of frenzy of murderous and loathsome revulsion that he might have felt in crushing a rat bare-handed. He struck and tore and strangled frantically; and the man, caught with one arm beneath him and still fighting to get out his revolver, was unable to protect himself from such an assault. When he got the weapon free he was blinded with his own bleeding, and Carey wrenched the revolver from him and beat him on the head with it. He went limp. Carey was kneeling on his chest, throttling the life out of him, when the lack of resistance and the choking under his hands brought him to his senses. For one horrified moment he thought he had killed.

Then the battered wreck under him drew a long gurgle of breath that sounded like water in a waste-pipe. Carey staggered to his feet. He took up the revolver and cocked it.

"Now, you dog," he said, "get up!"

The man rolled over, writhing painfully.

"Come here, Mary," he ordered.

She was standing erect in the doorway, her nostrils dilated, her hands clenched. She came forward slowly in that attitude.

"This is *your* dog," he said. "Do you under-stand?"

She nodded, without taking her eyes from the creature on the floor.

"Good! Shall I shoot him?"

The man undoubtedly thought he had to do with a maniac. Nothing else could explain the villain-ous ferocity of the attack. He began to whimper and snuffle in plaintive oaths and pleadings, smear-ing his bleeding face with his torn hands.

"Shall I kill him?"

Mary shook her head, wide-eyed.

"Come closer," Carey ordered.

She came.

"Now," he said to the man, "roll over and lick her boots. Do it, you hound, or I'll tear the heart out of you!" With a cruelty that he would never have used to a dog Carey turned him over with the side of his foot. "On all-fours," he ordered. "Do it!"

He did it—after a fashion. It was not a pretty scene.

"There!" Carey said. "Good! Now! This is *your* dog, Mary. Understand? See him. Your dog. Wipe your feet on him. Do it!"

She did it—with the expression of a child who is being encouraged to touch a cowed animal that she has been afraid of.

"Good! Now kick him!"

She shook her head. She said, slowly, "Let him go."

Carey looked at her. There was no fear of any one in her face. "Fine!" he said. "Here, you cur, crawl back to that door! Go on! Do it! Slowly! Grovel. Whine like the cur you are. Whine, or I'll shoot the ears off you. Now! If I ever meet you again, I'll kill you on sight."

He threw the door open. The man crawled out on hands and knees. Carey kicked the hat out after him and slammed the door shut.

They heard him stumbling frantically up the outer stairs.

Carey stood waiting—an unromantic figure—his collar torn open, his face scratched, one eye beginning to swell, and his complexion turning a delicate green with a seasick feeling that never afflicted his heroes after battle. She came toward him with her hands out, slowly, stiffly, tremulously confident, smiling, dry-lipped, pale. He laid the revolver on the table and took her in his arms.

4

"There!" he said. "Now! Good!" Then suddenly, in another voice, leaning on her heavily, he added: "Get me something to drink—quick. I'm all in."

And in that inelegant manner Mary Carey was reconciled to reality.

14

I say "Mary Carey," for he dropped the "Rosalind"; and though he married her under the name of McGillicuddy in order to escape publicity, she is known as Mary Carey to the few friends whom she has made—chiefly at summer resorts—since she has gradually emerged from her seclusion.

She has never emerged very far. She is too busy. She still acts as her husband's secretary, though a trio of silent Chinese have supplanted her as housemaid, valet, and cook. Carey has not emerged at all. He is, for one thing, too happy in his home. For another, he is—Owen Carey. He has taken refuge from all reality in his romantic art, and he devotes himself to it in the silence of a Trappist monk. How any one ever interested him in the Authors' League I cannot imagine. He resigned from the executive committee as soon as they began to talk about affiliating with the American Federation of Labor.

She is as silent as he, but she gives much more the impression of being a personage in her own right. She has a low-voiced air of grave young placidity, and she is slenderly graceful and well-dressed, with one of those Madonna-like faces that seem to show nothing of experience but its increment of wisdom. You could never imagine her starving in degradation on the streets. She seems born to be the successful wife of a successful author. And if his last novels have not been so successful as his earlier ones, it is, I think, because Mary Carey has become so interested in actualities that she is rather spoiled as an inspirer of the "literature of escape."

Not that it matters to either of them. He has saved a fortune. And she has an independent annuity of her own, which he bought for her with the surplus royalties from *The Queen's Quest, Sweet Rosalind, With Crash of Shield,* and *In Cloth of Gold.*

FROM THE LIFE

Jane Shore

JANE SHORE

SHORE, Jane (Frances Martha Widgen), actress; *b.* Phila., Oct. 27, 1883; *d.* Mathew and Martha (Deprez) W.; ed. Leslie Academy, Phila., etc. Made her début in "The Level of Pity," 1903; first starred in "A Woman's Reason," 1904; later starred in Thomas's "A Man's a Man," 1905–06; Shaw's "Satan's Advocate," 1906; Barrie's "A Window in Thrums," 1907–09; "Romeo and Juliet," 1910; Channing Pollock's "The World, the Flesh and Little Miss Montgomery," 1911–12; Galsworthy's "The Quality of Mercy," 1913; Shakespearian rôles and repertoire, 1914–16. *Address:* Hoffman's Theater, New York City.—*Who's Who.*

1

IT is not easy to do any sort of truthful portrait of Jane Shore. We are all, no doubt, different with different people, and at different times, but Jane Shore is wilfully so, particularly when she sees that she is being watched. It is difficult to choose any incidents from her life that seem wholly characteristic. And it is impossible to find any brief, connected series of events that gives her inclusively. The best that one can do is to offer one's portfolio of pencil studies and say: "Glance over these. You may find one or two that you'll recognize."

At one time I had a dozen photographs of her

tacked up together over a writing-desk; and invariably the stranger would say: "Who are all the good-looking girls? I recognize Jane Shore, but who are the others?"

Take, for example, the earliest anecdote about her that I have. It is the story of how, at the age of six, she rode her pony into a corner drug-store and demanded of the soda-fountain clerk that he serve her and her Shetland with ice-cream soda. She did it with childish seriousness, and the young clerk humored her by pretending to water the pony with fizzy drink while she had her glass in the saddle. And you might consider the incident typical of her imperious directness and unconventionality if there were not ground for suspicion that she knew exactly what she was doing, knew that the clerk would be amused by it, and knew that the story would be relished by her parents.

And the ground for this suspicion is found in the following consideration:

Once, when she was no more than eight, she was out driving with her father—behind the fastest and most vicious of the young horses that he delighted to fight and master—when the breeching of the harness broke, going down a hill, and the frightened animal, being butted into by the carriage, kicked back at the whiffletree, broke one of the shafts, put a hoof through the dashboard, and then bolted, with the harness breaking anew at every plunge and the hanging shaft prodding him on.

They were on a country road so deeply ditched that they could not turn out of it into a fence. They were approaching a bridge, and it was improbable that they would be able to cross it safely. "Well, young lady," her father said, through his teeth, "I think we're done." She clung to her seat in silence. He saw a shallower part of the ditch ahead, where there was an open gate into the fields. Fortunately it was on the opposite side from the broken shaft. He took a single rein in both hands and pulled on it savagely. The horse leaped aside, the carriage swooped into the ditch, a front wheel dished and broke at the hub, and they overturned.

They were saved from being kicked to a pulp because the tugs broke and freed the horse. When they picked themselves up from the mud, the girl, her face blazing with excitement, cried: "Daddy! Let's do it again!"

And the point is that she knew what she was saying and said it partly because she really had enjoyed the excitement, partly to reassure his anxiety about her, but largely for what you might call the dramatic effect. This she has admitted. She has admitted that by some duality of mind, even at the age of eight, and in such a moment, she was capable of a theatricality.

It is the more puzzling because she was evidently a frank and natural child. She was not precocious nor self-conscious. Nor was she ever paraded in any public way by her parents. They were not stage people. Far from it. Her real name is Fanny Widgen. Her father was Mathew Widgen, a Philadelphia business man, a rice importer, of Quaker descent. Her mother was the daughter of a Calvinist minister, of an old Huguenot family. And unless you blame the French blood of a great-grandmother, there is no inheritance to account for temperament, artistry, and the stage.

2

Jane Shore herself gives a curious explanation of the origin of her career—more curious than credible. She says that just before her birth her mother developed an unaccountable passion for the theater; and the staid Mathew, forced to humor her, took a box at every possible performance and sat stonily in the public eye, with his wife concealed behind him. The future Juliet was all but born in that box. After her birth Mathew Widgen's aversion to the stage—as one of the open gates to hell—prevailed again in his family, unopposed. And when, at the age of five, young Fanny was found standing on a chair in front of a mirror, whitening her face with flour, it was with horror that her mother cried, "I've marked her for the theater!"

That is all very dramatic. And it may be true, as far as it goes. But it omits to mention that Mrs. Widgen provided her daughter with lessons in singing and dancing and the parlor arts of water-color painting and piano-playing. It overlooks the encouragement that she gave her child in the imaginative games which they enjoyed together, secretly, in the attic—games that at one time included a miniature stage and elaborate costuming. It fails, in short, to understand what is quite plain in Jane Shore's recollection of her parents—namely, that her mother was a suppressed personality, kept pallid in the shadow of her husband's righteous domination and making an unconscious revolt in the person of her daughter. If she "marked" her child for the theater, she did it, I believe, as the mother of three solemn sons—and a prospective fourth—oppressed by the tight-mouthed Mathew, and turning involuntarily to the light and romance of the stage from the drab respectability of her smothered life. To understand her you have only to see Jane Shore's photographs of her mother and her father and their blank-windowed white-brick house with its black metal deer on either side of its entrance steps and the metallic-looking black pines surrounding it. Those photographs sufficiently explain why, as long as Mrs. Widgen lived, she never allowed the girl to be checked in any natural impulse or the expression of it.

It happened—as it frequently happens—that the father admired a spirit in his daughter which he would have crushed jealously in his wife. Fanny had inherited his strength of will; he was proud of it in her; and she had her way with him. In fact, she did as she pleased with them all, including her horse-faced brothers, whom she named after the three bears of the fairy-tale. She began life with the dominating spirit of privileged youth, and it carried her far.

Her mother's death, when she was only fifteen, had an abnormal effect on her. It put a shadow permanently into the background of her mind, established a peculiar tragic hinterland of thought into which Jane Shore retires at her most lively moments, unaccountably, with an air of almost cynical detachment when you would least expect it. But that came later. As the immediate result of her mother's death she was sent away from home, to the Misses Leslie's Select Boarding-school for Young Ladies. There she remained for three years, chiefly distinguishing herself as a leader in various dormitory escapades and in the school's amateur theatricals, in which she generally played male parts with a deep voice and a gallant stride. Her success in organizing mischief ended by the Misses Leslie demanding, with firm politeness, that her father take her home. And her success in the school theatricals gave her the idea of going on the stage. When her father received her, disgraced, in his library, she turned the flank of his wrath at her expulsion—characteristically—by announcing that she was done with school, anyway, that she was going to be an actress.

He sat grasping the arms of his library chair,

like a ruler enthroned, confident of his authority. "Never," he said. "No more of that. You'll take your mother's place here—"

"Dad," she cut in, "you've let me have my way too long to start bullying me now. I'm going on the stage."

"Never!" he said, with a gesture of finality. "Never!"

She folded her hands. "If *you* wanted to do it, nobody in the world could stop you. And I'm like *you.*"

His face hardened in a cold fury. "You'll not disgrace my name!"

"I'll change it," she said, cheerfully. "I'm going to call myself 'Jane Shore.'"

"Not while I live!" he shouted. "Not while I live!"

"Well," she said, "you can spend the rest of your life fighting me, if you want to. But I'm going to do it."

3

And, of course, she did it. She took her mother's place as housekeeper for a month, and during that time she secretly pawned or sold everything that could be removed from the house without being missed. She put in her own purse all the money that she could get for the household expenses, and she paid no bills. She sent her trunk unnoticed to the railroad station, with the aid of a young gar-

dener who was her slave; and, having dressed herself for a drive, she took her satchel in her dog-
cart, drove to an exchange stables where she was
known, sold the cart and her little mare for two
hundred dollars, and bought her ticket for New York.

That night she settled in a studio-room on
Twenty-third Street, with a former classmate who
was studying music. She had seven hundred dollars. She had left her father the pawn-tickets and
a letter addressed to "Dear old Daddykins" and
signed "Jane Shore." It informed him, gaily, that
as soon as her money ran out she would be back
for more.

She had chosen the name of "Jane Shore" because she had read Sir Thomas More's description
of the original Jane in a history of famous court
beauties—which she had borrowed from a school-
mate whose reading was secretly adventurous—
and she thought that the description fitted her.
So it did, somewhat. And, at least, it shows what
she was ambitious to be. It runs:

Proper she was, and faire: nothing in her body that you
would have changed, but if you would have wished her somewhat higher. Yet delited not men so much in her bewty as
in her pleasant behaviour. For a proper wit had she and could
both rede wel and write; mery in company, redy and quick
of aunswer, neither mute nor ful of bable; sometimes taunting
without displeasure and not without disport.

Her vitality, her will, and her high spirits carried her unwearied through the obscure hardships

of her first four years of struggle as a chorus-girl, as a gay young widow in a musical comedy, as an ingénue in a Washington stock company, and finally as the mother of a kidnapped child in a vaudeville act. She made a hit in the last by virtue of one nerve-shattering shrill scream with which she lifted the audience from their seats when she found that her baby had been stolen. She was then engaged to take a similar part, with a similar scream, in a melodrama by an author whom I knew. It was his first accepted play. I went to hear him read it to the company, on the stage where they were to rehearse; and I was struck by the fact that in the semicircle of actors who sat around him only two seemed to listen to the play. The others listened to the speeches of their individual parts, coming forward to these with their interest, so to speak, like children to receive their presents from a Christmas tree, and examining the lines that they received invidiously, with one eye always on what the others were getting.

The two who seemed to be hearing the play as a whole were a little girl, who was evidently to take the rôle of the kidnapped child, and a young woman in a dark street gown who listened with a consistent interest, her eyes always on the reader. She wore a sort of three-cornered hat, and she sat back in her kitchen chair, one arm outstretched to rest her hand on the knob-handle of her parasol in the attitude of a cavalier with his cane. She had an air of easy alertness, an air of intelligence, an air of personality. Her place near the middle of the semicircle indicated that she had only a small part in the play, for the principals sat at either extremity, near the footlights, by some stage convention of precedence; and the others had arranged themselves in order of importance in the arc. (The star, of course, was not present.) She did not strike me as remarkably beautiful—until I saw her properly made up, in the glory of the pinks and ambers of the foots. But there was, as Sir Thomas More said, "nothing in her body that you would have changed, but if you had wished her somewhat higher"; and greater height would have handicapped her in her beginnings on the stage, where the men are rarely tall and rarely willing to play opposite a woman who dwarfs them.

It was probably her hat that gave me the feeling she was a horsewoman; and this impression was confirmed when the reading was finished and she rose to walk about the stage with what used to be called a "lissome" carriage—a supple-waisted and firm-shouldered bearing—that obviously came from horseback-riding. I remarked her to the playwright, using some phrase about her "carriage"; and he repeated it, when he introduced me to her, as an excuse for the introduction. "Yes," she said, regarding us gravely, "it got me my start in the profession."

He was called away by the stage director, and I remained to ask her, "How was that?"—being already curious about her.

She replied, demurely, "I sold it for a hundred dollars." And with that she left me, puzzled.

It was not until I heard, later, of her selling her dog-cart to leave home that I understood the pert creature had been punning. She apologized for it, then, by explaining that she had been nervous. "I was frightened to death," she said. "It was my first engagement with a regular company, and I didn't know how to behave."

I do not believe a word of that. I do not believe that she was ever frightened in her life.

She left me, as I said, puzzled. She did not invite any further acquaintance, and I did not seek the invitation. My curiosity about her was lost, for the time, in a curiosity about the stage conditions that appeared to my astonished apprehension as the rehearsals progressed. And since those conditions have largely helped to make Jane Shore what she is, I should like to indicate them briefly.

4

In the first place, I had supposed that the rehearsal of a play, by a stage director and his company, was like the rehearsal of a musical composition by an orchestra and its conductor. I expected to hear it studied, practised, faithfully interpreted. I imagined that the author would rise at impatient intervals and say: "No, no. That isn't what I meant. Take it this way."

Nothing of the sort. Quite the opposite. The author proved to be as little important at the rehearsals of his work as a father at the birth of his baby. He was lucky if they did not order him out of the house. The producer, who had put up the money for the play, had the first right to say what should be in the play for which he had put up the money. The stage director, hired to rehearse the production, began immediately to suggest changes in the play in order to show that he was worthy of his hire. The star attempted not at all to subdue his personality to the part he had to play; he busied himself subduing the part to his personality. And not merely that. He did not care whether or not he was true to life; he considered only whether or not he was true to the sympathies of his audience. He was the hero, and he would not say or do anything that was not heroic. He had to dominate every scene in which he shared; the positions and the speeches of the other characters had to be arranged to show his dominance; and the whole play had to be remolded to that end.

It was one of those plays that have since come to be called "crook melodramas." The hero of it was a desperado who had stolen a child. He was in love with the Faro Nell of the gang. He contracted a salutary passion for the mother of the kidnapped girl, and under her influence he reformed and he converted his fellow-criminals. The author had been a police-court reporter—before he became a theatrical press-agent—and his crooks were real and their lines true, though his plot was "bunk," as he admitted. It was supposed to show the saving influence of a "good, pure woman" upon the criminal mind.

The star had already objected to talking "thieves' slang," and his lines had been rewritten. Now he objected to the unrequited ending of his devotion to the child's mother—so she was made a widow; she fell into his arms at the final curtain—and Faro Nell had to cherish the only unrequited passion in the play. This, however, left the star still a reformed criminal. The author improvised for him a noble motive of revenge upon a world that had done him wrong, but it was not sufficient.

"I'll lose them," the star said, referring to the audience. "I'll lose them if I steal that child."

The difficulty was overcome by making Faro Nell take the actual guilt of the kidnapping, and he assumed the responsibility in order to protect her, because she loved him—poor soul, she loved him. And then, in the second week of rehearsals, he arrived glowing with an idea. The hero should not be a criminal at all. He should be an honest, though desperate, man whose child had been kidnapped and whose wife had died of grief. He had joined the criminal band to learn their secrets and betray them to the police. Great idea! It was acted upon at once.

By this time the meaning of the play had been cheerfully obliterated. The curtains had all been changed. The characterization of the hero was a crazy-quilt. And the author was anxiously trying to add explanatory lines to account for actions that the recording angel himself could not have audited correctly.

"That's all right," the star would say. "Don't worry about that. They won't think of it till they leave the theater."

To do the author justice, he was not greatly worried by what was going on. Above all else, he wished his play to succeed; and these expert emendations were designed solely to achieve success. The producer seemed equally satisfied; he had seen such things done before; it was the way in which successes were written. And the actors, accustomed to the divine right and ruling egotism of stars, accepted their losses and their gains—as the alterations either reduced or fattened their parts—with Christian humility and resignation when they stood in the eye of authority, and with a fierce contempt and jealousy between themselves.

5

Throughout it all Jane Shore was wonderful. Whatever folly the star did, whatever absurdity he said, she watched him and listened to him with a deep-eyed admiration that was so meek and so trustful that it would have made a sick dove blush for its arrogance. Faro Nell had no such art. She argued with the star at the third rehearsal. And when her part began to dwindle—and Jane Shore's to grow—she knew it was because he disliked her and wanted to keep her down. She began to scheme against him. She even appealed to me, as a friend of the author; and I began to discover, behind the outward seeming of the rehearsals, a concealed activity of intrigues, stage politics, personal ambitions, plots, and counter-plots. Parties had been formed, influences had been organized. The resulting struggle, with its alliances and compromises, its victories and its defeats, was called a rehearsal. A detailed account of it would read like a court memoir of the days of a grand monarch. And the welfare of the play, that was to carry them all, seemed to be consulted as little as the welfare of the country that supports a grand monarch's court.

Jane Shore was obviously of the star's party and high in favor. He deprived her of some of her best lines—for various pretended reasons, but really because they competed with his own—and she merely said, studiously: "I see. Then I take the next cue, do I?"

He made her work down-stage, with her back to the footlights, so that he might face the audience when he addressed her; and she said: "Just a minute. Let me mark the position on my part."

He made her "noise up" her scenes with him, so that he might play at the top of his voice, which was his only way of expressing emotion. And she ranted diligently.

He made her stand as motionless as a dummy while he spoke lines to her, because he wanted the audience's undivided attention for himself—and he moved and gestured as much as he pleased while she replied. She obeyed him religiously, and with every look she called him "Master."

It was touching to see. When you consider that she knew exactly what he was doing and despised him for it, it was a masterpiece of art.

He took her out to luncheon with him. He took her home in a cab when it rained. They were seen together in a box at a benefit. They dined at his hotel. She was pointed out as his new leading woman—and then as his latest affinity. He was already paying alimony to three others, and the company began to bet on whether Jane was going to take the first step toward joining his Alimony Club. "He always marries them," they explained. "He's religious."

They were a respectable lot of hard-working men and women, but they had no illusions about their star. They admitted that he was a handsome bully, an egotistical cad, a bone-headed matinée idol, a strutting lady-killer with all the delicate impulses of a caveman. One of them said, "He's the kind of actor that ought always to wear a wig

—as a protection against woodpeckers." Faro Nell summed it up, "He's the lowest form of humanity I've ever had to associate with."

6

While they were betting on Jane's chances for the Alimony Club, it began to be evident that the producer had opened another competition. He had been seen at the opera with her. Some one whispered it around that he was calling on her in her apartment, which she still shared with her musical friend. He had not yet acquired the reputation for sexual rapacity that has since distinguished him, but he was not regarded as an ascetic bachelor. They began to watch Jane Shore with a new interest. What was her little game? How was she playing it?

As far as I could see, she was not playing it at all. At rehearsals she was entirely frank and natural, absorbed in her work, diligent, and biddable. It was evident that she had real imagination; she read her lines in the correct emotion, without fumbling, and her voice was rich and true. She had a good stage presence and some of the authority of experience, in spite of the meekness that made her appear unconscious of her art. Whatever game was being played, she seemed rather the innocent stake than the chief player. She deceived me completely. She certainly deceived the star. And I think she deceived the producer.

He had been an East Side boy, out of the Ghetto —an office-boy in a theatrical agency, a messenger-boy and assistant in a box-office, where he finally became treasurer. While he was still behind the ticket-wicket he rented the theater for a Hungarian violinist who had come to this country unknown, in the steerage. The violinist startled the critics with a brilliant and poetical virtuosity, and charmed a fortune into his own pockets and his manager's. The production of my friend's play was to be the entrance of this coming theatrical magnate into "the legitimate." And nothing less like a theatrical magnate could be imagined.

He was the embodiment of quiet, plaintive-looking, white-faced silence, with an unblinking eye and an impersonal voice. And he is still that, although he now divides the control of the American stage with what is left of the Big Three. He is a study. I believe his success is due to the fact that he is so pathetic, so apparently trusting, and so appealing, that the Big Three assisted him out of mere charity. As a matter of fact, he is as crafty in business as a society woman. He breaks contracts like a tearful widow when he is losing money by them. When it is the other party to the contract who is losing he can be as chalkily indifferent and implacable as a Chinaman.

Jane Shore discovered in him the soul of a musician. It had been his first ambition to be a violinist; all that he could save from his earnings as an office-boy he had put into a fiddle; and he still played it secretly, with much melancholy feeling, but no technic. Hence his original venture with the Hungarian violinist whose art he had appreciated instantly when he heard him in an East Side café. Hence, also, his visits to Jane Shore's apartments, where her friend played the violin and Jane sang to the piano.

"He was in love with me, I know," Jane has since confessed, "but I found out that he was mad about his mother, and she was so orthodox that it would have killed her to have him marry a Christian. And he never even hinted at anything else. He's really rather a dear. It's his mother's fault—the way he's going on, now, with chorus-girls."

There is no doubt that Jane Shore's beauty and culture and air of "class" reached some early marrow of subservience in his bones. When he was with her, as one of the company expressed it, "he looked as wistful as a sucked orange."

Her success with the star was another matter. "All he wanted," she says, "was a mirror"—a flattering feminine regard before which he could pose and admire himself. "He never talked; he boasted. He boasted of how much money he'd made with his other plays. How much he'd won on the stock-market. How he'd picked a twenty-to-one shot on the races. How he'd told Augustin Daly what he thought of him. How he'd pulled

Charlie Frohman's nose. What he said to a fire-man who tried to stop him smoking behind the scenes. How he'd thrashed a cheeky waiter, and an elevator-man who insulted him, and a cabman who tried to overcharge him. And even how he'd silenced Maurice Barrymore with the superior brilliance of his repartee."

He never boasted to her of his previous conquests. No doubt they had been merely mirrors, as she said. As long as they gave him a flattering reflec-tion, he treasured them. As soon as one grew tar-nished in the brightness of her complacency, he tossed her into the matrimonial dust-box, paid for the breakage like a gentleman, and looked for an-other glass. An audience was a sea of mirrors to him, and the image that he saw reflected there was that of a fine, upstanding, robust hero who never did a human thing on the stage or said a true one. He was an actor by virtue of the fact that he "put across the footlights" the fictitious personality that had made him popular. And he did not know it was fictitious. Obviously he did not know it. He saw himself in the eyes of admiration only, and never suspected the truth about himself.

7

At the dress rehearsal there began to appear one truth about him that few of us suspected: he could not act. He had almost no imagination. He had a certain easy grace, a confident manner, and a large voice. The rest had been done for him by good stage directors. In this case the stage director had been unable to control him, because he owned a fifty-per-cent. interest in the play—in lieu of salary—and the producer had let him have his way unchecked. As a consequence he had been so busy telling every one else how to act that no one had noticed his own performance. It was taken for granted that when the moment arrived he would open out like a magic rose.

At the dress rehearsal, when he opened out to nothing but resonant vacuity, we could not believe our ears. "I need my audience," he explained. "I'm dead without it." And we all accepted the explanation as sufficient—all except Jane Shore. She had endured much from him in the belief that, though he was an egotistical and selfish bore, he *could* act. After her first scene with him at the dress rehearsal she realized, with professional contempt, that "he wasn't there." Confronting him, with her back continually to the footlights, she allowed a mild withdrawal of her admiration to appear in her face, and that discouraged him.

When they came to the big scene in the third act—the love scene in which he returned her child to her—she suddenly let herself go. At sight of her little daughter coming through the door she uttered a scream of agonized joy so poignant that it stabbed into you instantly and struck tears. She fell on her knees and caught the girl to her in a sort of animal transport of maternal ecstasy, and instead of kissing the child on the face she kissed it on the breast, so that you saw the adored little body naked from the bath, and her nuzzling it, panting inarticulate endearments hysterically, choked with heart-easing sobs. It was a truly dramatic moment, and it came upon the dull mediocrity of the rehearsal like a flash of genius. It frightened the little girl, who began to cry. It took the stage away from the star; he stood staring at her in jealous silence. Behind me I heard a quaint sort of nasal moan, and looked around to see the little producer struggling to control the whimpering distortion of his face.

The star came down to the footlights and began to explain that the whole scene would be ruined if she overplayed it that way. It was a love scene. The point of it was: did *he* get *her*, not did she get the child. Her emotion should be one of gratitude to him for returning the girl to her. This cat-fit over the kid would kill the whole movement of the plot.

The stage director said, impatiently: "Yes. Go ahead with the act. We'll fix it after the rehearsal."

The scene went on. The director joined the producer behind me, and I heard him say: "There's nothin' else to it. She's immense." And—though I did not appreciate, at the moment, what had happened—with these words Jane Shore was launched on her triumphant career.

8

After the rehearsal there was a long and angry conference between the star, the director, the producer, and the author. The star said a great deal; the author said nothing; the producer said little, and the stage director said one thing over and over. It was this: "It's sure fire. We've got to have it. It's mother-love, I tell you. It's mother-love. Broadway 'll fall for it with a yell. It's sure fire. It never missed yet. Broadway 's always strong for its mother. Its wife's a joke. But its mother! Oh, boy! It's sure fire. We've got to have it. It's mother-love, I tell you. It's mother-love." And he struck his breast argumentatively every time he said "mother-love"—to indicate the seat of the appeal. And every time he struck his breast the producer nodded solemnly.

It was evident that Jane Shore had chosen the right scene to steal. "I knew it," she laughed. "I knew they'd never let him take that away from me." She had seen the producer's face, as I had seen it, contorted with emotion. "He's mad about his mother," she explained.

This was Sunday afternoon, in Atlantic City. The play was to open Monday night in a theater on the boardwalk. And when the star failed to shake the power of mother-love in the breast of the management he hurried to Jane Shore's hotel, in the hope of persuading her to give up the scene.

She had expected him. She was out taking the air in a rolling-chair. She remained out till after dark; and he did not find her till he caught her at her dinner, that evening, alone in a far corner of the dining-room, away from the music.

She rose, as she saw him coming, and she greeted him rather excitedly. "I'm so glad you came," she said in a low voice, clinging to his hand. "I've had such a fright."

"What is it?" he demanded, instantly protective. "What's happened?"

"It's all right now," she said. "A man's been following me." And she moved her eyes to indicate an adjoining table where a lonely diner sat reading his newspaper—or pretending to—and smoking a cigar.

Unfortunately for the decorum of the dining-room, as the star looked at him he lowered the paper and spied over the top of it at Jane Shore with an air of watching her from ambush. All the actor's rage at the stage director instantly focused on this peeping Tom. And his rage was reinforced by policy; he wished to do something to put Jane Shore under grateful obligation to him. He crossed at once to the table and struck down the paper, with an oath. In doing so he uncovered the proportions of a man whom he would never have challenged if he had seen him first. The man rose to his feet and struck back.

Jane Shore slipped quietly away.

When the waiters rushed in to stop the disorder the star was sitting on the floor, his nose bleeding and one eye closed, and the stranger was walking composedly to the door, with his cigar in his mouth.

He overtook Jane Shore in the hall. "You've forgotten me, Miss Widgen," he said.

She looked at him with bright intentness. "Oh, of *course!*" she cried. "*I* know! You're Tom! From the drug-store!"

He nodded, smiling. She held out her hand, delighted. He was the clerk who had given her pony a drink of soda-water the day that she rode into the drug-store and demanded refreshment for herself and her horse. Evidently he was no longer a clerk, but she did not ask for any explanations.

"Why," she cried, "I didn't know you! Why didn't you speak to me?"

She took his arm and hurried him away from the dining-room where the star, with his nose in a table-napkin, was explaining to a friendly head waiter that it was nothing, a private affair, a gentlemanly misunderstanding.

She was saying girlishly to Tom: "How strange to meet you here, after all these years! What are you doing? Come up and sit on the porch with me."

She did not ask what he had done with the star. She guessed it from what she had seen, over her shoulder, as she passed out the door. And Tom did not make any guilty explanations. He had not been following her. He had been finishing his dinner when she sat down at a neighboring table, and he had stared at her only a little more than she was accustomed to being stared at by solitary diners in such circumstances.

"Who was that fellow who—who spoke to me?" he asked, as they went up-stairs.

"Oh, he's a crazy actor," she said. "I'll tell you about him later. Tell me first about yourself."

He told her, on the balcony, in the moonlight, looking out at the misted ocean—while the star was having his bruised face washed and bandaged by his valet in the bathroom of his suite.

And what he told her was one of those fairy-tales of modern American business that put to shame the inventions of fiction. Briefly, he was no longer a druggist's clerk. A moment of prophetic thought had made him a millionaire. It had occurred to him, over a bottle of extract of pepsin, that the two American passions for chewing-gum and for patent medicine might be profitably combined if you put pepsin in the gum. He had sold the idea, on a royalty basis, to a chewing-gum manufacturer. And after successfully defending himself in court from an attempt to steal his rights he was now devoting himself to his health, his leisure, physical

[70]

culture, and the search for safe investments. He was not married. Fanny Widgen had been an unattainable ideal of his days behind the counter, and he still felt romantic about her. He did not say so. He did not need to. She knew it from his manner of recalling her and her pony and the sight of her driving past the blue and crimson bottles of the druggist's window in her dog-cart.

She explained, then, about the star, laughing unblushingly. "I didn't want to give him back the scene, and I didn't want to talk to him about it. I couldn't say I wouldn't, you know. That would have made too much trouble. So I let him think you had been annoying me. I hadn't recognized you, of course. I knew I could escape if he'd only start a row. And he'd boasted so much about 'beating up' waiters and elevator-men that I thought he'd jump at the opportunity to make a hero of himself for me. Did you hurt him?"

"I don't think so," he said, modestly. "Not much. I may have blacked one of his eyes."

"Blacked his eye!"

"They must have been all elevator-boys that he'd been beating up."

"He probably never fought any one in his life before," she said. And she added, reflectively, "Blacked his eye!"

That was serious. It was serious for everybody —the producer, the author, the whole company.

6 [71]

How was he to play his part with a black eye? And if he could not play his part, how about the opening?

9

He kept his room all the following day, and we had to be satisfied with second-hand reports. He explained that he had tripped on the boardwalk and fallen with his face against the railing. Rumor promptly added that he had been drunk. Jane Shore did not contradict the rumor. She contented herself with telephoning to thank him for his gallantry and his silence. "It was so kind of you," she said, "to protect me from gossip by not telling about that awful man. I suppose you nearly killed him."

He replied, grimly, "Well, he'll never bother *you* again."

She repeated that to us, weeks later, with gurgles of delight, as if it were a piece of boarding-school mischief.

He wanted to see her, to talk to her, and she invited him to be at the theater at seven. He was there. They had a long conference. She had another with the producer. I heard from the author that the star had threatened to give up the play unless it was played the way he wanted it. There were more conferences, while the audience gathered into the theater and the orchestra struck up a rusty overture. They were still conferring when I went out to find a vacancy in the back row, and the stage director, as I passed him, was saying: "I tell you he's a four-flush. You watch him to-night. Never mind her. Let her play to her limit. Watch *him*."

I watched him myself. And when he came on the stage—for an entrance that had been carefully built to—the chill that quivered over the house was almost an audible expression of perplexity. He was made up very pale, with his eyes darkened— both eyes—and one of them bloodshot. He wore a wig that came low on his forehead, to cover the lump of a bruise. He looked sinister, unwholesome, anything but the matinée idol that we had come there to see. And I offer it without apology: Jane Shore had done it. She had persuaded him that as a desperate man who had lost a wife and child—a tragic widower defying death among a band of criminals—he ought to be made up in this "interesting" manner. It would conceal his bruises.

His failure was unqualified—as unqualified as her success. Everything heroic that he said was contradicted by his appearance; and any one who has worked in the theater will understand how the eye will overcome the ear in such circumstances. He was immediately aware that the house was cold to him; and, not being able to see himself with the eyes of the audience, he did not know what was the matter; he thought that the part was "unsympathetic." He could not get any heart into it.

Jane Shore did not help him. She played in a low key, with repressed intensity, in a technic that he could not handle, and when they were on the stage together the audience went to her. Even with her back to them she dominated him. She clasped her hands behind her and in his emotional passages she opened and closed them, unknown to him, and they were as expressive as the dumb mouth of a gasping fish. She killed the biggest moment of one of his most thrilling speeches by dropping her handkerchief behind her, as if from fingers paralyzed with secret emotion. A shudder of her shoulders was more eloquent than his ranting. And when it came to the scene with the child she took the stage away from him, took the house away from him, took the applause and the curtain away from him, and topped it all by receiving across the footlights an armful of roses after a pretty play of girlish shyness and hesitation—as if to say: "For me? They can't be for me! Aren't they the star's?"—until the audience had to authorize and enforce the tribute with an ovation of handclapping and gallery whistles and the pounding of imperative feet.

The hesitation was affected, of course. The roses were Tom's and she had expected them.

She was almost compelled to make a speech. She did go so far as to shake her head in a refusal to make one.

"That finishes it," the author groaned in my ear. "He'll never play it again. Never."

The last act was entirely hers. The star sulked his way through it, saying mere words.

The author left me. I supposed he had gone to throw himself in the surf.

The audience crowded out, saying: "Who is she? Isn't she wonderful? . . . Charming! Such grace! . . . Well, she certainly takes that part off fine."

Out of a spirit of sympathy for the author, I went back to the hotel and to bed without joining in the post-mortem. I had felt all along that the play was a conglomeration of fatuous nonsense, anyway. One always feels that way about a friend's play.

And next morning I found that—as usual—while I slept all the really important things of life had happened. The others had been up all night. The star had left for Florida, with an incipient attack of press-agent's pneumonia, having broken his contract, abandoned his interest in the production, insulted Jane Shore, and had his other eye blacked by a little property-man named Fritz Hoff who hated him. An unexpected millionaire had "bought in" on the play, and this was the same millionaire who had been guilty of the barrelful of American Beauty roses across the footlights. "Tom the Gum-man" we came to call him. The author was busy rewriting again in order to make a star

part for Jane Shore. The stage director was helping by beating his breast like a gorilla and howling
for more mother-love. A young leading man, in
answer to a wire from Jane Shore, was coming
from Washington to rehearse the part in which the
star had fallen down. A New York manager had
agreed to take the Atlantic City theater off their
hands for the latter part of the week. And the producer was leaving for Broadway and the booking-
offices, to arrange for an out-of-town opening for
Jane Shore in "a new American drama" within
the month.

10

Her success in that opening is so much a part of
the history of our stage that I hardly need refer
to it. There is an accurate account of it in one of
William Winter's books. He hailed her, if I remember, as a young Madame Janauschek—for she
played her cheap melodrama with such eloquence
and distinction that comparisons with the old
school were inevitable. She showed, in her later
plays, that she was modern and naturalistic; and
Mr. Winter felt that she was a noble promise un-
fulfilled. She shrugged her shoulders and went
ahead. What her theory of her art is I do not know:
I suspect that she is largely innocent of any. Virginia Tracy has written of her: "I don't believe she
ever in her life gave two thoughts to anything except the smashing out of certain congenial dramatic

effects, quite unrelatedly to anything but her will to put those individual effects across." And in that respect she is certainly the creature of conditions on the modern American stage.

Her acting, I should say, is intuitional. It is not the result of any logical process of thought and study, although she pretends that it is. She acts with two lobes of her brain, one of which governs the utterance of emotion with sincere convincingness, and the other watches the audience, the stage, and her own performance with critical detachment. You will see her come off from a big scene with her lower face working hysterically and her eyes unconcerned and cold. When enthusiasm crowds into her dressing-room to congratulate her she receives it, like royalty at an audience, with a charmingly happy smile, but with a back-thought showing, if you look for it, in the attentive scrutiny of her gaze.

However, it is not her art that I am concerned with. She is a great actress, perhaps. She is certainly a fascinating character. I have done her injustice in this account of her first success if I have not indicated that, though she was incredibly crafty in her handling of the star, she was also impulsive, full of deviltry, a person of incalculable temperament. It was certainly an impulse of mischief that prompted her to start that dining-room fight, although she took such excellent advantage of the results of it. She is tricky. "Of course I'm tricky," she says. "Could any one who is not tricky get ahead in the theater?" She is deeply egotistic. "Well," she asks, "do you think it's possible to be as modest as a hermit-thrush and still make your living singing at the entrance to Brooklyn Bridge during rush hours?" She has faults of pettiness that seem impossibly opposed to her large and generous qualities; but with all the disintegrating impulses of variable temperament and contradictory moods, she has a strength of will that gives her character and direction.

11

My friend the author fell insanely in love with her. She petted him and encouraged him amiably until it came to a question of marrying him. "No," she said. "No. Never." Well, but why not? "Because it's impossible." She refused to see him. She would not answer his letters. He behaved like a lunatic, drinking and weeping in all the cafés of the Rialto. I went to her, to speak on his behalf; and she listened to me, sitting bolt-upright beside her reading-lamp, with her hands on the arms of her chair, as unmoved as a judge.

She said: "I can't help it. That's the way life is. He'll have to get through it the best way he can."

I begged her to see him. She shook her head. "I'll never see him again." And she kept her word, for years.

Tom the Gum-man came to a similarly violent end with her. "He's too possessive," she said. "He thinks he invented me. He'll be in court next, defending his royalty rights in me."

He went off in a rage and married the daughter of another prophylactic millionaire. She sent him a signed photograph of herself as a wedding-present, and apparently forgot him.

On the other hand, she never rested till she won her father back,

As soon as she made her first success she sent him the seven hundred dollars that she had "borrowed" to leave home. He returned the check without a word. She sent it back, and he returned the letter unopened. She made out the check to her brother Ben—who had a saving habit—and she wired her father, "Have sent Ben money with thanks." It did not come back.

She subscribed to a clipping bureau for her father and ordered every printed word about Jane Shore sent to him. He tried to countermand the order, but the bureau continued to fill it, and she paid the bills. The larger they were the happier she was. "Send him everything," she ordered, "even the advertisements."

She wired him good wishes on his birthday, on Christmas and New-Year's, on holidays and holy days. On Lincoln's Birthday she telegraphed, "Let us have peace." And on Washington's she wired, "Are you prouder than G. W.? He was the father

of his country and now look at the darn thing."
He replied, "Stop sending silly telegrams." She
wired back: "Letters did not seem to reach you.
Am writing."

She wrote without replies and sent him presents
without acknowledgments; and finally, when she
was playing in Philadelphia, she called on him
in his office and laughed him out of his resentment. He went to see her in "Romeo and
Juliet," and he was scandalized by the love
scenes, which she played with frank passion.
"All right, Dad," she said. "There was twelve
hundred dollars in the house. You know, you
have to be a bit scandalous to do that amount
of business in a godly town like Philadelphia.
Nothing has drawn as well as that, here, since
'The Black Crook.'"

"It's a disgrace," he scolded. "A daughter of
mine going on like that in public. A respectable
girl!"

"Respectable!" she cried. "I'm so respectable
I can't get my name in the papers without paying
for it."

And indeed she was so respectable that whenever
any one attacked the moral conditions on our stage,
Mrs. Fiske, in replying, never failed to refer to the
immaculate record and reputation of Jane Shore.
With whatever abandon she played Juliet or the
proposal scene in Shaw's "Satan's Advocate," she
was always primly chaperoned, off the stage, by

the inhibitions of her Calvinistic and Quaker ancestors. The nearest she ever came to scandal—

12

It was quite recently, at Madame Bernhardt's professional matinée, in the Empire Theater, on her last tour. Jane Shore was in the stage-box on the right-hand side with her old admirer, Tom the Gum-man. A wife and three children had not prevented him from returning to an apparently Platonic devotion for his first love. And from the rise of the curtain, from the first sight of Bernhardt as Hecube on her throne, Jane Shore wept quietly, continuously, without a word of explanation, without a movement of applause. She wept, not at the tragedy of the queen, or the soldier mortally wounded on the "field of honor," or Camille dying in her lover's arms; she wept for the greater tragedy of that indomitable artist, pinned down by bodily infirmity, with nothing left to her but her head and her hands, struggling—and with such heartrending success, with the voice of a young, unconquerable spirit, with an art that ought to be eternal— struggling to hold her little circle of light and brilliance against the dark stifle of oblivion that was closing in on her, that was creeping up on her, that had risen already to her throat. Here, after such a career as Jane Shore could never hope for, here was the visible end. When that voice ceased, when that unsubmerged, defiant head sank under the silence, what would be left of the fame and the triumphs even of Sarah Bernhardt?

"What's the matter?" Tom asked her in the auto on their way home. "Don't cry like that. You'll make yourself ill."

She shook her head. She reached out and took his hand blindly. They drove in silence through the evening drizzle.

She did not speak until they were in her front room. She was dry-eyed and tragic-looking. "Come here," she said, holding out her hand to him. He sat beside her on the sofa. It was the sofa from the proposal scene of "Satan's Advocate." She said, "Take me away from all this."

"What?"

"Take me away. You want me. You've always wanted me. Take me away, out West somewhere —where you can get your divorce."

"But my dear girl," he said, "do you know what you're saying? Do you know what it means?" He had released her hand, blank with amazement.

"Yes, yes," she cried. "I know. I want to end it all. No more. Not even to-night. Take me away."

He rose slowly. "But," he said. "But—"

She flung out her hands. "I know. I know. The talk—the scandal—I don't care. I don't want ever again to see their silly faces over the footlights. It's all— It doesn't matter. It's nothing. You've wanted—you've always wanted me. You're unhappy. We're both unhappy. I want to end it. I want to get—whatever there's left for me to get —before I'm old and—and pitiful. I don't want to be alone *then*—now—ever any more." And she began to weep again.

"My God!" he said. "If you'd done this ten years ago!"

"I know," she sobbed. *"But I didn't!"*

He began to walk up and down the room. "I wouldn't care for myself," he explained, "but I can't take advantage of a mood like this, to rush you into a position— You'd hate me. You don't appreciate what you're doing. With the people waiting for you, and the seats sold—running away like this, with a married man—and all the publicity and the scandal."

She sat up, staring at him. He was a big, dark man, black-mustached; and he stood uncomfortably, with his hands deep in his pockets, his head down, blinking at the floor, and talking in a rumbling, grumbling voice. "He looked," she said afterward, "like a fat boy who was being tempted to play hooky from school." And suddenly, in the midst of his perfectly reasonable remonstrances, she began to laugh.

He started as if she had struck him. He turned on her, red, ridiculous. "Have you been playing some damn game with me?" he demanded.

"No—no," she shouted, at the top of hysterical peals of laughter. *"No!* I was se-se-serious!"

"Then what have I done?" he cried. "What have I said?"

She was too hysterical to explain.

"There I had been," she told it, "for years pursued by these ravenous monsters, men. And you've no idea what a nuisance they are to an actress. They see you all beautifully made up, in the romantic stage lights, being everything sweet and noble and heroic that a playwright can make a woman out to be. And, of course, they go crazy about you —and come around offering to leave wife and family, and home and mother, and business and good name for you—and threatening to throw themselves into the Hudson if you don't instantly throw yourself into their arms. Why! They'd plagued me like a lot of wolves! The maiden pursued! And here, now, when I turned on the most ferocious one of them all— And you've no idea what a scene he'd treated me to only the day before— And when I turned on him and said, 'Well, take me, then! Here I am! Take me!' he began to make excuses. Funny! I laughed so hard I nearly fainted from exhaustion."

He grew more and more angry. He stormed and swore. She could only stammer, "It's—it's so funny!" And at last he stamped out of the house, enraged, humiliated. "And he'll never come back," she said. "Never. Because he knows that if he ever does come back, I'll never be able to look at him with a straight face."

And some of that perhaps explains one thing that seems to have greatly intrigued her public. It explains why Jane Shore has never married. Her suitors, she thinks, have *not* been in love with her; they have been in love with Shakespeare's Juliet, or Shaw's Patricia Beauchamp, or Barrie's Grizel, or some other ideal that is not Fanny Widgen. And they bore her. She will not marry an actor. "I won't marry one," she says, "for the same reason that I won't co-star with one. There isn't room for two of *our* egos in one house." A manager wanted to marry her, and she explained her rejection of him by saying in a Bowery voice, "I'm not goin' to be no man's white slave." The fact is she will probably end by marrying Fritz Hoff (now Hoffman), the property-man who blacked the star's other eye for her in Atlantic City.

He has served her like an adoring watchdog ever since that first defense of her. He was her property-man and stage manager in her first success. It was his skill as a stage carpenter that made her house so deliciously picturesque and theatrical with its window-seats and diamond panes and Belasco lights and Juliet hangings. He went with her when the most famous of her managers took her, and it was about Fritz that they had their famous quarrel, I understand. I know nothing about it. All I know is that after her last performance under that management I asked her, "Well, how do you feel about it now?" And she answered, "Feel!"

—raising her arms to draw a long breath—"I feel like a wax figure escaped from the Eden Musée."

Fritz became her personal manager, watched the men in the box-office like a prison guard, exercised her bad-tempered little Pekinese, tacked up dodgers for her in prohibited places, quarreled with her company for her, accepted summonses for bills he would not let her pay, let her scold and rage at him serenely whenever anything went wrong for which he was not responsible, and stood out across the street from the theater and enjoyed the glory of his name in electric lights over hers as his only apparent reward.

It is Fritz Hoffman who has made possible her whole later career. She will probably marry him. She will have to if he has ever sense enough to say, "I'll leave you, if you *don't*." And in the purely practical world in which Jane Shore has to live— the world of the theater—it would be the best thing that she could do.

FROM THE LIFE

Thomas Wales Warren

THOMAS WALES WARREN

WARREN, Thomas Wales, jurist; *b.*
Columbus, O., Feb. 21, 1851; *s.* John and
Esther (McCabe) W.; ed. pub. schools,
Univ. Law School; read law in office
Judge Stephen Wales; admitted to bar
of Ohio, 1880; *m.* Virginia Wales, June
10, 1881; member firm of Wales & War-
ren, 1880–92. Active in politics; twice
deleg. Rep. Nat. convs; mem. Rep. Nat.
Exec. Com., 1890–1902; state Attorney-
General; Attorney-General of U. S.;
Secretary of State; justice Supreme
Court of U. S., etc.—*Who's Who.*

1·

FOR the purposes of this portrait-study let us
take Warren before he was Justice Thomas
Wales Warren of the Supreme Court of the United
States. Let us take him before he was even Thomas
W. Warren, United States Attorney-General and
"Warwick the Kingmaker" at Washington. Let
us take him when he was still "Tom" Warren,
Attorney-General of his native state, unknown to
the national cartoonists, engaged obscurely in local
politics, and foreseeing his conspicuous future as
little as a man foresees the view from the top of a
hill which he is still climbing. And let us take him
on the day when he suddenly decided that he would
not follow the usual road to that hilltop, but make

an adventurous short cut to it over the most obvious obstructions.

That day was a Sunday and a hot July Sunday, but people have to be governed seven days in the week, and Warren was at his library desk. There is no need to describe him, because he had already the rather repellant features that have since become so familiar to the American public. But I should like to explain that some of his features quite belied him.

He had already begun to achieve his resemblance to a mummy, with Pharaoh's bony nose. He looked parched and his skin was dry and leathery. But that was not an indication of any moral evil. It was due to indigestion. Poverty had ruined his stomach in his youth.

He had also the deep furrow between his eyebrows which the caricaturists have made so sinister, but it was not really sinister. In its origin it was a harmless pretension. He had contracted it at law-school, listening to lectures with an intense young expression of attention that had been designed to impress the lecturer. He had long since ceased trying to impress any one. Quite the opposite. When he was most attentive, now, he looked most absent-minded.

And he had the weasel-mouthed weak look which the cartoonists exaggerate, but if you could have drawn back his lips to bare his teeth, you would have found that his lower jaw closed up inside the upper one, almost to the palate. And that was a malformation of the mouth which he had unwittingly forced upon himself in the struggles of his ambitious boyhood, when he had lived with his jaws clenched—literally—dramatizing to himself his wrestle with adversity, consciously assuming a pose of determination to succeed, and biting his jaws together as if he were fighting physically while he studied; or when he was threshing around his unheated room at night trying to get warm before he went to bed; or, in later years, when he was facing any opposition to his advancement. It was not a weakness in his mouth; it was rather a pathetic sort of strength. It showed, now, chiefly when he confronted any serious problem of policy that had to be grappled with in the secrecy of his private sessions with himself.

He was already growing bald, but he wore a toupee. This toupee he had taken off because he was hot, and it lay on his desk blotter before him, like the scalp of an enemy. He was apparently studying it, crouched forward on the arms of his desk chair, with his hands clasped in a loose entanglement of his long fingers. And his tight little skull shone with the gloss of a coffee-colored ostrich-egg in the warm gloom of his old-fashioned library.

The windows were covered with Venetian blinds that showed between their slats the green glow of locust-trees and sunlight outside on his lawn.

There he was, then—Tom Warren, about to cross the Rubicon! A historical moment! Fraught, as the historians say, with mighty consequences.

2

If you could have put your face down between him and his toupee, you would have seen that his eyes were focused on nothing nearer than the center of the earth. He was concentrated on an invisible perplexity. And his problem was this: A county sheriff in the town of Middleburg, in the southern extremity of the state, had telephoned to the Governor that the farmers of the district were arming to come in to Middleburg, that night, to break open the jail and lynch some negroes. The Governor was out of the state, on his way east to a political conference, and the sheriff's warning had been sent to Warren from the State-house. Warren, having elected the Governor on a law-enforcement platform, was busy with a campaign to have him nominated for the Presidency, with the reversion to himself of a place in the Cabinet. Middleburg was the Governor's home town, and a lynching there might be used by his political enemies and his party rivals to give him "a black eye" nationally.

How? Well, if the Governor was to show himself a man of conspicuous strength before the nation, he would either have to prevent the lynching with armed force—and perhaps kill some of the embattled farmers of the county—or he would have to make a grand-stand play of prosecuting the lynchers vigorously after the event. And by either act he might alienate the support of his home district, for it was far enough South to be on the border of parts where the white voter administered lynch law as an extra-judicial form of law enforcement against the black; and the solid South might even be persuaded to turn solidly against the Governor as a nigger-sympathizer who was playing for the Jim Crow vote.

Some one once asked Warren, "How did you ever think of *that?*" when he had outwitted a threatening situation instantly, without a moment's pause of hesitation. Warren replied: "You don't have time to think. It has to *be* there—or you can't do it." And, in this case, he remained staring at his problem—through his toupee and his desk blotter—a much briefer time than it has taken you to read of his doing it, unless you have skipped.

He pressed a call-button to summon his secretary, put on his toupee, and began to walk up and down his library with the long, slow strides of a wading-bird. As he walked his mouth relaxed into a sort of pout of dreamy satisfaction, and he played with a loose button on his coat, sliding his thumb under it and around it incessantly while he mused.

That unconscious habit, and the protrusion of the lips which accompanied it, had an illuminating origin. His mother had died of privations and malnutrition before he had been weaned. His spinster aunt, a dressmaker, had raised him from infancy; and his only "comforter" had been a bone button sewed on a rag. It had been on a button that he had cut his teeth. Even as a growing boy he had gone to sleep sucking a button on his night-shirt—secretly, of course. And there was still, for the Attorney-General, the satisfaction of a repressed instinct in this button play, although he was ignorant of the reason for it or the origin of it.

He stopped it as soon as he heard his secretary at his door, and, turning, he stood in the center of the room and watched the young man enter.

It was characteristic of Warren so to turn alertly to any new-comer, and it was characteristic of him to regard even Pritchard with a mechanical habit of scrutiny as he regarded every one who came to interview him. He used to say that he could tell if a man was going to lie to him by the way he crossed the room. And he was aware at once— though his mind was on another matter—that there was something not quite right about the boy.

To the casual glance Pritchard was merely a good-looking youth with smooth black hair that may have been pomaded, a small black mustache that looked petted, long black eyelashes, a dimpled, plump chin, and a dark mole on his cheek that touched off his girlish complexion like a beauty patch. He was somewhat flushed. As soon as he came in the door Warren said, abstractedly, "Shut that, will you?"

Pritchard, as he closed it, turned his back to Warren, looking down at the handle.

Ordinarily he would have closed the door with a hand behind him, his eyes on Warren inquiringly. Warren noticed something unnatural in this difference, without really formulating what the difference was. He had already observed that Pritchard was in high color.

"Get your note-book," Warren said in the same thoughtful tone, "and take this down."

Pritchard went to the desk, found his note-book, sat down in his usual chair beside the desk, and prepared himself to take dictation. He looked at his hands a moment, waiting. And then, looking up quickly at Warren, he watched the Attorney-General and, at the same time, furtively turned a ring on his finger so as to conceal the setting.

Warren was apparently not noticing. He was gazing meditatively ahead of him. But he saw Pritchard's action with the ring out of the corner of his eye.

If he had expressed the matter to himself—which he did not—he would have concluded: "This boy feels guilty toward me. He has something to conceal from me. It's connected with a ring, which he doesn't wish me to recognize. He's wearing that ring instead of his seal ring. He has probably changed rings with some one, and he doesn't want me to know it. Why?"

He said to Pritchard, still thoughtful: "One of our detectives, Ben Teague, is down in Middleburg on a case. He's probably at the Mansion House there. Under the name of Bert Todd. Make a note of it: 'Bert Todd.' I want to get a message to him without disturbing his cover. Understand?"

"Yes, sir."

"Well. Go out to a telephone-booth—in the Holman Hotel—and get him on the wire. Bert Todd. Representing the Consolidated Farm Implement Company. Say to him— Take this down: 'I have some confidential information to give you, on behalf of the president of the company, who is temporarily out of the state. And I cannot give it explicitly over the telephone.'" (He was dictating in the tone of a business communication.) "'The counsel of our company has just received this information from an officer of the company whose name is Steinholtz—the same name as the sheriff of your county there. He informs us that a competitor by the name of Lynch is likely to make trouble for us in his district. You understand it's the president's home district, and any such disturbance of our prestige in that locality might seriously affect the re-election of the company's present management by the stockholders. It is therefore imperative that Mr. Lynch shall be headed off.

"'Mr. Steinholtz has asked us for assistance. You must make arrangements to see him at once. Instantly. There's not a moment to lose. As soon as you have seen him, 'phone, on his private office wire, to our head law-office. Our lawyer will be there till you report. He'll be there all night if necessary. You understand the importance of it. The company depends on you.'

"That's all. Now, read that over to me."

Pritchard read it, monotonously, following the lines of shorthand with his pencil. Warren studied the thin gold band of the ring on the young man's finger. He had, of course already begun to suspect that the ring belonged to his daughter Meta.

When the reading was finished he said: "All right, Will. Go ahead, now. I'll be at the State-house. I'll 'phone here for you, if I want you."

Pritchard hurried out, with eager alacrity. Warren sat and considered him—and Meta.

3

Warren, as an orphaned boy, inadequately supported by an underpaid sewing-woman, had gone on the streets to "mooch" and sell newspapers as soon as he was old enough to walk. By working after school-hours, delivering newspapers, running errands, doing odd furnace jobs at night, and generally foraging like a stray cat, he had contrived to get an elementary public-school education. Then at the age of twelve he had gone to work as an office-boy for Judge Stephen Wales, and the judge in the end had practically adopted him. (Hence the "Wales" in "Thomas Wales Warren.") He sent Warren to law-school. He took him as a partner in his office. He even accepted him as a son-in-law, proud of the boy and his ability. And when the judge died Warren and his wife were already living in the old Wales home as the accepted heirs of it.

This was Judge Wales's library in which Warren now sat, thinking. It was Judge Wales's granddaughter Meta of whom he was sitting there to think. And she was much more the judge's granddaughter to Warren than she was his own child. She looked like a Wales. She spoke and moved like a Wales. She had all the high, impractical ideals of a Wales. And Warren felt, before her, the same class inferiority that he had felt with her dead mother.

He had always been, in his own mind, Tommy the office-boy to the judge's daughter; and still, subconsciously, with the judge's granddaughter, he was Tommy the office-boy grown old. It was some sort of arrested immaturity in him—like his playing with the button. Neither the mother nor the daughter had ever suspected it. They had never suspected, when they looked at Tom Warren, that they were not looking at a husband or a father, but at a devoted, adoring, confidential servant, who understood them affectionately and protected them shrewdly from the predatory world to which he belonged—the world that would have destroyed Judge Wales and his fine old benevolence and his unworldly idealism, if Warren had not defended him.

Warren had now to defend the judge's granddaughter. That was how he saw the situation and his duty in it. He had nothing against Pritchard —except that he was a subservient, inoffensive, secretarial valet who would never be anything else. He considered that Pritchard was no man to take care of a gentle girl and protect her children from the dangers of a cruelly competitive social system. If it was *she* who had given Pritchard the ring—

He first arranged the necessary machinery for finding that out. He removed a paper-fastener from the corner of a typewritten report, put a box of cigars on the edge of his desk-top, and laid the loose sheets of the report on the box. Then he went to his door and called, "Meta!"

She answered from the front room. He returned to his desk and began to gather up some papers.

She came to the door and stood there, not quite smiling, but with the happy recollection of an interrupted smile still lingering in her face. She was of the type of dark Southern beauty that matures young, but she was still girlish, and she waited in a girlish attitude, with her hands clasped behind her.

He said, looking for something in his desk: "Tell Fred to bring the car around. I have to go to the State-house. They're having trouble down at Middleburg, and I'll have to handle it in the Governor's absence. I'm afraid I'll not be back till late."

"Yes," she said.

He had reached out as if to open the cigar-box. He upset the typewritten pages. They slid with a rustle to the floor and scattered widely—assisted by his clumsy effort to catch them. "There!" he said, disgustedly.

"Let *me*, father." She crossed the room with a graceful quickness and knelt among the papers in a whorl of white skirts. He looked down at her hands as she gathered up the pages, and he saw that her ring was gone—a little single-ruby ring that her dead mother had given her.

He began at once to maneuver against that conspiracy of events as he had begun to maneuver against the menace from Middleburg. And his tactics in these two cases were typical of the man and his methods. They can be more briefly reported and more readily understood than the more complicated intrigues of some of his national manipulations, but they were just as astute and subtle in miniature as any of his later strategies have been in the large.

4

"I'm growing old," he said. "It makes me dizzy to stoop." He began to pace up and down the room rather dejectedly. "And I'm working too hard. At thankless work. People don't know how to govern themselves, but they revolt against any man who tries to govern them. You have to do it without letting them know you're doing it. That's what makes our politics so hypocritical."

He may have believed that, or he may not; he was not considering the truth of what he said, but its effect on her. He asked, as if casually, the question to which he had been leading: "Did you read the attack that this man Miller is making on me? 'Wardrobe' Miller."

"Yes, father," she confessed. He never discussed politics with her. She felt—as he intended her to feel—that he was appealing to her for a sympathetic understanding. She did not quite know how to give it.

"Well," he said, cheerfully, "Miller's turn will come. He'll satisfy them for a time with this pretense of 'letting the people rule'—with their direct primaries, and their initiative, and their referendum, and all the rest of it. But there has to be a captain to the ship; and as soon as they find out that Miller's the captain they'll mutiny against *him*, too, and throw him overboard."

"Are they going to defeat you?" she asked, distressed.

"No," he said. "Not this time, I think. But *they* believe they're going to do it. And the parasites are beginning to desert me already and fasten themselves on Miller." And that last was the significant statement to which all his preamble had been directed.

"It isn't pretty, is it?" she said. She had put back the loose sheets of typewritten manuscript on his desk, and she stood looking at him with a wistful desire to aid him showing in her large eyes.

"It's a strange business," he went on as if philosophizing idly, walking up and down. "When I first came into office, before you were old enough to remember—at the head of a reform movement —of business men—we turned out the thieving politicians and professional officeholders who were looting the treasury, and we put them in jail—many of them. And I was a popular hero. Your mother was very proud that day.

"And now they're in revolt against our 'business administration.' They can't say we've not been honest. We've given them good government. And the state's been prosperous. But it's labor that wants to rule, now, and the working-man. And they say I represent business and the corporations and the trusts.

"It all amounts to this: A man is born with the ability to rule as he's born with any other ability. It happens that, during his life, some one class is governing, and he governs for them. Then another class surges up, with a new ruler. And then another. But the people never govern. They can't, any more than an army can command and direct itself. They're always killing one king to put his crown on another. Yesterday it was King Birth. To-day it's King Money. To-morrow it will be King Labor."

He may have believed that, too, or he may not. He was saying it with a purpose, not with a belief.

He smiled at her. "Well, I'll soon be out of it all, I hope, and begin to live like a human being. I haven't had any life—home life or any other. I'm going to get a holiday. How would you like to go to Washington with me?"

"Oh, I'd *like* it," she said. Then her face changed. She looked down at her hands. She hesitated. And he was afraid she was going to confess her affair with Pritchard.

"Well," he put in, hastily, "run along and call the car. They're probably preparing their riot in Middleburg while I chatter. That's a very becoming dress."

"Do you like it?"

"I like it very much, my dear," he said, "and I like you in it."

"Thank you, father," she said, shyly. She went out in a little flutter of pleased embarrassment. He put the typewritten report in his pocket. It was a summary of all the direct-primary laws that had been passed in the Western States and of the court decisions that had confirmed or voided those enactments.

He stood a moment in deep thought. The girl, certainly, was not out of his reach, and he had given her mind an impulse in the direction that he wanted it to take. He could manage her if he could manage Pritchard.

He shut his door noiselessly. He sat down to his desk 'phone and called a private number. "Is that you, Robert?" he asked, in a low voice. "Know who's speaking? It's Tom Warren. Can you come at once to my office in the State-house? The side entrance will be open. And my private door. I'll be alone. . . . Yes, right away, if you can. I'm going right down. . . . I have a personal favor to ask. . . . Yes. Thanks."

He hung up the receiver with a quick click. The man with whom he had been speaking was Robert Wardrup Miller—the "Wardrobe" Miller of whose attacks upon him he had spoken to his daughter—the Miller to whom the "parasites," as he had said, were already beginning to attach themselves.

He went out to the hall. She brought him his soft felt hat. He bent to give her his usual perfunctory kiss; but she wished to show her loyal sympathy with him in the worries of political life and the defections of the parasitical, and, instead of turning her cheek, she took the caress full on her lips, as if it had been her lover's, avidly. Warren understood that Pritchard had been kissing her. She smiled up at him, and it was the assured smile of a girl whose ears were full of her lover's praises of her.

"Good-by," he said. "I'll 'phone you."

5

He hurried to his automobile. "The State-house, Fred," he directed his chauffeur.

The chauffeur nodded in the informal friendly manner of Warren's servants. They always liked him and served him and were proud of him. In fact, his ability to obtain loyal and righteous support was one of the significant attributes of "the most sinister figure in our national life," as one of his political opponents afterward acclaimed him.

It was necessary, perhaps, for him to have such an atmosphere of friendliness and private credit in which to live. At any rate, he had an instinct for obtaining it. He played politics as a club gambler plays poker, sociably, with a sympathetic geniality, winning by any means, without a scruple, but always as if he were more interested in his opponents than he was in his own play. It was characteristic of him that he would not openly interfere between Pritchard and his daughter, as he would not openly interfere between the people and their desire for the direct primary, the initiative, the referendum, and the other reforms proposed by the Direct Legislation League. But he believed as confidently that he knew what was best for the people of his state as he believed that he knew what was best for his daughter. He believed that in either case it was unwise to arouse opposition by asserting his superior wisdom. And he moved against Pritchard, as he moved against "Wardrobe" Miller and his Direct Legislation League, secretly, without showing any ill-will and without exciting any.

When the "wild-eyed reformers, agitators, and demagogues" of the state first began to demand measures of direct legislation—"in order," as they said, "to destroy the moneyed control of political machines and make the elected representatives of the community responsible to the electors"—Warren had watched the agitation interestedly, wondering how the men who should have to rule in the future would be able to rule over a people equipped with independent lawmaking powers of their own. He had studied it as one might study a chess problem with a dummy for opponent. When the agitators organized he saw the problem with an opponent sitting behind it. He had arrived at no solution, so he took his opponent "into camp." He insinuated machine men into the Direct Legislation League; they got control unostentatiously of the executive committee, and the League nominated for the governorship Mr. Robert Wardrup Miller, whom Warren had privately chosen for that empty honor.

Miller had accepted his nomination in good faith. He was a wealthy young idealist who had become an ardent follower of a national leader in reform, and he knew as much about practical politics as a nun. He was a member of the City Club to which Warren belonged, and it was Warren who had encouraged him to enter public life. "Mr. Warren," he replied, to that encouragement, "if I do, I shall have to oppose *you*." And Warren said: "Robert, a healthy opposition is the life of party politics. Oppose me by all means, and I'll oppose you. I'll enjoy it, and it will be a good training for *you*."

Miller frowned determinedly. He felt that he was a strong character asserting his independence and compelling even Warren to bend to him with assumed jocularity. When he was nominated by the Direct Legislation League he defied the lightning in a speech in which he named Warren as the man most responsible for preventing the introduction of a direct primary law into the last Legislature. And now, when Warren telephoned to ask him to come to the State-house, Miller showed his fearlessness—as Warren had hoped he would—by accepting the invitation instantly.

It was Warren, by the way, who had had him nicknamed "Wardrobe" Miller by privately starting the story that Miller had three hundred and sixty-five neckties and thirty-one pairs of trousers in the clothes-closets of his bachelor apartments.

6

Warren arrived at the State-house, passed the doorkeeper with a hasty greeting, and climbed the flight of stairs to his office in long strides of two steps at a time, taking out his keys as he went. His telephone was ringing as he entered his private office. He caught it from his desk and said, "Yes?"

It was the detective, Teague, in Middleburg, and he was calling from the sheriff's office, where he had no need of cover. Warren's face, as he listened, settled into its mask of concentrated impassivity. He sat down.

"I see," he kept saying. "I see. Yes. I see." He cleared his throat. "Are the Sunday-closing laws enforced in Middleburg? . . . I thought not. . . . Those saloons along the river-front will be pretty well filled, won't they? . . . I see. Well, Teague"—he cleared his throat again—"just go down to those joints, get together all the roughs and gunmen you can find, and tell them that a lot of Rubes are coming in to Middleburg to rough-house the town. Understand? Work up their natural antagonism to the hayseeds. And tell them if this lynching is pulled off in Middleburg we'll have to start a campaign of law enforcement that 'll end in a strict closing law and a dry Sunday. Do you get me?

"Well, enlist as many of them as you can, and then tell the sheriff he's to swear them in as deputies. Post them around the outskirts, with orders to arrest every farmer they see coming into town— and search him—and lock him up if he's armed. Now listen. This is important: You have to do

this on your own. You mustn't mention me, or
the Governor, or any orders from here. Understand?
"Yes. . . . Yes. Report to me whenever you can.
It's imperative that this lynching be prevented.
If the jail won't hold them all, take their guns away
from them and turn them loose—the least danger-
ous-looking of them. . . . Yes. I'll be here. All
night if necessary. . . . I say, I'll be here all night
if necessary. Good-by."

He hung up the receiver hastily. He had heard
some one at his door. He took his typewritten report from his pocket, slipped it into a drawer, and
went to the door, looking suddenly worried. When
he was really worried he showed no signs of it.

7

"Well, Robert," he greeted Miller, holding out
his hand, "I'm obliged to you for coming. It's a
personal matter. I won't bore you with politics.
Sit down."

Miller was a baldish young man with a rather
intense flat face. He was well dressed in light-
gray clothes with a white waistcoat. His mouth
was tightened in an expression of solemnly de-
fensive self-importance. "Anything that I can do,"
he said, "of a *personal* nature"—and he emphasized
the word "personal" invidiously.

"Yes, yes," Warren interrupted. "I knew I
could rely on you. It's a family matter. I have a
daughter Meta. You know her, I think?"

Miller said, unnecessarily, "A charming girl."

"Exactly; and I have a private secretary named Pritchard. Know him?"

"I've seen him—when he came to the club for you."

"I've just found that there's practically an engagement between them. Without my consent or my knowledge. They're not even aware that I've heard of it yet."

Miller looked puzzled. Warren explained, apologetically, "I have to tell you this in order to account for what I'm going to ask you."

He had begun to walk up and down the room. Whenever he was "finessing" in an interview he moved about in this way distractingly.

"The girl," he said, "has her mother's spirit; and if I oppose her I'm afraid I'll drive her into his arms. As a matter of fact, I'm not opposed to her marrying any honest young man—such as Pritchard seems to be—if it will make her happy. But Pritchard has no prospects. He's a clever stenographer and a trustworthy private secretary, and I suppose he aspires to promotion in the public service. I like him. I'd be glad to trust my daughter's future to him if his own future weren't so uncertain."

He turned abruptly. He said, with an almost pathetic paternal distress, "I need hardly say that this—is altogether confidential."

"Oh, surely, surely," Miller replied, embarrassed.

Warren continued pacing his carpet. "It's his future. That's what worries me. If he stays with me he'll become a machine politician—a practical, professional politician. He'll have to make compromises. Unless he's an exceptionally strong character he'll become involved in things that aren't—well, pretty. You know what our sort of politics means. I don't want my daughter to marry that sort of politician."

He sat down and leaned forward on his desk to look the astⱱ ished Miller straight in the eyes. "The future is with you men. *We're* fighting a losing fight here. I want you to give this boy a chance with *you*. I want you to offer him a place as stenographer, either for the League or for you personally. I'd prefer the latter. I know I could trust him with you. I haven't so much faith in your executive committee; I know some of those men of old. But try him. If he's not what I think he is, discharge him."

Miller began, "Well, Mr. Warren—"

"I know what you're going to say," Warren interrupted, rising again to walk. "With my influence in this city I could find him a dozen places without imposing on you. But if he has any training at all it's for political life. And if he's to go into politics I want him to go in with ideals among men who have ideals. I'm not speaking to you as a politician now, you understand, but as a father. If this boy's to have my daughter's future in his hands I want them to be *clean* hands. I'd be willing to pay his salary while he's with you. . . . I know. I know. That couldn't be done without scandal. I don't propose it— And, you understand, I can't appear in the matter at all. I can't even let *him* know that I've asked this of you; because I don't want to seem to interfere in their love-affair in any way. I can't let my daughter know. I can't tell her that I'm aware of her little romance without saying either 'Yes' or 'No' to it—which I'm not prepared to do."

"Well, Mr. Warren," Miller said, "it can be easily arranged, I think. I can use a good stenographer. We're rushed with work."

The Attorney-General sat down. His face cleared with relief. "I knew I could depend on you. You see," he said, smiling benignly, "I may be too much the anxious parent. It may be just a passing boy-and-girl fancy, due to proximity. And if it *is* it 'll solve itself if we separate them. That's another reason why I want him to leave me. I'll miss him. He's a good boy. I've confided in him." This was certainly untrue. His smile broadened playfully. "I'm putting all my secrets in your hands, Robert, if you can get them from him."

Miller started to protest.

"No, no." Warren stopped him. "I'm only joking, of course. What I really want to say is this: my daughter showed a disposition to tell me of her engagement this morning. That's why I intruded on your Sunday afternoon. I want the boy to go before she tells me. Otherwise it would look as if I had got rid of him. And if you'll write him a letter offering him the position, and send it here by messenger this afternoon, you'll help me out of a difficulty that has worried me more than a campaign. Will you do it?"

"If you wish it."

"My dear boy, you put me under a great obligation. I daren't keep you here any longer, for fear he might come in and see you. It makes me feel like a conspirator." He rose, smiling. "I hope you'll not avoid me at the club, now that we're political enemies. I see you're giving me some sharp raps. I wish I were a good public speaker; I'd come back at you."

Miller held out his hand. "Mr. Warren," he said, "I'm free to confess that this little affair, this afternoon, has given me a better opinion of you than perhaps I had."

Warren patted him on the shoulder. "It hasn't changed the opinion I had of *you*, Robert. I'm a pretty good judge of character. Better, perhaps, than you are." He added, at the opened door: "And in my capacity as a judge of character let me whisper something: 'Keep an eye on your executive committee.'"

Miller lifted an eyebrow. "I'm watching them."

That was what Warren wished to know. "Good!" he said. "Good-by and good luck."

When he had closed the door he returned to his desk, got out the report on direct primaries, and began at once to read it with methodical and patient care.

8

It is obviously difficult not to misrepresent Warren in this matter. He had to get rid of Pritchard or allow his daughter to marry badly. He could not discharge the secretary without precipitating a crisis which he wished to avoid. It was wiser to provide Pritchard with a better place to which he could go. True, he had told his daughter that the parasites were deserting him to go to Miller, and if Pritchard went to Miller it would certainly outrage the girl's ideal of loyalty. But he was not compelling Pritchard to accept Miller's offer. He was leaving that to the boy's own choice. Pritchard might refuse it. He might endear himself to the girl by refusing it. He might— He might do many things if he were not what Warren thought he was.

The success of the whole stratagem depended— as Warren's success usually depended—upon his insight into the character of the man whom he was outwitting. And that insight was so accurate that it was, I think, intuitive. He knew where to reach a man as the wasp knows where to sting a beetle so as to paralyze a nerve center that nothing but careful dissection under a microscope would seem sufficient to locate. He had never dissected Pritchard, and it is scarcely worth while to do it here; but to that well-dressed and good-looking young "secretarial valet" the offer of a place with the rich and "classy" "Wardrobe" Miller would be a flattery and a temptation hard to withstand.

9

As soon as Miller's letter arrived Warren telephoned to Pritchard, put the letter in the outer office, and returned to his work. Having absorbed the report on the direct primary, he was engaged in drawing up alternative bills to be introduced at the next Legislature, if the popular demand for a direct primary became too clamorous. One of the bills provided for a direct primary with a convention that should preserve to the party machines the control of nominations. The other was a direct primary bill that would surely be declared unconstitutional by the courts because it contained no provision to prevent Republicans from voting in a Democratic primary, or *vice versa*. He was making drafts of these two bills in his small, neat handwriting—to file them for future use—when he heard Pritchard in the outer office.

He listened.

Pritchard evidently read the letter over several times. Then he brought it in hesitatingly. "Here's a funny thing," he said, giving it to Warren.

The Attorney-General glanced through it. "Well,

Will," he said, handing it back, "I'll be sorry to lose you, but I don't want to stand in your way, and this salary is much higher—to be frank with you—than I could get the state to allow me for a secretary."

"It isn't the salary," Pritchard put in.

"No. I understand that, of course," Warren said. "But the salary should be considered. And added to the greater prospects of advancement—"

"It's the idea," Pritchard said, "of going over to Miller."

Warren looked surprised. "Miller? Oh, I see. Yes. I see. Of course, in a sense, we *are* opposed to each other; but Mr. Miller is a man whom I greatly respect, though we differ in our opinions of what is wise in matters of public policy. And I don't suppose for a moment that he had any idea —or thought that you would lend yourself, if he *had*, to any betrayal of confidence—"

"No, no. I didn't mean *that*," Pritchard cried in confusion.

Warren glanced at his watch. "Have you consulted any of your family?"

"No-o."

"You should talk it over with *them*. They're the ones best able to decide. And if you give me twenty-four hours' notice, I'll have Miss Davis relieve you until I can find some one to take her place. I'll be sorry to lose you, Will," he said, in the tone of an employer accepting a resignation, "but I've long felt that a boy of your abilities should be seeking a larger field. In a few years you'll be thinking of marrying. I know, of course, that it can't have entered your mind yet." Pritchard flushed. "You're still too young—and unable to support a wife. But you must prepare for such things while there's time, so as not to be taken unawares. To marry such a girl as a boy of your character would naturally aspire to you'll have to be something more than a stenographer." He was reaching for his pen. "I'll be here late, but you needn't come back. I'll see you in the morning."

Pritchard folded and refolded the letter. "Well," he said at last.

"And put the catch on the door as you go out," Warren dismissed him.

10

He knew that if Pritchard consulted his family they would use every argument to persuade him to accept the higher salary. He knew also that Pritchard would have to go home to dinner before he saw Meta. That is what he had been calculating when he glanced at his watch before asking, "Have you consulted your family?" And if he was practising some duplicity, he had the excuse that Pritchard had begun that game.

He went back to his work on the direct primary bills. Every now and then he was interrupted by messages from Teague, the detective, who 'phoned to report progress. The roughs of Middleburg had enlisted under the sheriff eagerly. "Say, Ben," Warren asked, "how about that river-front gang that you've been after? You know them when you see them, don't you? . . . Then why can't you manage things so as to have some of them sworn in as deputies, and grab any one of them that brings in a prisoner, and lock *him* up, too? Eh?" And later, when Teague reported not only that the Rubes were being gathered in, but that two desperadoes of the river-front gang had been held, on John Doe warrants, with their prisoners, Warren chuckled: "Good work, Teague. Look out, now. Be careful or you'll have both parties storming your jail."

He telephoned to his daughter to say that he would not be home to dinner, and the cheerfulness of her disappointment seemed to betray that she was counting on his absence for an opportunity to see Pritchard. He telephoned again some hours later, when he hoped that Pritchard would be with her, and her voice was shaken with an agitation that he understood. By this time he had finished his work on his direct primary bills and he locked them away in a private drawer. He even allowed himself a cigar, and sat back smoking it with a misered satisfaction, his eyes on the shining metal of his telephone, waiting.

When Teague reported that the lynching had been averted—that thirty-odd of the would-be lynchers were in jail, with five members of the river-front gang—and that the negroes and these five criminals were being taken out of the county for safe-keeping—Warren said, heartily: "Teague, you've done a good day's work. Have Judge Keiser hear those cases in the morning, and have · him fine them for carrying weapons. Nothing must be said about the attempted lynching or about your part in preventing it. You understand me? The situation is too delicate for publicity. Good night."

He called up his daughter immediately and asked her to have a late supper prepared for him, and invited her to come for him with the car. Her voice was toneless and dejected. He went back to his cigar and his waiting.

11

When he heard her knock he threw away the cigar, passed his handkerchief across his lips, and opened the door in an absent-minded manner, looking back at his desk.

She came in with a black lace scarf on her head, holding herself stiffly erect.

He began to gather up his papers. "Sit down a minute, my dear," he said, abstractedly.

She sat down on the edge of a chair. She did not look at him.

"Pritchard is leaving me now," he announced. "He's going to Miller, too." She did not speak.

9

He glanced at her quickly and appraised her set expression as a girlish look of high tragedy. He said, with cheerfulness: "I suppose he thinks the old ship is sinking. I imagine we'll disappoint him there. I'm not done yet."

"Father," she said, in an unexpected voice, "I want to go away."

He sat down. He asked, "What has happened?"

She replied, simply: "I'm not happy here. I want to go away."

"Well, my dear," he temporized, with a patronizing suavity, "you're to do whatever you wish. We're going to see that you *are* happy. What's the trouble?"

But suavity did not succeed. She shook her head, looking away from him as if to evade his insincerity. "I can't talk of it. I want to go away."

He tried another trick. He asked, "Are *you* deserting me, too?"

She kept her eyes averted.

"You're all I have," he said.

She did not reply. He got up from his desk, crossed the room to her, and took her hand paternally. His face did not betray his gratification in feeling her missing ring on her finger. He said: "I don't want to ask you anything that you don't want me to know. But—perhaps I could help."

She turned away from him to hide her tears. "No," she said, choked. "No. It doesn't matter."

"You've been disappointed in some one?"

"Ye-e-es."

"Some one you were fond of?"

She nodded her head, unable to speak.

"One of your girl friends?"

"No. No. I don't want to talk about it."
She wiped her eyes hastily. "I should have told
you long ago. I couldn't. He knew you wouldn't
—approve."

"And you? You knew it?"

She said, "I didn't understand."

"Is that all?" he asked. "Are you concealing
nothing else?"

"Yes," she said, "I am. We quarreled because
he said you weren't—honest—in politics."

"Ah!" He dropped her hand. "That's it."

She waited, without speaking, watching him.

He began to walk about very slowly. Then he
sat again at his desk and gazed at her thoughtfully.

"Tell me first," he asked, "do you want him
back?"

She answered at last: "No. . . . He's not what I
thought he was."

"If he *had* been," he said, "he wouldn't have
been afraid to tell me of your engagement."

"Yes."

"You don't like cowards?"

"No," she said, deeply. "No."

"You're not a coward yourself."

"I *have* been."

"And you want to go away because you can't

be happy here if what he says of me is true. Is that it?"

She caught her breath. "Yes," she said.

"You're afraid it *is* true."

She stared at him, her lips trembling, white. "No."

"Don't be a coward," he said, rising to confront her.

She tried to swallow the catch in her throat and her eyes were full of pain.

"He told you the truth," he said, harshly. He took his papers from his pocket and tossed them on the desk. "Now we can go away together."

"Father!"

He turned on her. "My life here has been what the necessities of my position have made it. It hasn't been honest in the sense that *you* mean. And it can't be if I continue here. Very well. Let's be done with it, then. Let some one else struggle and scheme and be the scapegoat. I've sacrificed—a great deal. I'm not going to sacrifice my daughter's confidence."

She had stumbled across the room to him, weeping, with her hands out to him. He took her in his arms.

"My dear," he said, patting her on the shoulder, "give me a week to wind up my office here—to get the Governor to accept my resignation—to make my plans to go East. He's been wanting me to take charge of his campaign for the Presidential nomination. I'll do it. Politics in this state are small and corrupt. We'll escape from them into the national field and the larger issues. You'll come with me to Washington, and if you never reign like another Dolly Madison in the White House, at least you'll be the friend of the Dolly Madison who *does*. And you'll never be ashamed of your old dad."

"I'm not ashamed of him," she sobbed.

"No," he said, "but you might have been if I'd stayed here. Come along now. I'm as hungry as if I'd been to a funeral."

12

And that was why Warren resigned from the control of his native state and went to his career in Washington. Moreover, it is why his career in Washington followed the lines that it did. Warren never philosophized; he handled facts as an artisan handles his tools; but if he *had* philosophized, his theory of life would probably have been something like this: "There is no justice, there is no morality, in nature or in natural laws; justice and morality are laws only of human society. But society, national life, and all civilization are subject in their larger aspects to natural laws—which contradict morality and outrage justice—and the statesman has to move with those laws and direct his people in accordance with them, despite the lesser by-laws of morality and justice."

His daughter abided by the by-laws. He had to conceal from her that he did not abide by them. He had to conceal it from the public. "The American people," he once said in confidence, "still believe in Santa Claus. They believe that if they're good, and wash their faces every morning, and do as teacher tells them, prosperity and well-being will come down the chimney to them. They don't realize that some one has to pay for the full stocking, and that they're that *some one*."

Consequently, in his first participation in national affairs, he kept behind the scenes. He was the stage director of the convention that nominated his Governor for the Presidency, but Warren's name was not even on the program. After he had accepted his place as Attorney-General in Washington he remained unknown, except to the inner higher circle of politics. It was not until he became Secretary of State—in the third year of his President's administration—that he grew conspicuous. Then his daughter married the son of a man who was certainly able to protect her from the dangers of a competitive social system (the real danger was that the social system would not be able to protect itself from *him*) and Warren was at once violently criticized and viciously lampooned. It was for his daughter's sake that he ascended from this persecution into the perpetual felicity and peace of the Supreme Court. Since that translation—concerning Thomas Wales Warren—"nothing but good."

There he sits, listening benignly to an eternity of argument, with his jaw peacefully relaxed and with a curious protrusion of the lips occasionally when his mind wanders and—under cover of his judicial robe—he fingers blissfully a loose button on his coat.

FROM THE LIFE

Benjamin McNeil Murdock

BENJAMIN McNEIL MURDOCK

1

MURDOCK is not yet in *Who's Who*, though he ought to be. He has produced a potato as big as a turnip, the "Murdock Manitoba," and a huge peach with a stone no larger than a cherry-pit, the "Cantaloup Alberta." These alone might not entitle him to anything more than honorable mention in a seed-catalogue, but the experiments by which he achieved his potato and his peach have had another issue—they threaten to modify the Darwinian theory of the origin of species.

This is a serious matter—more serious than has been apprehended by the newspaper men who have been head-lining Murdock as the "Burbank of New Jersey." He has obtained his new species not merely by cross-fertilization and encouraging "sports," but by opposing his plants with adversities which they have had to overcome in order to survive. He got the idea, I understand, by observing how flowers will grow a long stalk in order to reach sunlight; but from that beginning he has worked to the point of proving an adaptiveness in plants that amounts almost to unconscious intelligence. Consequently he appears to find the cause of variation—and hence the origin of species—less in the outer pressure of the plant's environment than in the inner effort of the organism to adapt itself to changing conditions.

That, as I say, is a serious matter. It casts a doubt on the whole mechanistic theory of evolution. It brings back into the non-sentient world a long-banished creative intelligence. It permits a pan-psychic view of the universe that is mystical. Unless I am much mistaken, the name of Benjamin Mc-Neil Murdock is likely to be one of the conspicuous names of the century, and his little farm in the Washington Valley may even become the storm-center of a controversy as world-shaking as the one that thundered over Darwin's pigeon-houses fifty years ago. You may care nothing whatever about the mechanistic theory, the origin of species, or the cause of evolution, but before long you will probably be as curious about Murdock as your father was about Darwin—as curious as I have become about Murdock since I found out what he was at.

2

For two years, from my summer windows on the southern slope of Wauchock Hill, I had looked down on the Murdock Farm below us and seen him pottering around, with his "Dago" assistants, among his hothouses and his cold-frames. I had watched him with an intent but idle observation.

You know, from your school-days, that when you are trying to write, on a blond June morning, at a task that drags and dawdles in a springing world, there is nothing too insignificant to take your eye and captivate your interest. I had watched Murdock as absorbedly as if he were a red spider making a web on my window-screen. Yet I never intelligently saw what he was doing.

I saw merely a lank, commonplace, and simple-looking farmer, going about his chores in faded blue overalls, a seersucker shirt, and a straw hat of the kind that is called a "cow's breakfast." I was aware that his neighbors thought him crazy. I had heard it said that he talked to his vegetables in order to make them grow in the way he wished. I knew that he could not talk to his vegetables less than he talked to his neighbors; that if it were not for his wife, he would be as much cut off from human intercourse and understanding as one of his own prodigious potatoes. Everything about him—except her—seemed entirely ordinary and bucolic. We had only one question to puzzle ourselves with, "How did he ever come to marry *her*—or she *him?*"

Then I learned, from a chance reference in a technical review, that Murdock's experiments were professionally considered as important as those of Hugo de Vries; that Professor Jeddes accepted him as a successful exemplar of "a needed renewal of the rustic point of view," or, more fully, as "a naturalist who grasps not only the mechanical and urban viewpoint, but the rustic and physiological one, theorizing neither in terms of the mere mechano-morphism of the physicists and the chemists nor of the puzzled mysticism of the vitalist philosophers as yet befogged by their urban environment or bewildered by reaction from it"—whatever that may mean.

It meant to Jeddes, and to the reviewer, that "Pasteur was not the last thinking peasant." And the name of Pasteur put me to the blush. Had we been looking down, in ignorant superiority from Wauchock Hill, upon the profound experiments of a new Pasteur? Apparently we had.

3

I carried the review to Mrs. Murdock. She had already seen it. She was her husband's amanuensis, and kept the daily record of his experiments, and wrote whatever was procured from him for publication. She acted as his interpreter, at our meeting, very gracefully; and what she interpreted was chiefly his silence. In a *Mayflower* arm-chair beside the open door, with his garden behind him, he sat smiling amiably at us, unembarrassed, but as quiet as a sea-captain, his feet planted firmly on the floor in leather slippers, his hands resting on the chair-arms, his trowel in one hand and his haycock hat in the other, his bony head and shoulders as gravely immovable as a mountain, with an air about him of something elemental, sun-browned, weather-beaten, and placidly but incommunicably wise.

She had been trying to write for him, and she was worried by a sense of her shortcomings. She appealed to me for advice with that respect which you feel for a writer whose works you have never read. He listened to us as indulgently as Emerson contemplating a dancing-lesson, and I was relieved when he rose quietly and stole out.

It appeared that she was a college graduate, educated in modern languages, a studious reader, fond of serious fiction and able to pass judgment on it with cheerful common sense. She seemed to have an idea that there must be in writing, as there is in golf, a proper stance, a correct stroke, a championship method. She had evidently been an athletic young girl. She was now perhaps thirty, neither handsome nor graceful, but interesting and individual. I had seen her walking with a long-armed stride, in low heels, with the powerful shoulder slouch of a tennis-player; now she sat listening intently, leaning forward, with her arms folded on her knees, smiling apologetically at the eagerness and the ignorance of her own questions. Her eyes were spirited. Her face was not. It did not express her. She looked out from behind its too large and immobile features as if knowing that they came between her and your sympathy, and as if straining to hold you to her eyes, which I found frankly magnetic.

There was something aristocratic about her easy simplicity, yet she seemed not out of place in the homely room of that low-ceilinged farm-house. I guessed that she was responsible for its furnishings and decoration, because it was done in the flat tints and simple fittings of a sophisticated taste. I left with the conviction that she and her husband were a remarkable couple.

4

It was a conviction that did not endure. There was nothing in their past to support it. Imagine: he had been born on that farm some thirty-five years before; he had had no schooling until he was nine; then, a hulking, slow-minded boy, he had joined the infants' class at the Wauchock village school, down the valley, and, in the ordinary course of education, he had progressed to the public school at Centerbrook. When he left school he went to work in a grocery at Centerbrook, and he moved from there to New York City, where he became bookkeeper for the Perry-Felton Company on William Street. During the years that he lived in New York he returned to his home only once— when he came to the funeral of his parents and the trial of the hired man who was found guilty of having murdered them.

At the conclusion of that trial he sold all the farm stock and implements at auction, locked up the house, and returned to New York. Several years later he reappeared, evidently with money, modernized the old place, and settled down to an absurd sort of gardening, raising weeds in hot-houses, and generally behaving like a silent and unapproachable eccentric. Within a month of his return he married Ruth Young, a moneyed girl of Centerbrook whom nobody in the Washington Valley knew he had been courting.

And there was nothing remarkable about her past, either. She was the daughter of a Charles Washington Young who had owned the stone-quarry near Wauchock in Murdock's boyhood days. Young and his family had moved to Centerbrook while Murdock was still at the village school, and Ruth and he had been at the public school together, but it was not known that there had been anything between them. Her father had made a great deal of money, first out of ballast stone, then as a rail-road contractor, and finally as a banker and first citizen of the county-seat. He had sent his daughter to Wellesley. His death brought her home to the pretentious Colonial country house which he had built—after the model of Mount Vernon—on the top of the mountain between Centerbrook and the Washington Valley. From there she married, against her mother's wishes. None of her relatives came to see her as Mrs. Murdock. Her husband, it seemed, was not "accepted" in Center-brook, New Jersey.

Now I ask you, could anything seem more ordi-

10   [135]

nary than such a history? Could you believe that,
beneath the superficies of these incidents, there was
hidden one of those romances that life delights to
invent, perversely, in order to confound the realities of fiction? No. No more could I. Murdock
might be a great naturalist, a peasant genius, another Pasteur, but there was obviously nothing in
him to repay prospecting by a short-story writer.
I gave him up. And then, unexpectedly, in gossip
about the details of that murder trial, I came on
traces of fiction's precious metal, followed it, placer-
mining, up the course of his history, and located
an incredibly rich mother-lode.

5

Take, first, the story of the murder as I dug it
out—and found it pay dirt.

In the fall of 1910, during the hunting season,
two shots were heard from the Murdock farm about
midday. The neighbors thought nothing of it, or
supposed that old Murdock was killing rabbits.
In the middle of the afternoon the next-door neighbor, Mrs. Heins—a woman who was always "running the road," as they say in the valley—came to
the Murdock kitchen door to borrow some mustard,
as an emetic for her son, who had been eating
"musharoons" that were behaving as if they were
toadstools. She got no answer to her knock. In
her anxiety about her son she opened the door to
call through the house, and she saw old Murdock

collapsed in his seat at the table "in a mucks of blood," and Mrs. Murdock lying across an inner threshold of the room "all of a heap an' bleedin' like a pig-killin'." She ran screaming back to her son. He hurried to the Murdock farm, and she went spreading the alarm down the valley.

"By gosh!" he said, afterward, "it *cured* me, it did. I never knowed I was sick till it was all over —an' then I *wasn't*."

Murdock's hired man was missing. He was at once suspected. And naturally so. Murdock's hired men were notorious. He had been in the habit of engaging any tramp who came to his kitchen door, and, almost invariably, after working a few weeks, the man disappeared with anything that happened to be unprotected in the valley on the day of his departure. The news "Ol' Murdock's man's moved on" became the signal for a general stock-taking in the vicinity.

The last man had been caught with a stolen shot-gun under his mattress before he had time to flee, and he was sent to jail as a vengeance on all those others who had escaped. His successor was a half-witted wanderer who said he was on his way to visit "Roseyvelt." Old Murdock told him that Roosevelt was dead, and the man—with his mainspring broken—seemed unable to go any farther. Murdock hired him for his board and a package of fine-cut a week. Now *he* had "moved."

Hunting parties with shot-guns started out in

all directions to seek his trail. He was found in the Murdock wood-lot, innocently cutting cedar-trees for fence-posts. He had been there since early morning; the shells of four hard-boiled eggs showed where he had eaten his luncheon, and the trees that he had cut and stripped were numerous enough to occupy a day's industry.

Heins said, suspiciously, "That's more wood 'n I ever seen a hired man cut in *one* day."

The man replied: "I dunno. Some of 'em, mebbe, was yeste'day's cuttin'."

Heins grumbled, "I thought so." And that conversation, related again and again, was Heins's contribution to the solution of the murder mystery.

At first they did not tell the hired man why they were looking for him, and he resented their questions, sulkily continuing his work. But as soon as he heard of the murder he dropped his ax and ran through the woods to the house, and, coming suddenly on the scene in the kitchen, he fell back down the kitchen steps in a sort of fit. When he had been revived with a drink from a hunter's pocket flask his innocence was conceded.

He could not be persuaded to enter the house. He retreated to the barn, sat down on the wheel of a mowing-machine, and told and retold his story, over and over, to a constantly changing group of men, women, and children. By sundown the whole valley was there, and all the villagers from Wauchock. They wandered around the house, the barn, the front yard, the side garden, the woodpile, and the outhouses like a colony of disturbed ants, gathering in two large clusters around the kitchen and the barn, nodding, shaking hands, conversing in low tones together, exchanging opinions and passing on gossip. By the time the sheriff of the county arrived a complete theory of the crime had been gathered for him. It was this:

Murdock's old hound had died two days before. Poisoned, no doubt. By whom? By the murderer. Who was he? Well, Murdock had heard, in Centerbrook, that the hired man who had stolen the shotgun was out of jail and threatening him. Why? Because, according to the man's story, he had not stolen the gun; Murdock had stolen it and "planted" it on him.

"He's been drunk down there," Murdock told his neighbor, Heins. "If he comes bleatin' around here I'll blow him full o' buckshot."

But the man's threats and the death of the watchdog alarmed the household. Murdock bolted his doors and windows at night and slept up-stairs on the floor of an unfinished room of the attic, with his gun beside him. And he carried the gun with him when he went to work in the fields.

That gun—a double-barreled shot-gun—was nowhere to be found. He had evidently stood it beside the kitchen door when he sat down to dinner. And the murderer had crept up, under cover of the kitchen weeds, reached the gun unseen, shot Murdock in the back as he sat at the table, and shot Mrs. Murdock point-blank as she ran in from the other room to see what had happened. They had both been dead for hours when Mrs. Heins came on them.

The sheriff drove off at once to send out an alarm for the jailbird. A deputy took charge of the preparations for the inquest and cleared the house of sight-seers. They moved on to the Heinses', and the hired man went with them.

6

In all this there was no thought of Murdock's son, Ben. Or if any one thought of him it was only to wonder where he was and who would notify him. The whole valley knew that he had quarreled with his father, that he had not been home for years, that if his mother heard from him she did not mention it. And no one recognized him when, toward midnight, a tall stranger came to the Heinses' kitchen door with a suit-case in his hand. He stood scrutinizing the group of late-stayers in the lamplight around the kitchen table, looked from them to the hired man who sat alone smoking beside the range, and asked, abruptly, "Are you Murdock's man?"

They supposed he was a detective. He wore city blacks and a black felt hat and a starched collar. The hired man slowly turned his head—a classical head, the head and bronzed profile of a Cæsar on a

Roman coin. And the stranger said to him, "I'm Ben Murdock."

That was all Murdock *did* say. For the rest of the evening he listened. And he listened in a peculiar way. After the first quick glance at this one or that one with whom he shook hands he looked past them, with a troubled frown, as if dissatisfied, and thereafter he avoided meeting their eyes in a direct gaze.

It turned out to be a habit of manner. He had a trick of looking at the chest of the person that stood talking to him; and when they were all sitting again he looked at their knees or at their feet, with no expression of shyness or self-consciousness. Only the hired man's face he studied thoughtfully, in an absent-minded muse. And the hired man, smoking apart, with his air of distinguished vacancy, remained beside the greasy stove in silence, refusing to answer even when they spoke to him.

"He's sort o' dumb," they explained, in the idiom of the valley, meaning by "dumb" half-witted.

Ben Murdock showed little emotion over the story of the murder. Once, when they were telling about the man who had been sent to jail for stealing the shot-gun, he took out his handkerchief and wiped his forehead as if it were wet with perspiration. And a moment later, when they were telling how the other hired men had invariably turned out to be thieves, he suddenly raised to them a bewildered face of suffering. It moved Mrs. Heins to take him away from the visitors by offering to make up a bed for him on the parlor sofa. He accepted the bed without thanks and left the kitchen without saying good night.

No one was offended. They took it as proof that he was still one of them; that, although he had acquired city clothes and a city pallor, he had not descended to any city insincerities of formal politeness.

He was up and out before breakfast, wandering alone around the parental farm. He ate his breakfast silently, and no one intruded upon him with any social expression of sympathy. Mrs. Heins saw that he had food and drink; the others talked around him as if he were not there. They merely made it a point not to speak of the murder. When he had finished he asked where the nearest telephone could be reached, and went out to find it. As soon as he was gone the hired man drifted in from nowhere for his breakfast.

In about an hour Murdock came back with the sheriff and asked for this hired man. He had gravitated naturally to the barn. They went after him. "Come along, Jack," the sheriff said. "We want you to show us where you were workin' when this happened."

His name was not "Jack." He was anonymous. But he accepted "Jack," as he accepted "Bill" or "Bo." indifferently.

He struck out across the fields to Murdock's wood-lot, and they followed him. As they went Murdock pointed out significantly to the sheriff the fence-line between his father's farm and Heins's; it was a thick hedge of small cedars, sassafras, blackberry brambles, and poison ivy, and it ran from the Murdock garden-patch to the edge of the woods toward which they were walking. The sheriff looked at it and nodded.

They entered the wood-lot at a pole gate, came to a brook where cows were pasturing on a little clearing of grass and brambles, crossed the stream on stepping-stones, and followed a cow-path through the underbrush into the taller timber.

The hired man stopped at the first of the cedars that he had cut down. "Yep," the sheriff said. "Where's the rest?"

The rest were in a bend of the stream at the foot of a raw bank of red shale that confined the creek at flood-time. The sheriff looked them over. "Well?" he said, inquiringly, to Murdock.

Murdock pointed to a large flat stone at the foot of the bank. "Tell him to turn that over."

He spoke to the sheriff, but he was looking at the hired man.

"What for?" the sheriff asked.

"Tell him to do it."

The man apparently had not heard. He was standing aside, gazing strangely at a shrub of scarlet sumac in front of him.

The sheriff ordered: "Here! See that stone? Turn it over."

He got no answer.

"Here, you!" he said. "Look-a-here!" and took him by the shoulder.

He found the man trembling hysterically under his hand, and he cried, "What! What the hell?" looking at Murdock.

Murdock made a vague, unhappy, pitiful gesture, turning away.

The sheriff strode up to the stone and rolled it over. It covered the mouth of a rabbit-burrow and the shining butt-plate of a shot-gun that had been forced into the hole. There was a moment of deadly silence. Then the maniac, falling on his knees before the sumac, made the motions of washing his hands in the reddened foliage. "Blood!" he said, hoarsely. "Blood! He killed Roseyvelt!"

He made no attempt to escape. He let the sheriff take him back to the farm-house, hitch up a team, and drive him to the county jail. To all their questions he only mumbled, "He killed Roseyvelt!"

7

It came out at his trial that in the middle of corn-husking he had heard that Roosevelt was alive. He had wanted to leave at once on his pilgrimage to Oyster Bay. Old Murdock had said: "Alive nuthin'. I killed him myself. His body's hid in the attic over your bedroom." And, haunted insanely by that secret of the attic overhead, he had killed Murdock out of revenge.

What did not come out at the trial—though the whole valley knew it—was this:

The deputy sheriff, searching the hired man's bedroom after his arrest, climbed through the trap in the ceiling of the room and found in a corner of the loft a collection of farm tools, axes, dishes, crowbars, pots, and household articles that had been hidden there under a pile of old sacks. At first he thought that he had simply discovered evidence against the man who had stolen the gun. But when the neighbors were called in to claim their property it appeared that some of the things had been stolen years before. Murdock's words, "The body's hidden in the attic over your bedroom," established Murdock's guilt. He had been a kleptomaniac. He had stolen all the things which his hired men had been accused of stealing. He had been doing it for years, and no one had suspected him.

Except, possibly, his son Ben. Old Heins recalled that once, years before, when Ben was a small boy, a new sickle had disappeared from the Heins tool-house. He was looking for it in his fields when he saw Murdock and his son over the fence, and asked them if they had noticed the sickle lying about. Murdock said, "No," but young Ben said nothing. He, too, was "kind o' dumb" in those days. He went back to his father's barn and reappeared with the sickle. His father demanded where he had found it. He said he had found it under the corn-stalks in the barn. How had he known it was there? He said he hadn't known—he had "just guessed." His father cried: "Guessed! Did you steal that sickle?" And in the end he beat the boy in a rage, shouting: "I'll teach you to steal! I'll teach you!"

Now, in the account of the murder, there was one detail that had interested and puzzled me. When the sheriff asked Ben Murdock how he had thought of looking for the shot-gun under that particular stone in the wood-lot, Murdock replied that he had "just guessed" that it was there. And when I heard old Heins's story of the finding of the sickle I was struck by the coincidence. I guessed something myself. And I began to verify it by gathering together every anecdote, every reminiscence, every bit of gossip that I could get about Ben Murdock anywhere. When I had enough to establish my theory of him I broached it to Mrs. Murdock one evening, after dinner, and I got it confirmed, first by what she told of him, then by what he admitted—with an odd scientific detachment, as if he were talking of some one else—and at last by what they both related together concerning the incredible incidents that led to their marriage.

8

As far as I can make out, the whole thing began in the autumn of 1893, when Murdock was about nine years old. And it began with the visit of a patent-medicine vender who drove into Wauchock from the direction of Pluckamin, in a gipsy wagon with two pinto ponies, selling an "Indian Herb Remedy" that was guaranteed to cure all known diseases, including baldness. He, in buckskins, and his wife, in a Carmen costume, gave a free entertainment of songs and sleight-of-hand, roping, knife-throwing, and Spanish dancing, at night, by the light of their kerosene-torches, and in the intervals between their acts they sold their Indian Herb Remedy.

Young Ben Murdock had been sent to the village by his mother to get a stone vinegar-jug filled with kerosene for the household lamps. He found the yard in front of the school-house flaring with torchlights, and over the head of a silent audience he saw the long-haired Westerner, with a braided mustache, ballyhooing his medicine. The boy drew nearer. He ended by making his way into the front row, against the little platform on which Carmen was finishing a bored fandango to the castanets, while her husband praised his cure-all.

Nobody was buying. The faker, searching the upturned faces for a customer, saw the boy. Ben had been suffering all day with toothache; his face was swollen, and that may have attracted the man's notice. Mrs. Murdock had tried to ease her son's pain with horse liniment, a few drops of which she had put on the tooth itself; there had probably been some narcotic in the dose, for Ben had been feeling dazed ever since, and his dull-eyed, stupefied look may have struck the faker.

At any rate, he came to the edge of the platform and said: "Well now, here's some one needs this great nosterum. Eh, sonny? Come up here." And taking Ben under the arm, he lifted him to the stage.

The crowd laughed. Benjamin McNeil Murdock was then an overgrown young dolt, shock-haired and open-mouthed, in a torn shirt and a pair of his father's patched overalls, and nothing else. He had no hat. He was barefooted. The medicine man held him by the shoulder and he hung his head sheepishly. He was supposed to be half-witted, and he looked it.

"What's the matter, bub?" the man asked. "Sick?"

Ben did not answer. The man put a firm, cool hand under his chin, tilted his head back, and studied him.

"Toothache, eh?" he said. "Fine! This here's a suverin remedy for toothache. Also fer trouble with the eyes. This boy," he told the audience, "is near dead with toothache, an' it's afflictin' his eyes."

Ben began to blink. He was held facing a kerosene-torch that shone directly in his eyes.

"He can't look at a light without feelin' sleepy. He can't keep his eyes open. This here pain has worn him out. He's dog-tired. His eyes is tired."

Ben's eyes had closed.

"Bring me a chair here, Mirey." His wife brought the chair. "There! Sit down on that. You're dog-tired."

Ben sank weakly into the seat.

"Now," he said, "first we'll cure them eyes." And, pretending to pour some of his remedy into the palm of his hand, he began to stroke the boy into a mesmeric sleep. "This boy," he kept saying, "is worn out with pain. It's passin'. It's passin'. Just like he was fallin' asleep an' fergettin' it. That's it. Just like you was fallin' asleep, sonny. Fallin' asleep."

When he saw from Ben's regular breathing that he was unconscious he announced, "We'll now cure the toothache." And he proceeded to rub Ben's swollen cheek very gently with an application of the Indian Herb Remedy. "The results," he said, "is almost *instantous*. The sufferin' begins to stop. Like you'd slep' it off. Peelin' better?"

He bent down. Ben's lips moved inaudibly.

"Yes. He says he's feelin' better."

His wife was standing beside him, holding the bottle of medicine, watching anxiously, alarmed because the boy had "gone under" so quickly. She poured out a spoonful of the remedy and offered it to her husband.

"All right, now," he said. "This 'll do the trick. This 'll fix it. Open yer mouth."

Ben opened it, with his eyes shut.

"That's right. Open yer eyes, too. They're all right. They're better. That's the way. Now swallow this down. Tastes good, eh?"

Ben nodded.

"Good. Now you feel better. Don't you? Yes? Well, tell 'em how you feel."

And Ben said in a strange, high voice, "I feel a hull lot better."

"Good. Toothache gone, too?"

Ben nodded.

"Good. Now, to show you people this 's no fake—" He took the boy's swollen cheek between thumb and forefinger and pinched it till the spot showed white. Ben did not flinch. "Couldn't 'a' done that five minutes ago, eh? He'd 'a' howled. That swellin'—that 'll go down in about an hour er so. Now." He corked the bottle. "You take this, sonny, an' run home to yer mom, an' tell her if she ever has a toothache what to do with it. Go right to sleep as soon 's you get home, an' you'll wake up in the mornin' feelin' like a nest o' young robins, an' ready to start right off to school. Run along." He was helping Ben from the platform. "Right home. Get in out o' the night air. I don't want no neuraligy to strike into that jaw o' yourn. I want you at school as a proof to the great Indian Herb Remedy. Now, my Christian frien's, the price o' this suverin cure fer sufferin' is fifty cents, but on this occasion—"

He watched Ben making his way through the

crowd with the bottle of medicine clasped to his bosom.

"The price o' this mirac'lous med'cine to-night is a quarter *of* a dollar. Thank you, partner. Here we are. Who's next?"

And Ben stumbled off down the road toward his home in the dark, like a sleep-walker, while all Wauchock behind him reached out its hands for that mirac'lous Herb Remedy.

It was a very dazed-looking boy who returned to the Murdock kitchen, carrying a bottle of patent medicine instead of a jug of kerosene. And at his mother's cry of, "What you got there? Where's the coal-oil?" he put the bottle on the kitchen table, sat down unsteadily, and dropped forward, his head on his arms, in a sleep from which she could not wake him. She put him to bed, scolding him distractedly.

He woke up in the morning clear-minded, but with no recollection of what had happened after the man had offered to cure his toothache. No one suspected that he had been hypnotized. When Wauchock found that its Herb Remedy was no cure for anything—not even for thirst—they supposed that Ben, being a "plum' idiot," had allowed the faker to persuade him that his toothache was better when it wasn't. Moreover, the toothache returned, and his mother had to take him to the dentist in Centerbrook to have the tooth out. His reputation as the village idiot was entirely

11   [161]

established by the incident. He supported it in confirmatory silence.

9

And yet something had changed in him. As soon as he woke up that morning he said to his mother, "I want to go to school." She took him to the dentist instead. A few days later he went to his father and said, sulkily, "I want to go to school."

He had never been sent to school—and the authorities had not insisted that he should be sent—because it was understood that he was too "dumb" to learn. His father had given him that reputation; he wanted the boy at home to watch the cows; there were no secure fences on the Murdock farm, and Ben spent his days in the wood and pasture-lot as stupidly as a watch-dog. The father himself was "queer." He had not been quite right since he had fallen from a load of hay, struck his head, and been unconscious for three days "right smack in the middle o' the best hayin' weather."

He replied, now: "School nuthin'. Might 's well send those calfs to school. Go 'n' do yer chores."

The boy went back to his work, and nothing more was said about school. But the incident of Heins and the sickle followed; and that night, milking in the stable, Ben took up a pitchfork and said, menacingly, to his father, "You lemme go to school er I'll tell 'at you're stealin' things an' hidin' 'em in the hayloft."

He has explained, relating the incident: "I don't know what had come over me. I don't know how I knew what he'd been doing. I just said it —and then I felt as if I'd known it all along. I remember he looked at me as though I'd tried to stab him with the fork, and he dropped the milk-pail and ran out of the stable."

He was allowed to go to school. And very little good it seemed to do him. He was incurably dull at his books, although he was permitted to labor over them at home as much as he pleased. His father never interfered with him in any way; they hardly spoke. What his mother thought of it I do not know. Murdock has never talked of her. To the neighbors she seems to have been merely a lean, hard-faced, meager woman who struggled through a life of unceasing but inefficient drudgery, handicapped by the stupidity and shift-lessness of her "men-folk."

10

Of Ben Murdock in the village school I have found only one anecdote, and I got that from Sheriff Steiner in talking with him about the murder case. It appears that Steiner was rather a bully in his school-days, and he "picked on Benny" as a proper butt, until one day in the winter Ben said to him, "You hit me again an' I'll tell 'em you're wearin' yer sister's made-over underclothes."

As the sheriff says: "It knocked me all of a heap. I'd 'a' died rather 'n have any one know it. You know the way a boy feels 'bout things like that. Well, I let Benny alone after that, you bet."

And of this incident I could get no explanation. Murdock did not remember it. He did not remember that Steiner had "picked" on him. He believed that the sheriff was confusing him with some other boy.

What he did remember was this: When he began to study arithmetic he was unknowingly a "mathematical prodigy," like the famous Gauss and the more famous Ampère. He used to do a problem by first putting down the answer and then working back to the solution. How he knew the answers he cannot now explain. "I lost the trick after a while," he says. "At first I could do it sometimes, and then sometimes I couldn't. And then I lost it altogether. I can still add up a column of figures by running my eye up it and keeping my mind a blank. The figures add themselves for me if I don't interfere with them. That's how I came to be a bookkeeper."

He lost, for a time, even that small remnant of his ability as a "calculating boy" during his years at the Centerbrook school. And he lost it as a result of a whipping which the teacher gave him.

It seems that the class had been set an unusually

difficult problem to do at home, and Ben arrived with the correct answer for it. He was sent to the blackboard to write out his solution, and there was nothing correct in his demonstration except the final line. The teacher accused him of having found the example and its answer in some book of arithmetic, and Ben in self-defense had to explain that he had "just guessed" it.

"Well," the teacher said, sarcastically, "let us see you guessing. Turn your back to the board. Now tell me what are the three figures I've written on it."

Ben stood a moment, staring at the grinning class. The sympathetic face of a little girl in a back row caught his eye. And suddenly he gave the figures correctly.

"You're cheating!" the teacher cried. "You saw them reflected somewhere."

"No, I didn't," Ben pleaded. "I guessed them."

"Very good," the teacher said. "Keep your eyes on the floor and guess *these!*"

But by this time the boy was so bewildered and the class was in such an uproar that he could not have guessed his own name. He named three figures at random. Not one of them was right. "Hold out your hand," the teacher ordered.

When school was dismissed and Ben started, swollen-eyed, on his walk over the mountain to Wauchock, he was waylaid by the little girl from the back row. "I'm sorry," she said. "I got scared."

That did not mean anything to him. He hurried away, shamefaced, without answering her.

And for the rest of his career in school he avoided "guessing."

11

As a career it was neither long nor brilliant. At the end of his second term he went to work in Simpson's grocery, because he had no money to buy clothes that were fit to wear to school. He never got back to a class-room. Neither did he ever return to his home. He was given a bedroom over the shop, and he ate with the grocer's family, but he lived very much to himself, taking long walks in the evenings and spending his Sundays alone on the country roads. He was a slow, silent, methodical young man. At first he worked as a delivery-boy and general help. Then he was taken behind the counter, and there he found himself a "lightning calculator" again, and he was given the accounts to keep.

He remained in that position more than a year. And he does not seem to have visited his home at all during that time. I do not know why. He does not speak of his relations with his people. But it is apparent that he was pursued by a guilty consciousness of his father's kleptomania, and that the thought of it made him morbid, solitary, and afraid of impending disgrace. I infer this from the fact that he admits he left Centerbrook because of a dream in which his father, having been arrested for stealing, was tried in the school-house yard, after dark, on a platform under the flare of innumerable grinning kerosene-torches. Before all the evidence was in it was Ben himself who was being tried, by the mathematical teacher; he was condemned to have his teeth pulled out; and he woke in a clammy fright, haunted by the fear that his father's thefts would be discovered and he would be discharged from the grocery.

He left Centerbrook in answer to a want advertisement for a bookkeeper in a New York newspaper. He went to work for the Perry-Felton Company. And for ten years nothing happened to him more exciting than a raise of salary. He made no friends. He had no companions. For a time he lived in a boarding-house, and then, in answer to another advertisement, he took a room in a flat with a childless German couple who spoke almost no English. He remained with them as long as he remained in New York. He talked to no one. He says he had an unpleasant feeling that people were never sincere; they said all sorts of things that they did not really think; you could see it in their eyes. He preferred to read, and he read chiefly newspapers. Then he developed a curious hobby that led him to read science.

One of the clerks at Perry-Felton's brought a popular "wire puzzle" to the office, and after every one else had failed to do it Murdock solved it almost at a glance. The clerk, piqued, brought another next day. It was more difficult, but Murdock unraveled it quickly enough. All the clerks joined in the game, and Murdock began to buy puzzles in order to study them secretly in his rooms so as to be ready if the clerks produced them. It developed into a hobby with him. He became so expert that the whole staff gossiped about it. One day the office manager, having watched him do a Chinese puzzle that was supposed to be practically insoluble, said: "Well, I know one puzzle you'll never find an answer to. I'll bring it to you." And next morning he arrived with a book called *The Sphinx's Riddle* and laid it on Murdock's desk.

It was a volume from a popular-science series that stated, in a simple way, the mystery of the origin of life in terms of evolution. It gave Benjamin McNeil Murdock his start. Scientific books began to take the place of puzzles on his bureau. In a few months he was buying bookcases. He carried books to his office and read at his luncheon. He read till all hours of the night. Even on his Sunday walking-trips up the Hudson he carried a volume in his pocket and read under the trees. And between walking miles to his work every morning and miles back at night, and reading insatiably whenever he was not asleep, his time out of office hours was so occupied that during all those years in New York he never entered a theater, or heard a concert, or even dropped into a moving-picture show.

The funeral of his parents, and the murder trial that followed, made only a momentary interruption in his routine. After it was all over he returned to his office tragically depressed, but freer in his mind because the apprehension of disgrace had been removed by his father's death. He had saved twenty-one hundred dollars. He owned a farm. He began to figure on how much it would cost him to live in the country; what was the best rate of interest he could get on a safe investment if he withdrew his money from the savings-bank and bought bonds; and what were the possibilities of scientific farming if he took it up.

12

Turning these things over in his mind, he was walking back from his office one August evening about half past six, when he passed the restaurant windows of a Fifth Avenue hotel and saw a young woman dining there with an elderly man behind the flowers of the window-sill boxes. The window was open, and she looked up as Murdock glanced at her. Their eyes met. His was an absent-minded glance, and he had passed on before it occurred to him that she had seemed to recognize him. He decided that she had been looking at some one else on the street. Nevertheless, at the corner, instead of continuing on his way to his room, he turned quite automatically down the side street and walked along that front of the hotel to the side entrance.

He believes, now, that he had unconsciously recognized her, and that this recognition drew him into the hotel. He admits that nothing of the sort was in his conscious thoughts. It was a warm evening, and he was tired walking. He had planned to have his dinner in the cheap restaurant near his room, where he always dined; but that restaurant was small and smelly, and the hotel dining-room had looked invitingly airy and cool. He bought a newspaper and entered the hotel.

He was not as shabby as usual; he had just bought himself a summer suit—at a reduced price because it was late in the season. But the head waiter was not to be deceived by new ready-made clothes. He seated Murdock at the least desirable table in the room, far from the windows, near the pantry door, with his back to the girl whom he had seen from the street. And Murdock did not turn round for a second look at her. He occupied himself with his newspaper, and particularly with the stock reports, which he had begun to study in his search for a good investment.

He remembers that when his beefsteak arrived he was convinced that he ought to buy Bethlehem Steel. He does not remember when he got the idea.

The girl from the window, leaving the dining-room, paused at the door to look back at him, but he did not see her. She even returned, on the pretext of having forgotten her gloves, and stared at him as she came in, and glanced back over her shoulder as she went out; but he continued absorbed in his newspaper. After she had disappeared he looked up quickly, as if some one had spoken to him; and he gazed around him bewildered at the tables near. No one was even noticing him. He paid his check and wandered out. And next day he drew two thousand dollars of his savings from the bank and bought Bethlehem Steel.

Throughout that fall and winter the war orders from abroad kept his steel stocks rising, and he followed them cautiously, gambling on a margin, halving his winnings, and adding a thousand dollars at a time to his savings account. By the following May he had thirty thousand dollars in sight, and this, he figured, was enough for him to live on. He sold all his stocks. He resigned his position at Perry-Felton's. He packed his books in barrels and all his clothes in his suit-case. And, telling his landlady that he was going on a holiday, he walked out of the apartment-house at eight o'clock at night—empty-handed, but with five hundred dollars in his pocket—and turned toward the Hudson River and the Jersey ferry.

13

By ten o'clock he was passing the City Hall in Newark. By midnight he was lying under a tree beside the Seven Bridges Road, as happy as a country dog that had escaped to the open fields. He sat up to see the dawn, and he remained gazing about him for at least an hour, his knees drawn up to his chin and his arms clasped about them in the attitude in which he used to sit in his father's pasture-lot watching the cows. He had a curious feeling. He felt as if he had been imprisoned among people for all these years, and had at last escaped to the trees and weeds and grasses that were his proper equals and companions.

He made his breakfast of rolls and milk in Springfield, and, swinging along the road to the Washington Valley, with his hat in his hand and his coat over his shoulder—about half past eight—he saw a large automobile approaching. It slowed down. It stopped before him. He saw that the girl who was driving it was smiling at him. "You don't remember me," she said.

No, he didn't. But he continued to look at her, without surprise, feeling friendly and unpuzzled.

She asked, "Did you buy Bethlehem Steel?"

He dropped his coat and hat and came to the side of the machine, gazing at her with a deep-eyed, hypnotized interest. "How did you know about that?"

She continued to smile down at him. "Don't you remember? You saw me dining at the window, and you came into the hotel, but you didn't look at me."

Some recollection of the incident returned to him dimly while he studied her. She was bareheaded, and the morning sun shone full in her face. It seemed to him that he had known her—somewhere. "Of course," he said. "I didn't recognize you."

"You don't recognize me yet," she replied.

No. He couldn't really say that he did.

She explained, "I don't think you ever knew my name."

"No." He could not place her.

"Do you remember," she helped him, "once when you were whipped, in school, for guessing the figures on the blackboard?"

He blinked at her. She waited confidently. "Was *that* you?" he asked. "At the back of the room?"

She nodded, enjoying it, as soberly mischievous as a child with some little mystification of its own. "And I spoke to you, afterward, on your way home."

"I remember." His own expression had become boyish and frank and friendly. "Did you tell me what the figures were—the first time?"

"Yes. And then I got frightened and couldn't tell you what the second ones were. That's what I tried to explain to you—afterward."

"I remember," he said. "I didn't understand. I thought I'd just guessed them." And then, after a long smiling pause of thoughtful silence, he added, "And that's where I got the idea of buying Bethlehem Steel, is it?"

He was talking to her, now, as if their meeting were quite natural and commonplace—as if they were in a dream in which the impossible could happen as a matter of course.

She had that air herself. "I tried awfully hard in the hotel to make you turn around and look at me," she confessed. "I even came back into the dining-room, but you never noticed. Father had been buying steel, and when I saw that you were looking at the stock quotations I tried to give you a tip."

"I made thirty thousand dollars on it."

"And you're coming back to Wauchock?"

"Yes. Did you suggest that to me, too?"

"No." She opened the car door to him. "But when I woke this morning I had a funny feeling that you were on your way. I thought I might meet you."

He climbed in quite unconsciously and sat beside her. "I've left the city. I'm coming out here to farm."

"On the old place?"

"Yes. It's queer," he said, "that I don't remember your name."

"No," she assured him. "I don't think you ever knew it. The first time I saw you you were having your toothache cured by that Buffalo Bill man who sold the patent medicine. Then you came to school at Wauchock, but I don't think you ever noticed me. And then we moved to Centerbrook, and I didn't see you again till you came to school there. I'm Ruth Young."

He did not remember ever having heard the name before. "It doesn't matter," he said.

He was gazing at her in a way that he had never looked at any one in his life before. During all those years of silence and solitariness at Wauchock, at Centerbrook, in New York, he had never spoken to any one as he was speaking to her or found any one who could meet his eyes in complete and friendly sincerity as she met them. And the strange thing was that now it seemed as if she had shared in all those years as an invisible companion, who had suddenly appeared to him, who was sitting beside him and smiling at him as she had in some way been watching him and smiling at him, unseen, always, even from his boyhood.

Perhaps it was the thought of what had kept him solitary that made him ask, "Did you know about my father?"

And it was certainly the tone in which he asked it that made her, for the first time, glance away from him as she replied: "Yes. There was a lot of gossip about it."

He said, "I'm glad."

She understood; he was glad that there was not even this secret concealed from her; that she knew it and was not ashamed of him. She put out her hand to him blindly, to reassure him. He took it as simply as she gave it.

She settled back in the seat with a little trembling sigh. There were tears in her eyes, but she gazed through them, smiling, at the long empty road and the long empty past. "I've motored by your house," she said, "but it was always closed."

He had lifted her hand and bent down to it and put his cheek against it, with his face averted. She slipped her fingers out of his and turned his head to her and held him so, looking at him, all smiling tears and tenderness, with eyes that at once searched him and accepted him and surrendered to him. Suddenly, as if he were unable to bear it, he bowed forward, with his face in his hands. She patted his head, weeping happily, and distractedly stroking his hair.

"Isn't it strange?" she said. "The first time I saw you, alone, on that platform, under the torchlight, I had almost the same feeling for you. And I told you those figures on the blackboard just as if I were talking to myself, and I knew you'd hear. And then they sent me away to school and I lost you, but somehow I always knew you'd come back. Even when—there was some one else that— I don't know. I think it was only because he seemed like you. And the moment I saw you passing the restaurant window I knew I had been cheating myself. And I brought you into the hotel and told you to buy the stock. And then I began to worry because I hadn't been able to make you look around. And father's dead. And I've been so lonely. I began to be afraid. I was so happy when I woke this morning and knew you were coming." She even laughed brokenly. "Get your coat and hat. I want to see our— I want to see the house."

14

And that is their story. I don't know what to make of it, any more than I know what to make of Murdock's disproof of the mechanistic theory and his belief that the plants themselves have a creative intelligence and some sort of dumb world-soul of their own. But I know this: hearing those two, watching them, seeing the deep and smiling trust of their way of looking at each other while they spoke and listened—and remembering that weedy life of poverty and ignorance and murder and kleptomania from which he came—I felt that I could believe any miracle of the immortal spirit, any mysticism of the creative intelligence, any hope of the transcending soul. Science may say what it pleases of Benjamin McNeil Murdock. He is, to me, his own disproof of a dead mechanical world and the philosophy of the microscope.

12

FROM THE LIFE

Conrad Norman

CONRAD NORMAN

1

HIS real name is not Conrad Norman. It is Con Gorman, and he was born in Centerbrook, New Jersey. So, I think, was Flora Furness. At any rate, they both grew up there from childhood as neighbors—although they were by no means neighborly.

There are two kinds of human beings in Centerbrook. Each is sustained by a feeling of superiority to the other; and this feeling of superiority has doubtless been provided by an all-wise Nature to enable each to endure with indifference the other's self-conceit. The native Centerbrooker regards the commuter as a Parisian regards a member of the American colony in Paris—or as a member of that colony regards an American tourist there— or as any one who is comparatively permanent, and in possession, regards the passing and the transitory. And the commuter—living in Centerbrook because "New York is no place to bring up a young family"—regards the native Centerbrooker as the summer visitor in the Catskills regards the buckwheater and the local village life, or as any one who is progressively transient regards the permanent and rooted. Humanity, as the philosopher says, is "like that." It is one of humanity's compensations for being so human.

Con Gorman was in the rooted camp because his father kept the bakery on Front Street, near the railway station. Flora Furness was of the commuters' circle because her father took the 8.25 to the city every morning. But, as a matter of fact, neither the Gormans nor the Furnesses were spiritually at home in the tents of their respective factions. They were only more antipathetic to each other than they were to their economic kind. Nothing in the newspapers could have sounded less likely to Centerbrook than the possibility that a daughter of the Furnesses would ever look twice at a son of the Gormans. The head-line, "Screen Star Weds Peeress," would not have puckered many mouths in Centerbrook. But "Con Gorman Weds Flora Furness"! That would certainly have started whistles enough to bring out the Ivy Hook and Ladder Company.

For my part, the first time I saw Con even speak to her I thought that I had turned his head.

2

It was at a concert and dance given at the Centerbrook Country Club in aid of the Belgian Relief Fund. I had just seen him act in a little sketch that was part of the concert, and he played his rôle so engagingly that it was evident he had dramatic talent. There is no mistaking it in a boy of nineteen. It is too rare to be overlooked. When the concert was finished and the room was being cleared for the dance I hunted him out in the crowd on the club-house veranda and proposed that he should let me give him a letter to a play-wright who, I knew, was in need of a juvenile. We were still shaking hands when I said it, and his gratitude was so violent that he all but wrung blood from my finger-ends.

"Really?" he said, half choked. "Will you? Gee!" And the rest strangled in his throat.

I tried to explain that I was not doing him a favor so much as I was doing the playwright one; that the movies had taken so many presentable juveniles off the stage that there was little left but Romeos in false teeth and toupees. "If you do as well at rehearsals as you did here," I assured him, "Bidey 'll probably adopt you—to keep them from buying you away."

"Really?" he cried. "Was I all right? Gee!" He strained at my hand again. "Gee! Wait a minute!" And he turned to buck his way back through the crowd as if I had passed him the football in a scrimmage and he was going through the line for a touchdown.

He was a handsome boy, with an entire lack of self-consciousness. It was this lack that had struck me in his performance. It had shown not only in his voice, and his face, and his hands, but also in his legs, where the constraint of the young actor stiffens and struts even after he has eased it up everywhere else. When his friends in the audience applauded his entrance he grinned genially, and his grin was just as contagious then as it is now. As soon as he began to speak his lines his voice took all the innumerable sliding gradations of a conversational tone, and it seemed impossible that he could do such a thing without training, yet his accent was quite obviously untrained. His r's were ferocious.

They did not matter. I had understood that the rôle of the boy in my friend's play was not a straight part.

In a few minutes Con came rushing back to me to explain that he was not really an actor; that he had done only amateur stunts; that he sang and danced, chiefly; that he had never thought of getting a part in a real play—only in musical comedy—and he had never been able to "break in" there. I promised to write a letter of introduction and mail it to him early in the morning. He bolted away again. He was in a pathetic state of pale excitement.

"Too bad!" said the man with whom I had been talking. "Nice boy, too!"

"What's too bad about him?"

"No good for anything," he said. He was the proprietor of the coal-yards on Leedy Street. "Parents' fault."

"What's he been doing now?"

"That's the trouble. He's not doing anything. He's never done an honest day's work in his life, and I don't believe he ever will. Huh! I see we have the stuffed-heart aristocracy with us."

3

He was referring to the Furnesses as "the stuffed-heart aristocracy."

The entertainment was a charity affair, and therefore open to any one who had a dollar; but, for that very reason, we had not expected the Furnesses to come. We forgot that the Belgians might be regarded as under the special protection of the British flag. There was a copper-bronzed and curly-headed young Englishman with Flora. He looked like a naval officer. I heard later that he was Lieut. Cuthbert Williamson, of the Atlantic Squadron.

And my coal magnate referred to the Furnesses as "the stuffed-heart aristocracy" because they were known to be as poor as they were considered "snooty." They had no motor-car. They kept no servants. They were such notoriously "slow pay" that they could not get credit even at the news-stand on the railway platform when they were in a hurry to catch a train. They never entertained. The butcher reported that they bought chiefly beef hearts (hence the stuffed-heart aristocracy). The grocer added, "And bushels o' turnips." And, as if to make themselves wholly ridiculous, they always dressed for dinner. The town was full of stories of how Mrs. Furness cooked in an evening gown, and Albert Edward, her husband, after dinner, lighted a post-prandial clay pipe of army cut, and smoked solemnly in his "soup-and-fish." Some one, on a midwinter evening, had seen Flora, with her bare arms goose-fleshed in a frozen drawing-room, trying to keep herself warm by playing Beethoven sonatas, while her brother, Howard Hartley Furness, twisted old newspapers into solid wads and fed them into the fireplace to encourage the cannel-coal.

I suspect that the "some one" who saw this was a younger Gorman, spying through a crack in the closed shutters of the Furness front window. They lived under a common roof—the Gormans and the Furnesses—in the old Voss house, on the corner of High and Leedy streets, the Furnesses having a front door on High Street and the Gormans using what had once been a side door and veranda on Leedy. Their lawns were separated by a class barrier in the shape of an old lilac hedge, planted by the last of the Vosses, Miss Elizabeth Voss, when she had been compelled to rent half her residence in order to be able to live in the other half. She had divided the house with a series of sound-proof walls, filled with sawdust. She had cut the back yard in two with a spite-fence high enough to discourage any social aspiration. And although she was now dead, and buried exclusively, her work remained unchanged.

On the High Street side of the house there were still shuttered windows and a sun-blistered, weather-crackled, high-eyebrowed, old colonnade porch that was prouder than paint. Behind their street hedge the Furnesses could drink afternoon tea under the Voss elms, safe from the intruding curiosity of any but neighborly mosquitoes—and Mrs. Furness rather managed to make them part of the function by calling them "midges." (Have I said that the Furnesses came from Bury, near Houghton, in Sussex?) Their front door still had its prim Voss air of being unapproachable to any one who had not been formally introduced—an air of never having extended its bell-pull to the fingers of the great ungloved. Occasionally, as you passed the gate in the hedge, you overheard the antique Furness piano articulating faintly in a high, precise, soprano tinkle. There was not another sound. Whereas, on the Leedy Street side of the house— where there was no hedge—the whole brood of Gormans lived with unshuttered windows opening on a public veranda, and sang and pounded the piano, and danced to the phonograph, and quarreled and smacked one another and played rough-house games as noisily as a kennel of young Aire-dales.

High Street still had some claim to residential respectability, although one house had been rented for a public library, two were boarding-houses, and another had put on a false front and become a milliner's shop. But Leedy Street was beyond the pale. There was not only a livery-stable on it; there was a plumber's shop, a coal-yard, and a brick terrace where day-laborers lived. It was not to be expected that a family on High Street would associate with one on Leedy, even though their dormer-windows gabled out of the one roof.

And the Furnesses did not really associate with any one in Centerbrook. They lived in the same general world as the other commuters, belonged distantly to the same country club, played silent golf on the same club links, and prayed regularly to the same Deity. But, under Providence, all their aims in life were as palpably alien to the Centerbrook commuters as the Gorman aimlessness was repellent to the coal-yard proprietor.

4

To him the Furnesses were "the stuffed-heart aristocracy" and Con was "no good for anything." He had all a Benjamin Franklin's practical contempt for them both. Out of that contempt he proceeded to tell me why he had discharged Con after a week's trial in his coal-office. I was confused by a vague recollection of a report that Con had said he was fired for refusing to give a customer short weight. Centerbrook is full of such gossip about its shopkeepers. It is the way the impotent commuter takes his revenge on the high cost of living. I avoided looking at the coal-man.

Flora Furness caught my wandering eye, across the veranda, and she gave me not exactly a smile, but at least a facial movement of friendly recognition. Her mother had discovered that I had once visited a member of the artist colony in Amberley, which is beside the river Arun, opposite Bury; and, though I had never been in Bury itself, I had stood on the downs above Amberley and seen the spire of Bury church among the trees across the river and the weald. It gave me a standing with the Furnesses that no one else in Centerbrook could approach.

The next thing I saw was Con Gorman speaking to Flora Furness. And, as I say, I thought that I had turned his young head.

She was standing near the veranda door, between her mother and Lieutenant Williamson. The music had struck up, inside; the dancers were streaming past her in answer to its call, and Con had stopped, incredibly, to ask her for a dance. At least I judged that was what had happened. I could not see his face, but I could see hers and her mother's and Williamson's.

Mrs. Furness wore her hair like the Dowager Queen Alexander, whom she respectfully resembled; she was holding herself regally erect, high-shouldered, with her hands clasped on her stomacher, so to speak; and her expression had calmly obliterated Con Gorman from the surrounding cosmos by an act of will. Williamson's face I did not understand till I met him later; he had, in fact, the absent-minded eyes of young Europe, gravely condemned to death and watching contemporary America dance to rag-time. Having regarded Con a moment blankly, he shifted the same regard to a passing couple.

As for Flora Furness, she seemed, at first, naturally, surprised at Con. She smiled a formal, polite refusal. He persisted. She glanced at her mother and then darted a look at him that confessed— I did not know what. It was an alarmed, reluctant, warning look. It was a look as of conspiracy betrayed. And it was so evidently private that I turned away at once as if I had been spying.

I found that the coal-dealer was refuting an editorial allegation that coal-dealers had caused the rise in the price of coal. When I looked at Flora Furness again she was talking to Williamson, with her eyes fixed on me. Con had disappeared. For a moment I thought guiltily that she was studying me to see what I had noticed. Then I understood that she wished to speak to me.

I made a strategic retreat from the labor war in the Pennsylvania coal-fields and moved toward her with the current that was being sucked in to the music. It seemed impossible that Con could have told her what I had said about his acting. Why should he? And yet why, otherwise, should she summon me in this way? And—most of all—why the look that she had shot at *him?* What was going on between them?

When I had been recognized and greeted by her mother and her she said that she wanted me to meet Lieutenant Williamson. That was pleasant but unilluminating. The lieutenant was equally so. I was not piqued, but I had once talked to a silent Englishman about the Boer War for two garrulous hours before I learned that he had served as an officer through the whole campaign; and I promised myself that Williamson might be as amiably illuminating as he pleased, he should not betray me into trying to enlighten him about the British navy. I turned my intelligence on her.

We talked of the concert condescendingly. "I've just discovered an actor," I said, "a born actor."

That was an inspiration. There had been but one dramatic number in the concert, and her eyes at once betrayed her. She had a clear young pallor that did not speak well for stuffed heart and turnips as a health food, and that pallor slowly reddened. "Isn't it warm?" she said. It was not particularly warm. "Could we find a cool drink?" We could.

The Furnesses were stanch in their English aversion to ice-water, and her mother showed some incredulous surprise, but before she could move to arrest her daughter we were through the door.

The girl took my arm. "I saw you talking to

him," she said, quickly, under her voice. "What is it? What has happened?"

5

I was as much taken aback as if a marble Venus had suddenly turned its sculptured head to me and spoken breathlessly. It was Con Gorman of whom she was speaking. I could believe that Con might have stood outside the railing and gazed up reverently at the placid face of the goddess, but I could not believe that the Olympian eyes had ever been lowered to look at him. She held her head high while she asked me about him. She was of that statuesque type of gray-eyed English beauty of which Du Maurier loved to make architectural drawings.

I repeated what I had said to Con. It did not seem adequate to her. "But he was so excited," she murmured. We were making our way across the semi-baronial hall of the Country Club, in the general direction of the fruit punch. And suddenly she deflected me toward the side veranda. "It's so hot," she said, hurriedly. "I feel almost faint."

I understood that she had seen Con—as I had—coming to intercept us. She escorted me rapidly outdoors, and down the deserted porch to the back steps and out across the lawn toward the tennis-courts. "I want to speak to him," she said, "alone"; and she stopped me with a hand on my arm and went on into the darkness without me.

She must have known that Con was right behind us, although she had not turned her head, and he, in his dancing-pumps, had not made a footfall audible to me. He shot past me instantly and over-took her. I heard him say: "Is it true? Are you going to—"

Was it "marry him"?

It sounded like "marry him"! And his tone was agonized.

I turned back to the porch and sat down on the steps, under an electric light, and consulted a cigarette.

I did not share the prejudices of Centerbrook, but the more I thought over the situation the more impossible it appeared. Con was simply the ne'er-do-well son of a drunken Irish baker whose business was held together by his wife and his daughters. Con had once helped them by driving the wagon and delivering the bread, but of recent years he had not done even that. He had worked for a week in the coal-office. He had been a clerk for at least two weeks in the grocery. He had tended the soda-fountain in the druggist's for perhaps a month. And there had been a period when it was under-stood that he was employed in New York. But, though he had no conspicuous vices, he had a cheer-ful irresponsibility that unfitted him for commercial life. He treated the grocery, the coal-office, and the drug-store as if their businesses were suffering from a lack of gaiety that could be supplied by bright

13   [183]

impertinences and practical jokes. The till at the family bake-shop being open to him always, he was never without pocket-money. He dressed smartly. He was the spark of life in any party that included him. He was a high favorite among many of the young people of Centerbrook. But their wise elders waited, not too patiently, to see him come to his inevitable bad end.

Among those whose frowns were expectantly prophetic I could not imagine the Furnesses. They must have been merely unaware of his existence. And how he had managed to come to speaking terms with Flora Furness was not to be learned from a cigarette. Yet there they both were—dimly to be seen on a bench under the trees beside the tennis-courts—in the animated intimacy of secret conversation. She was seated immovably, with her back to me, and he was turned sideways toward her, talking rapidly and running his hand up through his hair. I tried not to notice them, but I could not help seeing his arm go up and then out, every now and then, in a passionate gesticulation.

It was undoubtedly some sort of clandestine love-affair. And yet, of course, it could not be. I could believe it was while I was looking at them, but when I looked away it was incredible. It was like seeing a ghost and turning from it to blink at its familiar surroundings and say to yourself, "There must be something the matter with my eyes."

I ended by keeping my attention fixed on my cigarette, as you might feel that if you did not notice your ghost it would disappear. After all, no one in Centerbrook would have credited the report of such an intimacy. If I refused to see it, it was as good as non-existent. I refused to see it.

I refused even when the girl returned alone, almost running, in an agitation which I could not avoid hearing in her shaken breathing. I rose without looking at her, and followed her up the porch, and hastened to open the screen-door for her, discreetly silent. She controlled herself with difficulty, facing the crowded hall. I did not try to help her. I was afraid of intruding. We crossed the room without a word.

As we approached the other door she said, after a struggle, in a tone of shamed desperation: "Please take him away. Don't let him come to—to speak to me again. I'll tell them I feel ill. Don't stay to talk to them. Take him home."

Her distress was painful. I hastened to assure her: "Yes, yes. I'll fix it. Don't worry. It 'll be all right"—remorseful because I had not offered some approach to the subject in order to make it easier for her to speak of it.

We were at the door. As I reached for it she faltered out, with extraordinary poignancy: "Be— Be—*kind* to him."

I was afraid that she was going to break down,

and I fumbled blindly with the door-knob, frightened and embarrassed, whispering to her, "Don't —don't—" unable to look at her.

She did not answer. I drew the door open. She passed me and went out. On the veranda she gave me her hand in a hasty parting, her eyes averted. "Thank you," she said, in a clear, controlled voice. "I feel much better. Good night." And as I turned back I heard her tell her mother: "I've been feeling quite faint. I think we'd better go."

6

I went, rather dazed, to look for Con. And I found him on the bench where she had left him, facing the night. I spoke to him, without reply, and sat down beside him, and struck a match to light another cigarette. I did not light it. Glancing at him furtively in the small flare of the match, I saw that he was crying—his face drenched with tears—crying silently, his mouth open, his jaws trembling, his eyes staring, unconscious of himself or of me. It was not the audible grief of revolt or self-pity. It was the mute suffering of complete bereavement and despair. And it so shocked me that I immediately blew out the match.

I could not think of anything to say. I could not imagine what was the matter. It was not like a boy's grief. It was widowed—tragic. I sat helplessly waiting.

And suddenly I was overcome with a sickening

depression. The sense of his unhappiness beside me, the sound of the dance-music from behind us, the sight of the desolate tennis-courts vaguely in front of us, the taste of the cold cigarette in my mouth— Life has such aspects. They are intolerable. The mind cannot endure them. It escapes at once into some future, some plan, some hope. I began, desperately: "I think I'd better go into town with you to-morrow and introduce you to these people. They want to start rehearsals right away, and I'd like you to get a copy of your part and run over it with you. A good deal will depend on the first impression they get of you." And so forth. I talked about salary, contract, the probable success of the play, his opportunity to make a hit—anything rosy that came into my mind, ignoring the whole situation. He did not speak, although I paused several times to wait for him. When at last I turned to him directly and demanded, "Well, what do you say?" he answered, "It's too late." And his voice was not tearful, but quite toneless, out of a tight throat.

I ignored that, too. I went ahead babbling about his acting, the fact that he plainly had imagination, that it was the great gift in acting, that I was sure he would make an immediate success, that I had seen So-and-so—of whom he reminded me—walk on to the stage in New York, in what was almost his first part, and get himself accepted by the critics as "the best actor in America under twenty-five years of age." And if So-and-so could do it—

"It doesn't matter," he said, hoarsely, more to himself than to me. "It's too late now." And he began to sob.

I could not ignore the sobs. I took him by the shoulder. "Look here," I said. "Pull yourself together. This is all nonsense. If you get all torn to pieces this way, you'll be good for nothing to-morrow. I don't know what you imagine's happened to you, but it probably isn't half so bad as you think. If you make a ten-strike in a part, it 'll change everything. Don't be a fool."

He broke down completely, collapsing in a huddle when I shook him, sobbing with a frightful laboring effort to get his breath, and gasping out that she was going, that she was to be married, that it was too late. I threw away my cigarette. I put my arms around his shoulders and pulled him over to me. He fell across me, his face in his hands, and lay there crying like a child. I gave him my hand-kerchief when I felt his tears soaking through my thin summer trousers. I didn't know what in the world to do with him.

"If I knew what was the matter," I said, "I might be able to help you." It struck me that he was crying as if he had lost something more than a sweetheart. "If it's Flora Furness—I don't think she's turned against you. She told me to take you home and to— Well, she asked me to be *kind* to you."

He sat up at once, frantically wiping his eyes. "Where is she? Where is she?"

"No." I held him by the arm. "You can't go and make a scene with her. You stay where you are till you've pulled yourself together. Besides, she's gone home with her people."

With that he began to curse her family like a truck-driver, even while he mopped away his boy's tears, abusing her mother in language that was beyond belief—delirious indecencies—the sort of language that you hear from a patient in a surgical ward coming out from under ether. I put my hand over his mouth, afraid that some one might hear him. "Shut up," I threatened, "or I'll throttle you."

He struggled with me a moment, trying to bite my hand, and then he collapsed again into hysterics. I scolded him in an attempt to get some backbone into him that way. "You young cad—calling decent people names like that! What 've you to do with a girl like her, anyway? Or any girl? You don't earn your salt—never did—never even tried to! If she's going to marry, she'll marry a better man than you—no matter who he is. I don't see how she ever came to look at you. Or how you ever had the—the effrontery to speak to her—to suppose that—that she—"

He had come back to himself with a sort of shudder. "I know," he said, abjectly. "I'm sorry. I —can't help it." He choked again with tears. "You—you," he gulped, "you don't understand."

"No," I said. "I'll be hanged if I do. How long has this been going on?"

"Always," he wept. "Always. Ever since I can remember."

"What? Why, you're *crazy!* Here in Center-brook!"

"Yes. Nobody knew. Not even her family— or mine."

And then the whole story began to come out pell-mell, every which way, wrong end first, the middle nowhere, and all confused with mixed emotions, tears and young despair and disorderly outbursts of vituperation against himself, Center-brook, his ill luck, her family, and everything and everybody but the girl herself. For a long time I could not believe him. Then, when I believed I could not understand, for much of it he did not understand himself and could not make credible. But what a situation! With a little of the pathos of actuality taken out and its place occupied by romantic motive and symphonic "bunk," what a situation for a fictionist! Well!

7

They had met years before, as children, in circumstances that were just absurd. He had been chopping kindling in the woodshed with his pockets full of bake-shop cookies. The Furnesses had, that day, moved into their half of the house; it had been for some time vacant, and a missing board had not yet been replaced in the fence that made the rear wall of the woodshed. Con, straightening up from the kindling in order to cram a cooky into his mouth, saw her watching him through this hole in the fence with an expression of hungry envy. He grinned and held out a cooky to her. She studied him between shyness and temptation. ("They never had enough to eat in the house," he explained, "but they were so proud you'd never guess it."). He went over to the opening and said: "Go on. Take one. They're good. My father makes them. We own the bakery. Go on. I got lots."

She took it and said, "Thank you," polite, but embarrassed.

He introduced himself. "What's *your* name?"

Instead of replying she said, unexpectedly, "Mother 'll not let me play with you."

"Why won't she?"

"She doesn't let me play with any one."

"All right," he said. "Then I won't ask her to. Have another."

He gave her a handful. She was more at her ease, having confessed that she could not play with him. She nibbled the cakes greedily, looking at him over them. "My name's Flora," she confided.

That was their beginning. "She wasn't so

pretty," he said, "but she wasn't like any girl I'd ever met before. She was so quiet. She'd just stand and watch you, and listen and look—look friendly, and never say a word. I was dead nuts about her in no time. I used to take all sorts of things in my pocket for her, and she'd slip out and get them when she heard me chopping wood. I used to make all the noise I could on purpose, and bang on the side of the woodshed when she didn't come.

"I don't know how she let me know—I guess she told me straight out—that she couldn't speak to me if she saw me on the street. I didn't care, but I pretended I was sore. I had some Scotch shortcake for her, but I said I wouldn't give it to her unless she let me kiss her. She said she wouldn't do it for the shortcake, but she'd do it because she couldn't speak to me on the street. It was the—the first time I kissed her." And then he began to sob again.

He must have been about eight years old at the time, and she ten. Her father had come to New York for an English publishing-house. He was an Oxford man and a younger son; he had not yet developed his destructive weakness for brandy and soda, and, although his income must have been beggarly, the family kept up appearances. She did not go to school; she was taught at home by her mother. And she was not allowed to associate with the neighborhood children because their accents were bad. There was, in fact, no accent in

Centerbrook that her mother considered it safe for her to hear too often. Her brother, Howard Hartley, was sent to a boys' boarding-school up the Hudson, after the English fashion. Mrs. Furness was secretly giving piano lessons in a girls' school in Plainfield. And Flora was left alone in the empty house every afternoon.

Con could not recall how the meetings in the woodshed were discovered, but he remembered clearly enough that he found the missing board replaced one day, and no one answered his industrious uproar among the kindlings. He was not outwitted. He had loosened that board himself in order to get into the Voss back yard before the Furnesses occupied it, and he had another way of entering; he had clambered out a dormer-window on to the roof and forced an entrance through a corresponding window on the Voss side of the house. And more than that. Miss Voss's sound-proof walls did not extend to the top story. There was a door from the Gorman attic into the Voss attic. It was bolted on both sides, but, having entered the Voss attic through the window, Con had withdrawn all the bolts. He had gone down through the house and unlocked the cellar door. And with a picked following of young burglars he had made the vacant house the resort of a gang of imaginary desperadoes of which he was captain.

The day that he found the woodshed repaired he went at once to the attic, took off his shoes and stockings, and crawled across the roof again into the Furness top story. He unlocked the attic door to open a quick retreat for himself—according to the best traditions of the criminal professions— and started tiptoeing down-stairs in search of the imprisoned princess. There was not a sound any- where. He reached the ground floor before he heard so much as a cough. There, through the hinge-crack of an open door, he saw her sitting in the parlor, reading a book. He made sure that there was no one else in the room before he put his head in and whispered, "Have a gingersnap?" She dropped her book and cried, "Con!" And she made so much noise about it that he knew she was alone in the house.

8

That began the second stage of their affair. They met in the attic thereafter, and talked and read and played together while her mother was away. It was easy enough for the girl; there was no one to spy on her so long as she remained in- doors. But Con had to practise all sorts of strata- gems and deceptions in order to escape from his small brothers and his boy friends, and at first he did not spend much time with her; he would just run up to see her for a few minutes after school was out and take her some cakes. When the novelty wore off, it was rather a deprivation for him to be shut up on a holiday afternoon with her, over a book or a game. If he had been another sort of boy he might have tired of it. But he was naturally gentle and affectionate and "sorry for the kid" (as he expressed it to me) and sufficiently out of tune with his surroundings to enjoy his escape into a hidden friendship with a girl like Flora Furness, and he was not proud enough to resent the fact that she could not know him publicly. He had in him a Celtic strain of poetry and imagination that kept him as secretive about her as if she were one of those invisible playmates that solitary children invent. She never asked him to come. She never reproached him if he were late or hurried. But she was always waiting for him, and she glowed with a touching pleasure, repressed, but flatteringly sincere, when he arrived; and she played his make-believe games with him, fascinated by an inventiveness that was beyond her. She was probably rather stupid as a child in everything but the depth of her feeling.

Apparently he did not realize how far matters had gone with him until she was sent away to a girls' school where she could not receive letters or write to him without it being known. He mooned around in a state of desperate loneliness for a long time before he returned to his proper associates. It was during this absence of hers that he took the Gorman attic room as his bedroom and study, with some boyish idea of being nearer the memory of her. He put the high head of his bed against the connecting door to conceal it, but sometimes, when he had locked himself in, he moved the bed aside and went into the other room and pretended that she was there with him.

Then she returned for the holidays and the thing began to be serious. She had been unhappy at the school. The other girls were all daughters of the well-to-do; she had put on the pride of poverty in her association with them, and they had retaliated as Centerbrook would have retaliated if it had had the opportunity. She had made no friends. She could not appeal for sympathy to her mother, whose ideal of character was not exactly sympathetic. And it was impossible to appeal to her father; her mother had always been between them in the family administration. So she poured it all out to Con. He took it greedily and consoled her with the whispers of adolescent love. They began meeting at night, after the others of the household were in bed. She came to his room.

<h2 style="text-align:center">9</h2>

Well, as I say, the middle of their story was missing from his account of it. The end of it came first; and it only ran back as far as the time when he left school to go to work. She tried to persuade him to continue his studies, but he was too impatient; he was eager to earn money, to make himself rich, so that they might be married the sooner. That was why he gave up driving the bakery wagon; there were no riches in sight along that route; and while he traveled it he had to deliver bread to her back door and be treated as a hired man by her mother. And that was why he left every other occupation that he tried in Centerbrook. He lasted longest at the soda-fountain, because the Furnesses had not the American weaknesses for cold drinks and proprietary medicines. The apparent cheerfulness of his irresponsibility was a humorous Irish mask for his distaste for commercial drudgery and the growing unhappiness of his divided life. He flung out impatiently against a situation which only the most deadly application of industry could have cured.

When he tried working in New York he was away from her all day; she had now refused to meet him at night after the others were asleep, and he could not endure the deprivation of not seeing her. She must have discovered, by this time, that their love-affair was becoming a guilty madness. While he was with her he had all sorts of plans, the most impossible hopes, the wildest dreams, but—away from her—he could not fulfil them. She was like a drug that left him enervated instead of a stimulant to spur him on.

For a year at least a silent struggle had gone on between them; and then, apparently, she gave it up. He began drifting aimlessly, and she did not reproach him. He took it for granted that she was satisfied to wait for the realization of his vague ambition to be a singer—he was the barytone soloist in the Choral Club—to "break into" musical comedy, to take to the concert stage. She had become patiently melancholy, but he attributed that to the war. Her mother's was a military family, and five of her relatives had been killed at the front. The letters from home were full of tragedy and discouragement. She tried to talk to him about it, but he knew very little about the war and cared less. His father was an irreconcilable hater of the Sassenach, rejoicing in the British disasters; and Con felt himself superior to both sides in his neutral indifference.

Now she had just returned from a visit to friends in New York, and she had returned most affectionate, but most depressed. Her brother, Howard Hartley, was going to England to enlist. She had even hinted that there was talk of the whole family accompanying him. But she had said nothing about Lieutenant Williamson, and it was only accidentally that Con overheard some one at the Country Club speaking of the Englishman as her fiancé. That had happened on the club-house veranda, just a few minutes before I spoke to him. It was the cause of his excessive emotion at my offer of assistance. It was the reason why he had tried to get a dance with her, and waylaid her when he saw me with her, and followed us to demand of her, "Are you going to marry him?"

She had refused to say that she was not. She

had admitted that she was probably going to England with Howard and her parents. "We're needed. We're all needed," she kept saying. "And what's the use of my staying here? I'm only ruining your life."

"And she's *not!*" Con cried. "She's not! She can't leave me now—after what there's been between us. I'll go crazy. I'll kill myself. It's all I've had to live for in this— If she's needed over there— Needed! I know. I know. It's her mother. She's— She's got her all doped up with this English stuff. She always did it. She's kept her away from everybody and everything. If it hadn't been for me she'd 've gone crazy, shut up that way, with no one even to talk to! She doesn't understand. She believes what her mother tells her. She's always doing things because her mother— She should 've— When I wanted her to— When I had a job in New York in that big clothing-store I wanted her to beat it and get married, and she wouldn't. She said it would be 'too terrible—for mother.' That old snoot! I'd like to know— I don't see what hold they've got over her. *I* can't make her— Half the time I can't even tell what she's thinking about any more. She just sat here to-night and shivered till I could hear her teeth chatter and said, 'No. No. I'm ruining your life!' And she's *not!* She's *not!* Oh— Oh —if I lose her— She *can't!* I can't let her! She's *got* to wait! I'm only nineteen. I'll find some way.

14   [199]

I'll do anything! I don't care, as long as she doesn't go and— O my God, I'll go crazy!"

And I was afraid that he might. I never saw anything like it. He would talk himself into comparative exhaustion, and then the thought that he was going to lose her would strike him like a physical pang, and he would bury his face in his hands and cry out as if he were contorted with actual pain. And then he would begin to rave again. He had an amazing capacity for suffering. He wore me out with it. I would certainly have given him an opiate if I had had one with me. For a long time I could think of nothing else to do.

10

I was convinced that she had made up her mind to break with him. It was the only course open to her. He could not marry her; he could not marry any one; and there was no prospect that he would ever be in a position to marry a girl of her traditions. She could not introduce him to her family and its conventions, even as a friend; it would have been torture for both him and her. She was returning to her own people. There was nothing for him to do but to return to his. That was obvious.

But it was equally obvious that if he realized what she was doing he would fight it in a scandalous frenzy. He would expose her to everybody as he had already exposed her to me. He was beyond the reach of persuasion, caution, reason of any kind.

He talked incoherently of going to her family and confronting her mother and "bawling them out." It was just frantic nonsense, but he seemed capable of doing it. And since, by her appeal, she had made me responsible for him, I could not simply walk away and leave him to run amuck.

I began to persuade him that his situation had been entirely changed by the fact that I had a part for him in a play. I assured him that he was an actor, with a career before him. If he could convince her of that—or if he could persuade her to wait a month while he proved it—even if she went to England she might be willing to wait for him. "Show her," I argued. "That's what you have to do—show her. Make good. Get her to give you time. She'll do it, I'm sure. Even if she goes to England she'll wait, if she sees any hope. She's that sort of girl. Show her that you have the backbone and she'll stand by you. Sure."

And I intended to find some way of reaching her and saying: "You can't go off like this. He'll do something mad. I can't hold him. Nobody can— except you. If you have to go to England, wait till you get there before you break with him. Give him some hope—and take it away from him gradually if you must. But, meanwhile, help me, some way. You'll have to. He's in a frightful state."

I persuaded *him* easily enough. He was ready to clutch at anything. But I persuaded him too well. I persuaded him so well that he insisted only *I* could persuade her.

"She won't believe me," he confessed, pitifully. "I've had too many plans that never came to anything. But if you told her that I can act—that you've got this part for me—that we'll go and land it to-morrow morning—she'll believe *you*. Yes, she will. 'Phone her. 'Phone her. Come on and telephone her."

"I'll do it," I said, "if you'll promise to go home, and stay there, and keep quiet, and get ready to come to town with me to-morrow morning."

"All right. All right." He grabbed my arm. "Come on. You can 'phone her from the drugstore. Hurry up. We'll be too late. They lock up—"

At least he was no longer in hysterics; there was that much gained. And he had given up his idea of bursting in on her family and demanding her out of hand. But in some unconscious need of physical action to relieve his impatience he tried to start me running to the drug-store instead of taking my car. "Keep quiet, you idiot!" I said. "This has to be done carefully. Get in the back seat there and keep quiet. I have to think of what to say to her."

I might as well have tried to think in a Bellevue ambulance, with a patient on the way to the psychopathic ward. He had gone from a frenzy of despair to an insane height of voluble hope. Certainly he would make a great actor if temperament could do it.

I left him in the car when I got out at the druggist's to telephone. And I had a moment to collect my thoughts while her brother—who answered the 'phone—went to call her. I began guardedly to explain to her that I needed help, mentioning no names; that I had succeeded in persuading him to go home, but he insisted that I must see her; that I had something to propose—

She cut me short with, "Tell him I'll come."

I did not understand. "Where?" I asked. "When?"

She repeated, "Tell him I'll come." And she hung up.

He understood.

"Come on. Come on," he cried. "Hurry up. My room. It's my room."

11

I was glad that Centerbrook went to bed at ten. He hung over me, from the back seat, urging me on, like the heroine of a movie race between a touring-car and sudden death. And when he had hurried me, stumbling through the dark halls and up the creaking staircases of the sleeping Gorman family, and pushed me into his attic room and locked the door behind us and switched on the light, he stood, with his eyes on the faded chintz curtains of a clothes-closet, panting with all the impatient emotions of a screen star with the chest heaves. It seemed to me that life had become amazingly melodramatic.

He began to pace up and down the room under the sloping ceiling, talking in low, eager, distracted tones, throwing out abrupt and meaningless gestures at me. He was vitalized with emotion to a degree that made him feverishly demonstrative, but inexpressive. He bewildered me. He filled the little dormer-windowed room with a noiseless clamor of incoherent whispers and incommunicable dumb show and jumpy shadows. I sat down on the side of the bed and felt dizzy.

Suddenly he stopped. He stood waiting in a breathy silence. The chintz curtains parted before her, over an open door. And with her entrance our movie melodrama became, at once, the tragedy of beauty and dignity and poignant repression.

She was draped in some sort of flowing dressing-gown that made her appear matronly and classical. Her hair had been hastily gathered up in a coiled disorder high on her head. She came in from the darkness to our light noiselessly, and found him with a slow, set look that pitied him and suffered for him and stood firm. It was a look of irrevocable judgment and unmerciful compassion; and it made her most movingly beautiful to see.

Con cried out at once and rushed to her and took her in his arms. I went to blink out a window.

I began to realize the seriousness of the situation

in which I had undertaken to help. She had more character than I had supposed. She was more mature. She was not sparing herself, and I had to persuade her to spare *him*. I did not believe that I could do it. But when she spoke to me and I turned she was sitting in an old arm-chair, bending over Con, who was kneeling on the floor at her feet, his face buried in her knees childishly; and she was consoling him, like a widowed mother, with silent caresses, herself in tears. If she had that maternal love for him—

I began to tell her about the part that I had for him, talking for *his* benefit and making conspiring signs to her. It is an amazing thing to look back on; I did not predict half the success that he has met with, and yet neither of us believed a word I said. He alone was convinced by me. He looked up at her while she listened, and she pretended to be interested and impressed. "All he needs," I said, "is a little time—a month, say—to show you." ("Just a month," he pleaded. "Just a month.") "Don't do anything final—even if you have to go to England. Wait. Give him a chance." ("I'll make good. I will. I promise.") "He has real possibilities—real imagination—a real gift for the stage." And so on.

She kept saying, in reply to him, "Yes, yes. I'm sure you will," trying to smile, and patting at him blindly. "Yes, yes. I know."

In the midst of it she turned to me—in response

to something in my manner of which I was unaware —and said, jealously: "You mustn't blame him. He's been so good to me. He's—he's such a dear. It has all been more my fault than his. I wasn't brave enough. I'm not now. We were just—just children—innocent. We didn't understand. And we were—so happy."

"Oh, Flora!" he sobbed. They clung together like the babes in the woods. I felt like the cruel uncle.

I went back to the window. The lights of my car were burning in the street below. When there was a pause in their pitiful endearments I said, "We want to be in town early to-morrow morning." I couldn't stand any more of it. "You come along with me, Con, and we'll run in to-night, in the machine, sleep in my room there, and get hold of Bidey before any one else is given the part. I can 'phone up to the house and say I've been called in to New York unexpectedly. It often happens." I made a sign to her. It was as if we both knew that she was dying and we were planning to get him away in ignorance of it. She took it with just that face.

"Yes, yes," she said. "Go on, Con dear. Does he need to take his things? Let me pack them."

"And I'll run along, and telephone, and be back in ten minutes." I was glad of the chance to escape. "I'll toot for you."

She held out her hand. "Good-by," she said,

simply. "Thank you." But the look and the clasp of the hand that went with it were secretly in the manner of a death-bed farewell.

Not merely haste and darkness made me stumble going down the stairs.

12

I took as long as I could at the telephone, and had the car filled at the garage, and dawdled returning. Even so I had to wait ten minutes before the light in his room went out and I knew that they had parted.

I could imagine what the parting had been when I saw him stagger down the steps with his suitcase. And I was sorry enough for him. But I had to pretend to be optimistic or betray her confidence. "Now, boy," I said, "get in, back there, and make up your mind to leave this trouble behind you till you've landed the part and landed it big." He dropped the bag and sank into the seat, exhausted. "There's room to lie down on the floor, if you want to sleep. You can put back that foot-rail." He muttered something feebly and shook his head. I threw in the gas. And Conrad Norman started toward his unbelievable success.

He did not arrive in *my* care.

I got him the part in the play with no effort whatever. He seemed ideal for it. He began to rehearse. And after watching him for a few mornings I left him to his fate. It was evident that he lacked training. Beside the cultivated "readings" of the professionals in the cast he sounded amateur, pale-voiced. His tones had no theatrical make-up on them. They did not carry his points. At the best it would take him three or four years to acquire the experience and authority needed to put him over with an audience. And even then would Flora Furness marry him?

How could she? All the years that we had been laughing at the Furnesses in Centerbrook Mrs. Furness had been instinctively molding her son and her daughter to a career that was now beginning. Like a queen in exile, she had kept her children reminded of their royalty, stanch to their class. She had preserved in them the accents, the manners, the conventions, the ideals of the governing English. Flora could no more escape from them— to marry Gorman—than if she were a crown princess whose whole family depended upon her to succeed to a throne. Her very beauty made escape impossible. I could foresee that much.

I did not foresee Con's complete failure at rehearsals.

For a week everything went fairly well. Apparently he tried to work and forget her. He tried to keep her out of his thoughts and learn his lines. And I judge that what he succeeded in doing was this: by a very common trick of the mind he inhibited not his memory of her, but his memory for his rôle. When every one else in the cast was letter perfect he was still stumbling and uncertain. He began to lose his self-confidence. He could not "read" a single line correctly, because he was trying to recall it, not trying to *mean* it. No one understood what was the matter with him. They thought that he was simply stupid. When they found him crying in the wings they accepted it as his despairing recognition of his own failure. (He was crying, I learned afterward, because she had sailed from Boston that morning.) The stage director "let him out," as they say. I did not hear of it for some days, and he did not come to me for any further help. He went to Los Angeles with a film company.

Three months later we got the news in Centerbrook that Lieutenant Williamson had succeeded to some sort of title by the death of his two elder brothers in France, and that Flora had married him in the church at Bury. And, as far as I was concerned, the story was complete.

When I saw Conrad Norman in "King Charles the First" I realized what fools we had all been and of what a young genius the spoken drama had been deprived. I realized, also, that the disastrous ending of his affair with Flora Furness had been the making of him artistically. He had qualities of repose and pathos that were marvelous in one so young. His salary was advertised as a thousand dollars a week. At that price he was irrevocably lost to the playwrights. I felt sorry for them. I even felt sorry for Flora Furness. As for the Centerbrookers, the joke was on them both ways. The daughter of the stuffed-heart aristocracy and poor Con Gorman, the ne'er-do-well, had both arrived at their distinguished goals by following the impractical bypaths which Centerbrook—in the person of the coal-yard proprietor—had so despised. Life has a way of playing such little jokes upon the wisdom of the too practical.

13

It has also a way of playing similar jokes upon the wisdom of the too unromantic.

I supposed, as I say, that their story was complete. They were separated by all the waters of the Atlantic, to say nothing of the even greater distances of social differences between them. When we heard that Howard Hartley, being invalided home from France, had married an English heiress the news made no point with me. It did not occur to me that the Furness family no longer depended on Flora to maintain their position in the world. I was equally blind when her husband's name was given among those who died aboard the *Queen Mary* in the Jutland battle. I still thought of Lady Flora Williamson as irrevocably committed to the aristocratic life and the war work of the Woman's Auxiliary Corps, of which she was an active patroness.

Even when I received a letter from her, asking how Con was doing, I took it merely as more of her "unmerciful compassion," sent her an account of him, and inclosed her letter in an envelope to Conrad Norman in care of the Domino Film Company. She wrote, it seemed to me, in a tone of war weariness; but that was natural. She said something about England being changed, life there a tragedy, the war a "dreadful oppression." I did not wish to blame her, but I felt that if she was unhappy she had no right to imply that I was responsible—by writing to me for sympathy.

What I did not understand was this: England had been to her a home of dreams, a place of refuge in her mind from all the realities of poverty and Centerbrook. Her father and mother talked of it as Adam and Eve might have recalled better days in Eden. All her English novels painted it in imaginative colors, in "the light that never was"; and she went to it as an escape from life, from the hopelessness of her affection for Con Gorman and the sight of his misery. And she found that England was "changed," that life there was full of the most terrible realities of death and war, that she had not escaped, that even the unhappiness of Centerbrook looked like comparative peace and quiet.

This, as I say, is what I did not understand. I did not understand it till she told me of it herself, not very lucidly, sitting over our coffee-cups after dinner in a suite at the Biltmore, a week after Con and she had been married, under such head-lines as these:

SCREEN STAR WEDS PEERESS

CONRAD NORMAN SECRETLY MARRIED TO SIR CUTHBERT WILLIAMSON'S WIDOW

Conrad Norman, popular star of the Domino Film Company, and Lady Flora Williamson, widow of Sir Cuthbert Williamson, late of the British navy and who was killed in the Jutland battle, were married by the Rev. Simon G. Montague, in St. Agatha's Episcopal Church, upper Broadway, last Tuesday afternoon, it was learned yesterday.   Lady Williamson is the only—

I had not been invited to the wedding. I should probably never have been invited to the dinner either, if I had not happened to encounter Lady Flora under the *porte-cochère* of the Biltmore after their secret was in all the papers. "We intended to start at once for California," she apologized, "or I should have called you up. You must have dinner with us. Con will be so glad to see you."

I suspected that Con would be about as glad to see me as to see the coal-proprietor from Leedy Street, and my suspicion was accurate. He was entirely polite, at his ease, and unself-conscious, but he scarcely looked at me. He kept his eyes almost constantly on his wife. He talked to me, as it were, through her. And he gave me the strangest impression of a complete withdrawal of interest, not only from me, but from all the outer world from which I came.

At first I thought he averted his eyes from Center-brook, as represented in my person, and from his past, of which I reminded him. But he had the same air toward the waiters who served him and the food that he ate. And when she spoke of both Center-brook and of their days there he had no change of face. He listened to her and watched her, deeply contented—too contented to speak or to smile. He was obviously a happy man, in a happy dream, making a fortune in a world of make-believe as a young actor and seeing in her the only reality that interested him.

As for her, she seemed more beautiful, more dis-tinguished, and yet more human than ever. Our dinner was served in the sitting-room of their suite, a room of French grays and gray-greens that had an air of luxurious delicacy, in which she reigned like a princess of Versailles. The waiters looked to her for their directions and she gave them without consulting her husband; she knew exactly what he liked and how he liked it served. A maid came to her with a telephone call, and she said, "Tell them he is at dinner." A man-servant brought her railroad tickets, and she explained to me, "We are leaving for Los Angeles to-morrow." They had seats for the opera that evening, and it was she who watched the clock and ordered the taxi.

I congratulated them on their happiness as I left. She said, "I'm happier than I ever deserved to be." And she put her arm through Con's and patted his hand, looking up at him fondly, as if to assure him that he, at least, had deserved his happiness.

In any case, he continues to enjoy it and his popularity and his income and his whole colossal success. Charlie Chaplin is now his only rival in the public eye, and even Chaplin has to take the second place which comedy must always accept from tragedy in the republic of art.

FROM THE LIFE
W. T.

W. T.

1

I DO not know who he is. And neither does old Captain Jim Johnson, who told me about him. We know only his initials. They were tattooed on his right forearm in blue ink and red—a blue anchor with a twist of red rope around the shank, and a red "W" over one fluke and a blue "T" over the other. But what we do know is his remarkable story, and it surely entitles him to a place in these portrait-studies, for it seems to me quite the most distinguished true story that I have run across; and if "W. T." is not himself immortally famous, it is only because he has not met a Eugene Sue to do him as another "Wandering Jew," or a second Coleridge to make another "Ancient Mariner" of him.

Moreover, Captain Johnson has begged me: "Put somethin' about him in the papers, an' if any one comes across 'm, tell 'em to write Cap'n Jim Johnson, Port Derby, eh? I'd like to get th' ol' crocodile back here an' look after 'm. I don't sleep well no more. Gettin' old. An' I—I kind o' bother about him at night. *You* know."

So, if only to keep my promise to the captain—

2

Imagine an old stooped sailorman coming into Port Derby one summer day in the late 'nineties, with brass rings in his ears and dusty to the waist with walking. Imagine him as bald as a toad—not a hair on his face, not an eyelash, not a bristle—and his scalp as bare as a dried mushroom below the sun-greened cloth cap that he wore on his skull-top. Imagine him wind-cured, sea-scalded, storm-toughened, wrinkling up his forehead to open his eyes, working his lips in a toothless mumble, shuffling along the road with the dust puffing up under his feet, and looking altogether like an old tortoise that had been driven out into the glare of the highway in search of a new "crawl."

And imagine Port Derby a mere cluster of houses at the mouth of Catfish Creek, with orchards and corn-fields behind them, a rotting wharf at the water's edge, some boats drawn up on the sands, and a number of great pound nets, raised on poles in a shore meadow, waiting to be mended. Imagine the little village lying in a hollow so quiet and so hidden that the hills of the shore-line seemed to cuddle it in the crook of an arm, with a haze veiling it against the midday sun and all Lake Erie glittering before it and all Lake Erie's little waves rustling quietly on the beach shingle.

Imagine such a weary old tramp, in the blazing heat of the hill road, looking down on such a peaceful refuge—so cool and so moist—and you will understand what Captain Johnson does not profess to know, namely, why "th' ol' crocodile happened in on Port Derby." As well ask why the alligators happened in on the Everglades of Florida.

The captain, sitting on the veranda of the little hotel, saw him come crawling across the wooden bridge of Catfish Creek. "Well," he says, "I seen at onct he was a sailorman. Rings in his ears, ol'-fashioned sailor ways. He was the color of a smoked ham that's been hung too long. Kind o' dried up an' drawn to the string. Bald as a peeled egg. Been trampin', I c'u'd see that."

And the captain greeted him, "Well, mate, where 're *you* bound to?"

3

The man stopped and looked up at him slowly, with a brow-puckered scrutiny, dazed and uncertain. He did not reply.

"Come in out o' the sun," the captain said; and he came into the shade of the veranda and sat down on the steps, with his back turned.

He had no pack. He was coatless, in a gray flannel shirt, a leather belt, and stained overalls. A bare toe showed through a break in his shoe.

Captain Jim tried him with various inquiries: "Come far?" "Purty tired, eh?" "Lookin' fer work?"

No answer. He did not even turn around. He sat looking, apparently, at the pound nets in the meadow across the road.

"Hungry?" the captain asked, and he replied with an unintelligible dumb grunt.

"Well," the captain said, "come along and have a drink first."

He rose painfully and followed into the bar, silent, looking at the floor. The captain decided he was either dumb or had "a button loose somewhere." He would not speak. He would not look at them. He gulped down his whisky straight, turned at once and shuffled back to his place on the steps. The captain ordered a plate of dinner sent out to him. He took it, as silent as a dog, and ate it from his fingers, discarding the knife and fork, his back to them all.

"Give 'm anything he wants," the captain ordered, shook his head—with pity—and went home to his own meal.

He was an old man himself, with a white head of hair and a white fringe of whiskers so fine and so fluffy that he looked like a "four-o'clock"— like a ripe dandelion gone to seed—with his pink scalp glowing through its aureole and his tanned skin brown under his beard. There are babies that look like wise and solemn old men. Captain Jim looked like one of those babies in a beard; and his favorite oath—"By damn"—came wonderingly from a small mouth of red lips that sucked on the stem of his pipe as if the bowl of it were full of modified milk.

He was the postmaster and the customs officer of the port; he owned the fishing-tug and the pound nets; and he employed all the men of the village who would work in his boats. He was building another tug and needed hands to help with her. The old sailor looked as if he might be of some use.

Captain Jim, after dinner, proposed it and was answered by a grunt which he accepted as assenting; and when the men, returning to their work, reappeared in the meadow where the tug's keel had been laid, Captain Jim led the new-comer to join them.

"What's yer name?" he asked, on the way.

He got no answer.

He said: "All right. I'll call you 'Sam.' I s'pose you can swing an adz?"

They came among the oak timbers that were being cut out for the boat's ribs. Captain Jim held out an adz to him. He drew away with a nervous shrinking from the tool, and when the captain asked, sharply, "What's the matter?" he looked down at his hands, held them out, open, and showed a deformity that he had been concealing.

The little finger of each hand was closed down flat on the palm, as if paralyzed.

"Huh!" Captain Jim said. "How'd you do that?"

The question was asked in a tone that was scarcely

more than mildly curious, but it had the most amazing effect on the old sailor. He had his hands still out in front of him, and his wrinkled gaze was fixed on them pathetically. They began to tremble in a shuddering palsy that crept up his arms to his neck and set his teeth chattering and fluttered his breath.

The captain caught him by the shoulder. "Sit down," he said. "You're dog-tired. There. That's all right. Now."

The old man sat down weakly on a log and took his head in his hands. He shook as if he had a chill.

When the tremor had passed Captain Jim said: "Better, eh? Well. When you feel like work come over an' help us on the steam-box. Know how to warp boards, eh? . . . Come away, boys. Don't bother him. He's a bit touched."

They did not bother him. They did not even appear to notice him. And, though they watched him and speculated about him all the afternoon, they did it with that cunning of village curiosity that seems so indifferent and is so secretly keen.

He took his place among them at the steam-box, and his crippled hands did not seem to interfere with his work. But he refused to wield an ax as he had refused the adz; he continued dumb; and when the afternoon was done he took his supper on the hotel veranda at the captain's expense, accepted a corn-cob pipe and a plug of tobacco, and wandered away up the beach in the fading light.

He did not reappear until the morning. Subsequently it was found that he had taken possession of a deserted shack in a hollow behind the captain's farm, where a bend in the shore-line met the trickle of a swamp.

"I seen a man had hands like that afore," Captain Jim said. "He done it handlin' grain-bags. Yeh. When they ust to team it down here an' load it into schooners—afore the railroad was built up yonder. But *he* 'ain't been a longshoreman. He's been a deep-sea sailor er I'll eat my hat. Wonder what he's doin' away up here, anyway."

4

Port Derby is hundreds of miles from the ocean and ten miles from a railroad, even. The mail arrived on a buckboard once a day. The fish were taken to a shipping port, on the tug, once a week. Between fishing and farming the little community supported itself in a contented isolation, and if old "Sam" had wished to escape the world he could not have chosen a better hermitage.

If he had wished to escape the notice of his fellow-men he could not have chosen a worse one. He was as much discussed as a murder trial in town. Was he crazy? Was he a criminal in hiding? Was he really dumb? How had he lost his hair? What had happened to his hands? Where did he come from? Why had he left his home?

The belief that he was an imbecile was weakened when it was seen with what ingenuity he fitted up his shack, making himself a sort of bake-oven of stones, taking useless blocks of wood from the boat-building and nailing planks to them for benches, cutting fir branches for a bed, mending his roof with rotted canvas from the wharf and painting it over with tar, unraveling old nets to make himself fishing-lines for rusty hooks that had been thrown away by the village boys, and in everything proceeding as rationally as a Robinson Crusoe. The suspicion that he was a criminal in hiding could not endure after it was observed that he avoided strangers less than he did the acquaintances of his working-hours and seemed more uneasy with the benevolent Captain Jim than with anybody else. His incredible hairlessness was explained by a young doctor—summoned to the village to set the broken leg of one of the boat-builders—who gave it out that Sam was the victim of a skin disease with a sesquipedalian scientific name. But on the mystery of where he had come from or why he had come nothing happened to throw any light.

One of the men stole up to the shack at night and peeped through a crack in the boarding. He came away with a report that the old man sat for hours by his lantern, looking at his hands. Certainly he used an amount of oil that was not accounted for until the village found that his light burned every night till sunrise. Some small boys, who hid behind the bushes at dusk and pelted his shanty with beach pebbles, were driven off, panic-stricken, by an unearthly bellow close behind them in the trees—a hoarse, inhuman noise which they could not describe except in terms of terror. When Captain Jim heard of it he threatened all the boys of the village—and their parents—with all the punishments of his wrath if any youngster so much as hooted at Sam on the street. And thereafter the poor wretch was left to his misery in peace.

Captain Jim gave him clothes and bedding, sent cooked food to his shack while he was away from it, "stood" him drinks in the bar, lent him a boat in which to go fishing for mud-cats up the creek, and paid him, as well, for his work on the boat-building or in the garden. In return for it all he did not get more gratitude than could be expressed in a grunt.

"He's got somethin' on his mind, that's all," Captain Jim decided. "It's got him a bit touched. Knowed 'n old sailor up to Duluth like that—on'y his was religion. He'll come through. He hangs 'round down to the hotel now, 's long 's no one speaks to him. Leave 'm alone."

They were willing to "leave 'm alone." Their curiosity, by this time, had died a natural death. They accepted Sam jocularly as a half-witted old mute who was amusing when he was not too pig-headed.

And then one morning, after the new tug had

been launched and the work of calking the deck seams was in progress, Captain Jim, while overseeing the men, stepped back against a loose timber, lost his balance, and fell backward into the creek. Before the others could more than drop their tools Sam screamed, "Cap'n! Cap'n!" and dived overboard. And the men were so amazed at the sound of his voice that they stood staring at the pair in the water as if they had seen a dead man come to life.

The captain had been a good swimmer in his day, but he was dazed by his fall, and for a moment, when he came to the surface, he beat the water feebly with the palms of his hands, gasping. Sam had him by the collar in an ·instant and held him out of water to the shoulders till he caught his breath. Then they struck out together for the bank.

When they had found bottom and stood up dripping in the water-weeds Captain Jim turned on his rescuer. "Well, by damn!" he cried. "You old mud-turtle!" and thumped him on the back. "It was you, was it? What d'you mean! Get up out o' this. D'you want to kill yerself?" He shoved Sam up the bank before him, calling upon all the men to witness the ancient folly of this reprobated old son of a sea-cook. "What d'yon think o' that!" he cried, wiping the trickle of water out of his eyes and grimacing in a doubtful attempt to grin down an emotion that was not acknowledgable. "What d'you think— Th' old— Well, by damn!"

Sam ran his hands down his sides, squeezing the water from his shirt. He stooped to wring out his trousers legs stolidly. He said nothing.

Some of the men came down the plank, with the clumsy inquiries of an awkward solicitude for the captain. He did not understand the way in which they looked at Sam; he had not heard the scream that had betrayed the old sailor's voice.

"Are y' all right, Cap'n?" they asked him.

"All right," he quavered. "O' course I'm all right. Little water. Come on here, Sam. Come on an' have a drink an' get off them wet clothes. Course I'm all right. Go on with yer work."

They went back to the deck, and Captain Jim, still unaware of Sam's return to the use of his tongue, took him to the hotel. It was late in the afternoon; a chill wind had begun to blow, and the captain, for all his jovial and hearty gratitude, shivered so much that after a brief glass he sent Sam to his shack and hurried home. Very much shaken and chilled through, he went to bed.

5

"Sophy," he said that evening to his daughter, as he sat up, smoking, among his pillows, "that old boy can't winter it in a shack. He'll freeze stiff. Better give 'm the room over the kitchen. He'll carry wood an' do chores fer you, anyway. Eh?"

"Well," she said, taken aback, "he's pretty feeble, ain't he?"

"No!" the captain cried. "Feeble! I thought it was Johnny had me by the neck. Feeble nothin'! He works 's good 's the best o' them—where he knows how."

"He won't chop the wood," she said. The whole village had discovered his aversion to the use of an ax.

"No," he reflected. "He's a bit queer about that. He ain't strong in his top story. But he's harmless, girl. An' we've treated him like a dog—leavin' him live in that swamp—"

"He wouldn't let you do anything else."

"That's so. That's right. Well, I'll make him come if I have to move the shack to do it."

The captain's house was a relic of the ante-railroad days of Port Derby's prosperity. It was a building of some pretensions, with a Colonial pillared porch and a roof-top belvedere. And his daughter was a middle-aged spinster of precise habits who was a neat housekeeper and proud of her house. She did not relish the prospect of admitting this uncanny old outcast to a place in it; the room over her kitchen was her sewing-room, stored with blankets, winter bedding, household linen, and a thousand things that she did not wish to remove. Moreover, one fanciful old man at a time was all she desired under her care—for the captain had his peculiarities.

It was not that she objected to having all the inner door-sills painted twice a year, as if they were aboard a ship, and she let him use a lantern in his bedroom, although a lamp surely would have looked better, but she had noticed of late that he had begun to be careless about his clothes, that he slept heavily in the afternoons, that he depended too much upon the stimulants at the bar. And when she found, treasured up under his bed, a big tin biscuit-box filled with misered plugs of tobacco of which many had gone moldy, she realized that the captain was failing. She would have a happy life as the captain grew worse and Sam was added to her burden!

But the captain had an obstinate temper. It was bad policy to oppose him outright. She had to humor him, to wheedle him, and to get her own way while pretending to give him his. It was for this reason that when the story of how Sam had spoken came to her—from one of the men who called to see how the captain was—she went straight to her father with her indignation. "A nice old man! After all you've done for him! Why, he's been making fools of all of us."

"What's the matter, girl?"

"Why, that old Sam—pretending he couldn't talk."

"What?" The captain sat upright. "Is he talkin'!"

"Yes! All the men heard him."

"Where? When?"

She told him artfully, working herself into a fine resentment against "the old scamp." And the captain listened, staring at her like a snowy owl.

"I wouldn't trust him!" she cried. "I wouldn't put anything past him. He's no fool. He's bad. Of all the double-faced— I s'pose he's been laughing at us behind our backs all the time. He's done something wrong. That's what he's done. Why, you could tell it by the look of him! I'd be afraid to have him near the place. He might murder us all in our beds. I never heard of such a thing. The old liar—if I do say it." And so endlessly, while the captain listened with a "Huh!" that sounded as if he were really half convinced, but signified merely that there was matter for new thought in the affair and that he was reconsidering it.

He made no reply to her then nor later in the day when he rose for dinner, and she supposed that he had weakened in his kindly feeling for the hypocritical Sam. He did not go down to the boat that afternoon, but sat smoking and thinking and taking "cat-naps" in his chair. Once he remarked that the cold weather would be coming on and inquired about the woodpile. "Ought to get a couple o' loads o' that driftwood fer the fireplace," he said. "Wonder if there's much of it on the beach this year."

She did not know. It was a peculiarity of the

beach that there was one spot where the wood came ashore in abundance—great trees that had been uprooted by the rains and carried out into the lake, ships' timbers, the loosened planks of derelicts, and all the wreckage of storms and freshets. The natives of Port Derby went there to gather their winter's firing, saving their own trees.

The captain, after an early supper, while it was still light, filled his pipe and started .off across his fields to see the cove where the wood came in. And it was not till he had gone that his daughter remembered that Sam's shack stood near the edge of this same cove. Even so, she was in doubt whether the captain had deceived her with a rather senile cunning or whether the whole thing was an innocent coincidence.

It is probable that the captain did not quite know, himself. But it is certain that when he came upon Sam, sitting on a scoured log at the water's edge, he was not surprised to see him.

"Well, Sam," he said, "they tell me you've found yer voice."

6

The men at the boat had been nagging the old man in Captain Jim's absence, venting upon him some of that same spleen which the captain's daughter had felt when she learned that they had all been "made fools of"; and Sam was obviously worried and dejected. He did not look up at the sound

16

of the captain's voice. He continued gazing out at the sunset, his elbows on his knees, his chin supported on his cramped hands, smoking sadly.

The captain struck a match and sat—to relight his pipe—on the other end of the log. "Well," he said, "I come down to see if there was much wood here fer the winter. Pick up more logs here in a day than you could cut down in a week. Cold weather's comin', Sam. You'll freeze stiff in that shack. I was tellin' my girl to get a room ready fer you—over the kitchen, where it 'll be warm. You can do her chores fer yer board—if you want to."

Sam stopped puffing at his pipe, but he did not turn around.

"We're gettin' old," the captain went on. "Got to have a warm bed when you're old. I ust to be able to sleep on cargo an' never notice it. Well, well. I remember once—" And he rambled off into reminiscences of his rough youth when he had sailed the Great Lakes and been a "terrible feller."

They were reminiscences of the easy love-affairs of an able-bodied seaman, of sailors' fights in water-front "dives," of smuggling adventures in the days when he had run a schooner between the mouth of the Niagara River and the Canadian Port Credit—before the use of the telegraph put an end to that sort of "skylarkin'"—and of "bounty-jumping" in ports along the American shore during the Civil War. If there was a noticeable strain of moral obliquity running through them all, it was not because the captain was uncon-scious of it. He had been thinking about Sam all day, and these apparently idle recollections were given artfully.

Sam's pipe went out; he sat with it in his hands, staring at the darkening water and listening like a man mesmerized. The sun had set; an early autumn moon rose behind them. Once or twice Sam muttered to himself. And once he began in a dry squeak of a voice, "Cap'n"—but the cap-tain did not pause. Sam sighed and moved un-easily. The captain continued his amiable confes-sions in a friendly, soothing tone.

"Cap'n," the old man said, hoarsely, "what 'd you 'a' done if—" His voice fell away into silence irresolutely.

"If they'd ketched me?" the captain asked. He was at the end of his story of the bounty-jumping. "Well, I s'pose I'd been rushed to the front on the first train. But they didn't ketch me." He chuckled. "Not them."

Sam shook his head. "If you 'd been out 'n a boat an' the water near all gone, an'—"

"What boat?"

"The *Bristol's*."

The captain leaned forward, intent. "Ship-wrecked?"

Sam sank in upon himself again; he fumbled at

his forehead with a hand. "Ay, shipwrecked. Me —an'—" He either could not remember or his mind wandered. "In the boat," he said. "An' the water all gone—an' the heat till yer brain 'd ache." He shook his old lizard's head again weakly. "Hot—hot."

The captain signified a professional understanding. "Yeh?"

"An' we had nuthin' but the end o' one keg o' water," he said, staring ahead of him as if he saw in that vast expanse of lake the scene that was in his mind's eye. "It was goin' by thimblefuls. Seven of us. An' our tongues swollen so we couldn't shut our jaws. An' the mate says: 'Boys, it's time to draw lots. There's too many of us. Take yer choice. We'll all die together if we don't,' he says. 'All of us!' An' my mouth so dry I couldn't eat the biscuit no more than it was sand."

The captain waited, listening, with his head on one side, watching him. The moonlight had grown strong enough to make a faint shadow on the beach. When Sam continued silent he said: "Well, in a case like that there, I s'pose there's nothin' else to do. I remember once—"

Sam licked his lips. "So we drawed lots—the long one an' the short one. An' young Tom got the long one—an' then, when it come to me, I got the short one. An' nobody said a word, except one o' the men sort o' laughed."

He turned suddenly. "What would you 'a' done?"

he cried. "With the wife home—an' the baby—waitin' fer you? An' young Tom with nobody dependin' to him."

The captain replied, coaxingly, "Well, what 'd you do, Sam?"

"'Mates,' I says, 'I'm a married man. I got a wife, mates,' I says, 'an' a little one. Is it fair,' I says, 'that I go, that's got them dependin' to me, an' Tom here's got no one? Is it right?' I says. An' they didn't say a word. We was all played out. I could scarce speak, my mouth was so. 'Is it right?' I says. 'No! If any one goes, it ought to be Tom,' I says. 'He's got no one. He's near dead now. What good is he? He can't help none. 'Tain't right! I'm a strong man. I got a woman to keep. I got a little one—'"

"Sure, sure!" the captain soothed him. "What 'd they do?"

"It was Tom. Tom did it. He was sick. He didn't care what happened to him. He said he'd sooner go than do it—than shove me off. We'd nothing to do it with but the ax. So we changed lots—Tom an' me. An' he said if we'd do it while he was asleep— That's all he asked—to do it while he was asleep."

"Asleep?" the captain cried. "Do you mean to say he could go to sleep?"

"Asleep. He was sick."

He had begun to tremble. "U-up in the nose o' the boat," he said in a low, shaken voice. "He crawled up there an'—an' laid down. An' after it was dark—"

"Well, Sam," the captain cut in, quickly, "that's the way those things happen. A man's got to fight fer his life sometimes. He ain't accountable. In a boat like that—dyin' o' thirst an' you with a wife an' fam'ly to think o'. It couldn't be helped, I guess. It just had to be. You want to ferget it. It's—"

Sam said: "I couldn't do it. I sat there all night—an' couldn't do it. In the dark. I heard him turn over. He was talkin' crazy to himself —wantin' water. It was hot—hot—an' still. An' no one said a word."

The captain clucked his tongue commiseratingly. "Tut, tut! It's all past an'—"

"An' then a little breeze sprung up, an' it got a little light, an' I thought if I didn't do it mebbe he'd wake up an' go back on what he said. An' so—" He clutched his hands in front of him agonizedly. "I—I—"

"Sam!" the captain cried. "Now never mind! Never mind! I don't want to hear. You don't want to be thinkin' about it. That's what's the matter. You been thinkin' about it too much. You—"

"Listen!" Sam screamed. "Listen! He wasn't cold before they seen a sail. Right against the sun when it come up! A sail! A brig that took us all aboard—him, too—an' me—with the blood onto my hands—" He held them out to the lake, clenched, shaking them fiercely as if they were not a part of him, but something hateful, something criminal, and guilty against himself.

The captain grasped him by the arm. "Stop!" he said. "Stop it! You've got to stop it. You've got to ferget it. Listen to me. It wasn't your fault. Case like that. Man's got to fight fer his life. When he's got a wife an' fam'ly—'"

"Ah!" Sam groaned. "Wife an' fam'ly. They didn't think o' that. In the fo'c'sle—they turned against me. Them that 'd been in the boat with me. Yes! From the day they dropped him overboard with their prayers an' their caps off. They didn't think o' that. It makes a might o' difference when yer tongue ain't swelled up like a boot in yer mouth an' achin' so you'd go mad. Yes! Wife an' fam'ly. She turned against me. Her, too. Ev'ry one. All o' them."

"What? Yer wife, too?"

"Ay, an' my wife, too. It was all right the first night I got back. An' then one o' the boys told her." He dropped his voice to a broken breathiness. "He was her brother. Tom was her brother."

"Good—!"

"Tom was her brother—an' she took the little one an' went back home without a word. Not a word. An' when I went to tell her—to tell her how it was—her father came out. He was like to killed me."

The captain let him be. He sat, crouched, a figure of despair in the desolate moonlight, his mouth in his hands. The waves broke and broke before him, falling forward in a hissing sprawl on the pebbles.

"I went away," he said, talking to the water. "I shipped an' went away—an' no one knowed about it aboard an' I lay awake nights thinkin' of it—because no one knowed. An' they was hot nights—hot an' still. An' I heard some one turnin' over an' talkin' to himself. An' no one said a word, an' I had to bite into my blanket to keep from— There was a man named Durkin. Him an' me had a watch together. An' I wanted some one to ask. I wanted some one to—to— No one knowed about it. We was frien's—him an' me. An' I told him. I told him. An' there it was again. I could hear them whisperin' behind my back. I could see them lookin' at me when they thought I wasn't takin' notice. An' no one said a word about it. An' the little spot on the back o' my hand kep' spreadin' —bare—till the hair was all off. An' off my arm."

He held his hands out and looked at them.

"There, on the back—like where there'd been— there'd been blood—a little round spot, it began. Greasy." He clapped his hands to his face again, as if to cover his eyes against the sight of them. "An' they seen it!" he cried. "They seen it an' knowed what it was. An' I went ashore an' got away an' I didn't come back. But I knowed it!"

He threw out his arms. "I knowed it. I had it. Ev'rywhere I went I had it. I had to ask. I had to tell. I couldn't ferget it. I was marked. Head an' hands." He tore off his cap and raised his leprous skull to the light. "Look at me," he wailed as if to the night and the heaven and the indifferent waves. "Look at me! Head an' hands an' face an' body—marked! Marked! An' ev'ry one seen it. Ev'ry one knowed it. Ev'rywhere!"

The captain wiped his neck and wrists in his hand-kerchief and swore feebly. Sam had collapsed upon himself, huddled on the log.

"Sam," he said, "part of what happened—it—it's happened. There's no more to be said about it. It's past an' done. But part of it's nothin' but yer own damn imagination. There's somethin' wrong with yer skin. It's a—a disease. Any doctor 'll tell you the name of it. Cure it mebbe. An' yer fingers you hurt handlin' heavy weights. You've been roustaboutin'—workin' on the docks, 'ain't you?"

Sam said, sepulchrally: "I been ev'rywhere. All over the world, I've been. Doin' ev'rythin'. An' ev'rywhere I went there was some one that wouldn't let me be till he'd found out. An' then—"

"Well," the captain put in, guiltily, "that's what I say. That's what it is. Now here's where the thing ends. I don't say a word to no one—an' you don't. Not a word. You've had this thing on yer mind, an' now you've got rid of it. I'll see that no one bothers you. You needn't speak to a soul if you're afraid o' what you might tell. Just keep quiet an' mind yer bus'ness an' ferget all this—this stuff."

He patted Sam on the shoulder. "It weren't your fault. It might 'a' happened to any one. It might 'a' happened to me. An' here we are, now, a pair of old hulks together—me an' you—on'y I've got into a snug harbor an' you've been batterin' around crazy-fashion. You come up to my house an' I'll see you have enough t' eat, a warm bed, an' ev'rythin' to make you comfort'ble. No one 'll bother you. No one 'll speak to you 'less you want it. An' 'n a little while you'll ferget about this bus'ness, an' ev'rythin' 'll be all right again. Eh?"

He picked up Sam's cap and put it on him, found him his pipe in the sand, and coaxed him to his feet. "Come on, now. We'll make you snug's an ol' cricket. You'll be settin' by yer fire, come winter, with a glass o' grog in yer hand, happy 's —happy 's a cat. Come on. Eh?"

Sam was holding back. "Wait," he said, hoarsely. "Wait till to-morr'. I'll—"

"Will you come then?"

Sam nodded.

The captain remembered his daughter. "Well, then, all right. P'raps that's best. The girl 'll have to get yer room ready. That 'll give her time. Now you go to bed, Sam, an' have a good sleep. In the mornin' you'll feel better. This 's where this thing ends. You're going to be all right after this."

"G'night," Sam said, and staggered off through the sands toward his shack.

The captain watched him go—through the serene moonlight toward the shade of the willows that draped black along the edge of the swamp. There, suddenly, he threw his hands up over his head—and at the same instant disappeared in the shadows. The captain, having stood a moment gazing after him, turned and went home to his bed.

7

In the morning, after a scene of anger with his daughter, he posted down to the boat and found that Sam had not appeared for work. He waited an hour, and then hurried off to the shack. The door was open. The place was in disorder—the lantern thrown upon the floor, the bedding dragged aside, the bench overturned under the table—and Sam had gone.

Sam had gone. And all the efforts of the captain to learn in what direction he had gone, to find any one who had seen him on his way, or to hear anything of him in any of the neighboring villages—all were unavailing. He had gone. He had told his story again—and he had not waited.

"It was my fault," the captain says. "I oughtn't to made him tell it. But there it is. That can't be helped. He says himself he tells it ev'rywhere he goes. No use pretendin' he's dumb. Any one can see he's got somethin' on his mind an' they pump it out of 'm. No use beatin' around the way he's doin'. Get him back to me here. I'll look after him. Put somethin' in the papers about him, an' tell 'em to write Cap'n Jim Johnson if they've see 'm. Cap'n Jim Johnson, Port Derby. Eh? They'll know him by that 'W. T.' right here on the inside of his arm. A blue anchor fouled with a 'W' over one fluke an' a 'T' over th' other. Don't ferget *that*, now. That was his name—'W. T.'"

FROM THE LIFE
Hon. Benjamin P. Divins

HON. BENJAMIN P. DIVINS

DIVINS, Benjamin Parmalee, banker, politician; *b.* on farm, Sullivan Co., N. Y., Apr. 15, 1853; *s.* John Edward and Sarah (Parks) D.; ed. common sch.; *m.* Mary Johanna Van Slack, of Danville, N. Y., Nov. 21, 1888. Began commercial career as clerk in P. L. Boulton's general store, Cappsville, N. Y., 1870. Started in business for himself at Danville, 1875. President Danville First Natl. Bank 1895–1900; v.-p. 1901–08; p. 1909–   ; del. Nat. Convn., 1884; candidate N. Y. Assembly, 1890; state senator 2 terms, 1901–05; Dir. Ulster Electric Co., Ltd., Public Service Power Co., Ontario Suburban Ry. Co., Sullivan County Land and Investment Co., Catskill Mortgage Co., etc., Trustee Danville School, Schuyler Trust Co., Meth. Orphan Asylum, Hope Cemetery, etc. *Address:* 310 Walnut St., Danville, N. Y.—*Who's Who.*

1

IT is not difficult to choose the most significant day to chronicle in the life of the Honorable Benjamin Parmalee Divins, nor to decide what are the illuminating incidents to use in a brief portrait-study of him. The red-letter day of his life was the day that he drove over from the railroad at Cappsville to his brother's farm among the foothills of the Catskills in Sullivan County. And the illuminating incidents occurred after he arrived and met his brother.

He had hired a livery rig in Cappsville—a buggy that was decrepit and stiff in the springs, and a horse that was shaggy with its winter coat and as slow as rheumatism. The six miles of hill roads had been washed down to bed-rock by the April rains, and the drive would have been a long boredom of jolted discomfort to the Honorable Ben if it had been anything at all to him. As a matter of fact it was nothing. It did not register on him. Although it was a road that should have been full of memories of his youth, he drove it blindly, his eyes focused on empty space over the horse's ears, the reins slack in his hands, his collar turned up, his hat pulled down, leaning forward in his seat, his mind occupied. His unbuttoned overcoat showed that he was wearing broadcloth and clean linen, as became a man of his position in life. Under the brim of his hat his eyes were a cold blue, pinched in wrinkles.

It should have been one of the romantic moments of his life. Here he was—the most successful man that the neighborhood had ever produced—coming back, for the first time in twenty years, to revisit the scenes of his early hardships. And it would have been romantic to him if it had not been that he was thinking of his future, not of his past. And that was characteristic of the Honorable Ben. He was "a go-ahead man," his admirers said. His critics put it that he was "always on the make." His victims expressed another view of the same quality when they accused him of having no conscience.

He drove steadily, indifferently, up hill and down, past the wood-lots, the rocky meadows, the shabby farm-houses, the weather-beaten barns. The spring had come late, and, though a May sunlight was fitfully warm on the road, a March wind was hoisterous in the upper branches of the wayside trees and came plunging across the woods like the sound of surf. He ignored it.

He showed no interest in anything until he came to the Divins woods and saw ahead of him, on a cleared hillside, the Divins homestead. The reins tightened mechanically in his hands. The horse stopped.

Down the path from the farm-house to the road there was approaching a tall, gaunt man who walked like a moving frame of bones, lifelessly. He was dressed in clothes that had been worn and washed and sun-faded down to the essence and common nature of all cloth—an old felt hat the color of mildew, a brown cotton shirt, stained trousers, and dried cowhide boots. The house from which he came was an unpainted frame wreck that had been bleached and rotted by the inclement mountain seasons until it looked as broken and dejected as the man himself. He had an alder pole in one hand and a rusty tin can in the other.

The Honorable Ben studied him. He studied the house. Remembering it as he had known it in his boyhood, he might have looked at it with disgust for his brother's shiftlessness. He looked at it rather as if it were a property on which he was compelled to take a mortgage. He looked at it obviously with an eye to his own interests. He looked at it predaciously, speculatively, but with distaste.

Distaste was uppermost in the way he looked at the man. He had not seen his brother for fifteen years, but he had no doubt that here was Matt himself. It might have been a hired man, but he knew that Matt could not even pay the wages of such a slouching "buckwheater" as this. It was evidently Matt—going fishing.

He waited, watching him approach. Matt did not raise his eyes till he was close. Then he took in the horse first before he turned his mild attention to the driver. He accepted the challenge of Ben's keen stare with no sign of recognition.

"Well?" Ben said. "Don't you know me?"

2

He got no answer. Matt looked at his clothes, at his hands, and then at the horse again in a silent acceptance of him that was worse than indifference. It was the sort of acceptance that you might get from a friend's dog that dislikes you and lets you pass without a sound, without so much as a sniff at your heels, regarding you inscrutably.

Ben's mouth was sufficiently tight-lipped at its

best. It tightened perceptibly at his brother's manner. He snapped out, "I want to see you."

Matt did not reply, "Well, here I am." He had apparently recognized the horse; it was one that he had sold to the livery-stable, and, shifting his fishing-pole to the hand that held his bait-can, he patted the animal's flank thoughtfully.

"I want to see you alone somewhere," Ben said, with a growing impatience.

Matt nodded. He did not say, "Come along up to the house." He did not even give the invitation tacitly by moving to get into the buggy so that they might drive together to the barn. He stepped back from the horse, took the can of worms in his free hand, and said, "I'm goin' fishin'."

He said it placidly, and he met Ben's glare with an impenetrable mildness of melancholy brown eyes.

Ben caught up the reins. "Geddap!" he cried. "Get over there." He jerked the horse aside into the ditch.

Matt seemed more interested in the patient bewilderment of the horse than in the irascibility of the driver.

He was known to his neighbors as something of a philosopher. He had a theory of the earth's electric currents from which he predicted the weather. He knew the medicinal properties of some of the local plants, and dosed himself, for liver chills and rheumatism, with his own prescriptions. He knew enough of law to keep out of litigation with a quarrelsome neighbor who let his cattle run wild, and enough of politics to vote independent of his party and to despise the campaigns of the Honorable Ben. On account of his ill health and his meditative habits he was the least successful farmer on the ridge, and his wife and his neighbors did not respect him for it. But his dog and his cattle always made a friend of him, and so did his son—who had recently died of a gunshot wound. Matt had been suffering with a chronic dejection since the accident.

Ben tied the horse to a tree, took a small black bag from the buggy, and came back with it. "I want to see you alone somewhere," he repeated.

Matt looked at the bag. "I'm goin' fishin'. If you want to come along—"

"Fishing!" Ben cried. "D'you think I came up here to go fishing! My time's valuable, if *yours* isn't."

"Well—" Matt took off his hat and rubbed the back of his head indifferently. He had a thatch of thick hair, like the pelt of a wild animal, rusty brown in spots and shaggy. "I promised the missus I'd get some perch fer dinner—if they'll bite. Water's cold yet fer perch."

"Here!" Ben shouted. "I've got no time to fool. I've got something to say to you, and I want you to hear it."

Matt shouldered his pole. "You kin stay here

if you want to. Er you kin come an' sit down in the punt an' not waste my time." He turned away unperturbed. "I got to catch some fish," he said as he moved off down the road.

The Honorable Ben stood in a helpless rage that was nearly pitiful. Pale, his lips trembling, he glared after Matt with a despairing ferocity. He blinked as if his eyes were burning. He set his teeth and swallowed, breathing through dilated nostrils, with a sound that was almost a moan of plaintive fury. But he did not turn and fling his satchel into the buggy and drive away. No. He stood there, watching Matt down the road and slowly gaining control of himself.

When Matt turned off into the woods and disappeared he put down his satchel, wiped his forehead with a shaking hand, pulled his hat down to his eyes, picked up his satchel with a jerk, and followed.

3

In the fields, on one side of the road, the first strawberry blossoms were as white as wedding wreaths in the grass. On the other side, in the warm wood shade the anemones were May-Daying, like picnicking children in holiday muslins, delighting in the breeze that set them dancing. And where Matt turned off on a narrow path among the maples the spring beauties were already coyly hidden, awaiting some sentimental rendezvous, in coquettish blushes, pink and white.

The Honorable Ben had no eyes for them. And if Matt had noticed them as he passed it would only have been to observe the progress of the season by them, as automatically as a city man notes the hour on the street clocks. He was deeply ruminative. He did not look behind him to see whether Ben was following. He did not need to. He had a woodman's ears, and Ben's footsteps rustled and crackled on dead leaves and fallen branches.

The path joined an old wood road that led through a second-growth forest of beech and maple—a forest of gray tree-trunks and green underbrush, where the sunlight was caught in a net of low-hung branches and tossed among entangling leaves. Matt went placidly toward the glimmering streak of water at the end of the vista. Ben followed in a furious silence.

He could hardly have expected a more friendly reception. His relations with his brother had not been friendly—not since their school-days—not since Ben had hired himself to the owner of the Cappsville general store and Matt had remained at home to work his father's farm. When the father died he left the farm to both of them, and Ben had deeded his half of the property to Matt in return for a mortgage on the whole of it. He had taken advantage of Matt's impracticality in order to saddle him with a much larger mortgage than the place was worth, and then he had sold the mortgage to the Sullivan County Land and Investment Company, of which he afterward became a director. They squeezed the interest out of Matt implacably. When he could no longer meet it they foreclosed. Matt was now paying them rent. He was allowed to occupy the farm only because no one else wanted it. And he might well have regarded his brother as the heartless leech who had bled and impoverished him all his life.

Curiously enough, he did not so regard him. "Well," he would say, "that's the way Ben is" —with a sort of philosophic and superior contempt. It was the contempt of a wronged man who knows that he has done nothing to deserve the injustice that has been done him. All the anger was on Ben's side. He felt toward his brother as if Matt had been an opponent who had lost to him in a card game, and who blamed him instead of blaming his own unskilfulness or his ill luck. The game was over. He had come to Matt—with his winnings in his little satchel—prepared to talk sense to him. And Matt, walking away from him like a contemptuous dumb animal, compelled him to follow ignominiously. Every step that he took added to the insult.

Matt came to the swampy edge of the lake where there was an unfinished landing-place made of stakes driven in like a row of piles to hold a filling of loose rocks. And tied to one of the stakes was a flat-bottomed punt, unpainted, coffin-shaped, home-made, as crude as one of those "stone-boats" in which the Sullivan County farmer sledges the stones from his fields.

Matt was stooping to grope for a pair of oars in their hiding-place under the trunk of a fallen hemlock when his brother came to the wharf, saw the punt, and saw it as shiftlessness and poverty made manifest in the shape of a boat. He scowled at it. He scowled at the unfinished wharf. There was a gruesome fatality connected with the history of the wharf and he knew it, but he did not intend to refer to it—not yet. He was holding that, to lead up to it as his climax.

He began suddenly in a blustering voice: "Why don't you fix up your place? Your house 's a disgrace. No fence. No steps. Not fit to live in!"

Matt said, calmly, as if addressing the oars in his hands: "It ain't my house any more, an' *you* know it. Besides, I don't need a fence there. The fields are fenced an' the dog stays 'round the front door. He keeps out the cattle. I never got 'round to fixin' the porch steps. We don't need 'em, anyway."

"You get 'round to going fishing."

Matt untied the boat and put his fishing-tackle into it. "I promised the missus I'd get some perch."

Ben said, "Hell!" with the grunted disgust of intelligence balked by stupid reiteration.

Matt climbed into the boat and held it to the wharf, waiting for Ben to take his place in the stern.

"How far are you going?"

Matt moved his head in the direction of the lower lake. Ben hesitated a moment, his lips working. Then he got in and sat down, muttering profanity, and put the bag on the seat beside him because the bottom of the boat was wet and dirty.

Matt fitted his oars to the rowlocks and shoved off. A gust of wind helped him to get under way. A burst of sunlight was blown across the lake in a sudden glory with the flying clouds. He began to row, beaten from his course by sudden side buffets of wind and bringing the head of the boat back mechanically without looking 'round to see his direction.

"Where 're you going?" Ben demanded.

Matt replied, "Down to Alder Point."

4

They both had boyhood memories of Alder Point, and it may have been these that kept Ben silent and preoccupied for the rest of the way. Or he may have been thinking of what he had to say and how he was to say it. In either case he was so deep in thought that even when Matt had dropped his anchor-stone off Alder Point and shipped his oars and taken up his fishing-pole Ben did not speak. Matt looked up at him a moment from his can of bait and began to crowd his hook with a bunch of wriggling worms. He said, smiling grimly, "Been doin' purty well, Ben?"

It startled Ben. "Who?" he asked, hoarsely.

Matt did not reply. He flung his line. "Boys growin' up?"

Ben made as if to speak, checked himself, looked at his watch, and asked, in a harsh tone: "Well, what about your place? What do you want? Money?"

"What's that to you?"

"They're throwing it up to me for letting one of my family live here in this sort of way. It isn't my fault, is it? What's the matter with you? Don't you care how you live? I'd think your wife 'd want to do better if *you* wouldn't."

Matt replied: "I didn't have your luck, Ben. I didn't marry money."

"If you think I got anything out of my wife's money— She's given more to her church than she ever had when I married her."

After an interval of thought Matt observed: "She's took to religion, eh? Well, that's better than rum."

"What's rum got to do with it?"

"Nuthin'," Matt said, "'cept that I hear your boys are goin' in fer it pretty strong."

Ben did not reply.

Matt fished. "People nowadays," he reflected, "they don't seem to think there's any hell—so I guess we'll all be happy in heaven, uh? Think you're goin' there, Ben?" He added, in interpretation of his brother's eye-puckered silence: "Don't

care whether you do er not, uh? Not botherin'
you any."

"My religion's my own concern."

"I guess that's right." He nodded. "I guess
that's right."

The boat swung 'round on its anchor-line with the
shifting wind. Matt drew in his hook to see if it
had caught on any of the brown lily-pads that had
not yet lifted themselves to the surface of the water.
"No perch comin', I guess."

The reference to perch was too much for Ben's
irritability. He broke out: "I tell you what's
the matter with you—you're lazy. You'd sooner
sit in a boat all day waiting for a five-cent fish than
go out in the field and earn an honest dollar. That's
why you're living the way you are. It's shiftlessness. It's laziness—sheer, damn laziness!"

Matt had put the butt of his pole under his leg
and taken out his pipe. "Well, Ben," he said,
"*you've* worked hard."

"You're damn right I have."

"You've worked hard, an' your two boys have
gone to the devil with drink—"

"That's none of my doing."

"An' your wife's trying to buy fergiveness fer
you with the money you sold yer soul fer. An'
you're just about as happy as if you'd gone to hell
already. You've worked hard, an' you've got what
you've been workin' fer. Well, you can have it. I
don't want it."

Ben controlled himself, in a white rage. Matt lit his pipe deliberately.

"You folks that make money call us failures. You're the failures." He puffed. "You remind me of the bees in a hive—workin' yerselves to death to store up honey that's no use to you. The bumblebee's got more horse sense. When it gets enough fer its family it's satisfied. You tell me I'm lazy because I'd sooner be a bumblebee. An' I tell you you're just sort o' foolish."

Ben said, sneeringly, "I'd like to buy you at *my* price and sell you at *yours*."

Matt nodded. "You can't buy what ain't fer sale. That's been your trouble right along. You've been so busy gettin' money you haven't got any o' the things that money can't buy—the things that 're worth more than money. You're a failure, Ben. I'm sorry fer you. That's the feelin' I have. I'm sorry fer you."

"Is that all? Is that all you have to say?"

Matt took up his rod again. "That 'll do me."

"Good." Ben stretched out his arms to bare his wrists like a man about to deal cards. "Now," he said, in a cold passion, "listen to me. There were some people over on the other side of the lake last summer. They used to row over here to get milk and eggs and so forth—from you. Do you remember?"

Matt nodded.

"They complained to your wife one day about

that wharf of yours. She said it was your wharf, and like everything you did it was a failure. She said you never finished anything you started and never started anything you could put off. She said she was ambitious when she married you—a girl of good education—wanted to be a school-teacher. You were studying, then, at night, and she thought you were going to be another Abraham Lincoln. You were studying law. A little later you were reading medical books. Then you took to reading newspapers and talking politics. You studied everything but farming and did everything but attend to your work. She saw she'd never escape from poverty unless the boy pulled her out of it. And she kept him at school, and slaved for him and pushed him along, and let you do as you liked. . . . Well?"

Matt looked up, with the gaze of a man whose thoughts are turned inward upon himself and his past.

The brother clenched his hand. "That boy tripped on your wharf and shot himself! On your wharf—the wharf you were too lazy to finish. He tripped on one of the stakes you were too lazy to even off—and killed himself! Those people told me about it when I saw them in town. They told me your wife was as good as crazy—that she went around like a madwoman, stone dumb—that she never even shed a tear—that you'd killed the boy and worse than killed her. They found out that you were related to me and they asked me to come up here and try to do something for your wife." He sat back with a contemptuous gesture of withdrawal from the discussion. "You tell me I'm a failure. You!"

Matt said, hoarsely: "You don't understand. She don't, either. I've been— All my life—" He looked down at his feet, clumsy in their "cowhides." "The boy was an accident. It might have happened, anyway. A woman isn't responsible fer what she says like that."

It was as if he had found his tongue as clumsy as his feet, as fumbling as his hands, and struggled within himself, futilely, without expression, bewildered by this new and terrible view of himself as a criminal failure in life. He, who had always thought of himself as above his circumstances and better than his neighbors, as a thinker and a superior man!

He looked up at his brother pathetically. "I couldn't do the way you did. I couldn't go on workin' except I knew what I was workin' fer. I didn't want to live like a cow. I wanted to know what we were all livin' fer. I didn't want to make money just fer the sake o' makin' money, like you fellas in the city—"

"Look here," Ben said, fiercely, "I want you to understand that I went after money because I had brains enough to see that no one could live a healthy life without it. Poverty—it was poverty that killed your boy, because you hadn't money enough to build a decent wharf. It's your poverty that makes your wife despise you. You want money—that's all! You're a failure because you tried to live without getting the means to live on."

Matt shook his head, humped over his knees. "What's the matter with things? Why 'm I— what you people think I am, when I tried to be—what I *did?* Why are you what you are when you used to be"—he choked up—"you used to be 'Benny'?"

That fond little name of their childhood came upon them from their past with a tender appeal that silenced them. They stared at each other, and Matt had a mist of tears in his eyes.

Ben glanced aside quickly at the green edge of Alder Point. "That's got nothing to do with it," he muttered.

The sunshine burst upon their silence with a sudden light that seemed to make their emotion public and improper. The Honorable Ben thrust his forefinger down between the back of his neck and his shirt-collar and made a pretense of easing the pinch of the linen. "Look here," he said, with a determined gruffness, "I came up here to say this: I'm looking for a bit of land to build on. The wife likes the country. I want a place for her to live—in case of trouble. We could get this land around here for a song, if you'd run the farm for us or see that the natives didn't steal the whole damn place while our backs were turned. What's the land worth up here?"

"Seven to ten dollars an acre."

"You could make farming pay here as well as anywhere if you had the capital behind you. You could work it on shares if you liked."

Matt said nothing.

"Who owns this?" He waved a hand to the shores of the lake.

"A man named Coddington."

"Would he sell the whole thing—lake and all?"

"Yes. I guess so."

The man of large affairs nodded curtly. "Take me ashore yonder and we'll look it over."

Matt drew in his forgotten line and lifted his anchor-stone aboard. Under cover of the action Ben said, "I want you to help my family, now, Matt—and I'll help yours."

Matt looked at the stone. "It ain't that," he reflected, dully. "There's something wrong. If a man don't make money, he kills his children. An' if he *does*, they kill themselves. There's something wrong. Look at you an' me. Look at any young uns an' then see what they grow into. Look at how a man starts out to do the right thing—an' can't."

"Nonsense!" Ben said, impatient of all this moralizing. "Nonsense! Let's look at the land." He rubbed his hands together, chilled by the wind. "I want you to buy it for me. I'll put up the

money—and more, too—but I don't want my name
to appear. Understand? I want this to be between
us two. See? Just— Who's *that?*"

5

Matt was bending forward, busy with his oars.
The boat had swung around so that its nose was
pointing toward the home shore again. There was
a man in a topcoat and a derby standing at the
landing.

"Who is it? Who's that?"

A note of alarm in the voice startled Matt to
attention. He caught the direction of Ben's eyes
and turned in his seat to look.

The man was a stranger to him. "I dunno," he
said. "What's the matter?"

Ben reached a hand to his satchel, put it on the
bottom of the boat between his feet, and said,
quietly: "Wait. Wait a minute. I think I know
him. Don't row in." He had opened the bag.
"In case anything happens I want you to buy that
land for me. Understand?" He drew out a package
of bank bills the size of a brick, strapped with
elastic bands. He stooped to conceal his action
from the man ashore, and threw the money along
the bottom of the punt to his brother. It struck
Matt's boot. "Whatever there's left over I want
you to just put away safely for me. I'll trust you."

"What's the matter?"

"Nothing. Nothing. It's just the financial

18   [263]

stringency. There's been trouble at the bank. Things will be tied up for a while. I've saved this out. Understand? I want you to buy the land. Just hide that somewhere and say nothing about it."

Matt looked down at the money, without loosening his stiffened hold on the oars. "What's the matter? Why can't you buy it yerself?"

Ben glanced at the shore. The wind was carrying them slowly toward Alder Point. He said: "I'm in a little difficulty—for the time. That's my wife's money. I've saved it out of the smash." His impatience showed in his voice. "She'd be fool enough to give it up. Understand? I want you to buy the land for her and keep what's left over until I see you again."

Matt drew back his foot from the package.

Ben said, anxiously: "I want you to work the place for us on shares. That's what I came up here for. Anything you need you're welcome to, too. Understand? Just take what you want yourself. I'll trust you. You're honest." His voice had begun to grate in a dry throat. "It's money. That's what you want—money. Understand? Fix yourself up. Make your wife happy."

Matt did not move.

"Listen! I can't keep that money myself. The bottom's dropped out of everything for me. I've lost everything but this. They'll take it. They'll take everything. I want you to keep this for me. I'll trust you. We'll all go in together. You're getting too old to work. I'll see that you don't have to.... They can't touch me. I'll get out of it, I guess. But they'll pluck me to the last cent. I want you to keep this for me. Take it! Take it!"

Matt sat motionless, his eyes on the money, as if he did not hear. The water lapped and chuckled along the side of the punt maliciously as a puff of wind hurried them toward the shore.

"Say! Say, Matt. Look here. For God's sake! It's all we have.' Everything's gone to smash. They've been watching me while they—they've been going over the books. That's one of them at the landing. He's come to— Matt! Take it! Don't let them get it! Matt!"

Matt shook his head, without raising his eyes.

Their progress had put the Point between them and the landing. The Honorable Benjamin, seeing that he was hidden from the man on the wharf, crouched, half risen from his seat, grasping the thwarts. "G— damn it!" he cursed in a fierce undertone, "aren't you good for anything? Won't you even save yourself and all the rest of us from the poorhouse now that you've got the chance? That man's come here to arrest me! Matt! Hide it! Hide it!"

Matt did not move. Ben looked back over his shoulder at the lake, reached one hand toward the money, and then said to himself, desperately, " It 'd float!"

There was a long pause and silence. The crackle

of a trodden branch sounded from the laurel-bushes. Ben sprang from his seat in a passion of angry despair, snatched off his hat and flung it at his feet, plucked from his pocket a bright metal object that flashed in the sunlight, and put it to his mouth in both hands, holding it as if it were a flask from which he was to drink. Then a little cloud of yellowish-blue smoke exploded from it and blew him backward, stiffly, over the stern of the boat—and his face was still distorted with an expression of anger as he fell, but his eyes, meeting the blaze of sunlight, looked surprised, startled, as if he had suddenly realized what he had done.

And when the man from the landing burst through the laurel-bushes—with his warrant for the arrest of the president of the wrecked Danville National Bank—he found an old farmer with a pair of oars still grasped stiffly in his hands, sitting in a coffin-shaped punt, staring, horrified, at a spot of blood and bubbles on the water a few yards from shore—with a small fortune in bank bills lying in plain view at his feet.

FROM THE LIFE
Sir Watson Tyler

SIR WATSON TYLER

TYLER, Sir Watson, K.C.B., *b.* Coulton, Ont., May 24, 1870; ed. pub. schools, Univ. of Toronto, grad. 1891; *m.* Alicia Janes, 1893. Pres. Coulton Street Ry. Co., Coulton Gas and Electric Co., Farmers' Trust Co., Mechanics' Bank of Canada, Janes Electric Auto Co., etc. Donor Coulton Conservatory of Music, Mozart Hall, etc. Founder Coulton Symphony Orchestra, Beethoven Choir, etc. Conservative leader. Senate, 1911. Privy Council, Minister without portfolio, 1912. Knighted 1915 for services to the Empire.—*Canada's Men of Mark.*

1

THE stairs that Wat descended—
(He had been christened "Wat," not "Watson." He made it "Watson" later. I am writing of the fall of 1892, when he was twenty-odd years old.)

The stairs that Wat descended on that crucial Sunday morning had been designed by an architect who had aspired to conceal the fact that they were, after all, stairs. He had disguised them with cushioned corner-seats and stained-glass windows, with arches of fretwork and screens of spindles, with niches and turns and exaggerated landings, until they were almost wholly ornamental and honorific. They remained, however, stairs—just as the whole house remained a house, in spite of everything that had been done to make it what *The Coulton Advertiser* called a "prominent residence." And to Wat, that morning, those stairs were painfully nothing but stairs, leading him directly from a bedroom which he had been reluctant to leave down to a dining-room which he was loath to enter. In the bedroom, since daylight, he had been making up his mind to tell his family something that must soon be told to them. He had decided to tell them at the breakfast-table; and he could have forgiven the architect if the stairs had been a longer respite than they were.

In a dining-room that had been made as peevish with decoration as the stairs he found his father, his mother, and his two sisters already busy with breakfast and a Sunday paper, which, in those early days of Coulton, was imported across the border from Buffalo. His sisters were both younger than he and both pertly independent of their elders, and they did not look up from the illustrated sections of fashion and the drama which they were reading, aside, as they ate. His father seemed always to seize on his hours of family leisure to let his managerial brain lounge and be at rest in the comfortable corpulence of his body; he was stirring his coffee in a humorous reflectiveness that was wholly self-absorbed. Mrs. Tyler smiled apprehensively at her son, but she did not speak. She did not care to disturb the harmony of the domestic silence. Both the harmony and the silence were rare and pleasant to her

Wat sat down, and humped himself over his fruit, and began to eat with an evident lack of zest. The dining-room maid came and went rustling. Mrs. Tyler brushed at a persistent crumb among the ribbons on the ample bosom of her morning wrapper, and regarded Wat from time to time with maternal solicitude.

He had once been a delicate, fat boy—before he took a four years' college course in athletics—and she had never been quite convinced of the permanency of his conversion to health. He had come home late the previous night, and he looked pale to her. His lack of appetite was unusual enough to be alarming. He did not begin his customary Sunday morning dispute with his sisters about "hogging" the picture pages of the newspaper.

She broke out at last: "What is it, Wat? Aren't you well?"

"N-no," he stammered, taken by surprise. "I'm all right."

His sisters glanced at him. He was unthinkingly afraid that they might see his secret in his eyes. They had all the devilish penetration of the young female. And he looked down his nose into his coffee-cup with an ostentatious indifference to them as he drank.

Naturally they accepted his manner as a challenge to them. Millie remarked to Ollie that he seemed thin—which was far from true. Ollie replied, with her eyes in her newspaper, that he was probably going into a "decline." He pretended to pay no attention to them; but his mother interfered, as they had expected her to.

"You've no business, now, making fun of Wat about his health," she said. "You know he isn't strong. He's big—but he's soft."

"Soft!" the girls screamed. "Paw, maw says Wat's soft!"

It *is* incredible, but—at that day, to everybody in the household except his mother—Sir Watson Tyler was a joke. And it *is* incredible, but—in spite of all the honorable traditions of convention to the contrary—these were the family relations in the Tyler home.

Mr. Tyler turned an amused eye on his wife, and she appealed to him with her usual helpless indignation. "Well, I think you ought to speak to the girls, Tom. I don't think it's very nice of them to make fun of their mother."

"But, maw!" Millie laughed. "You say such funny things we can't help it."

'I don't. You twist everything I say. Wat *isn't* strong. You ought to be ashamed of yourselves."

She scolded them in a voice that was unconvincing, and they replied to her as if she were an incompetent governess for whom they had an affectionate disrespect.

Wat began to fortify himself with food for the announcement which he had to make. He ate nervously—determinedly—even, at last, doggedly. His mother retired into silence. His sisters continued to read.

When they got to discussing some of the society news he saw an opportunity of leading up to his subject; and when they were talking of a girl whom they had met during the summer, at the lake shore, he put in, "Did you ever meet Miss Janes there?"

They turned their heads without moving their shoulders. "*Lizzie* Janes?"

The tone was not enthusiastic. He cleared his throat before he answered, "Yes."

Millie said, superbly casual: "Uh-huh. Isn't she a *freak!*"

His face showed the effort he made to get that remark down, though he swallowed it in silence. His mother came to his rescue. "Who is she, Wat?"

"A girl I met this summer. I went over there with Jack Webb."

His sisters found his manner strained. They eyed him with suspicion. His mother asked, "What is she like?"

"Well," Millie put in, "she has about as much style—!"

Wat reddened. "She hasn't *your* style, anyway. She doesn't look as if her clothes—"

He was unable to find words to describe how his sisters looked. They looked as if their limp garments had been poured cold over their shoulders and hung dripping down to their bone-thin ankles.

"I'm glad you like her," Millie said. "She's a sight."

He had determined to be politic. It was essential that he should be politic. Yet he, the future leader of a conservative party, retorted: "It 'd do you good to know a few girls like her. The silly crowd *you* go with!"

"Lizzie Janes! That frump!"

He appealed to his mother. "I certainly think *you* ought to call on them, mother. They've been mighty good to me this summer while you were away."

"Well, Wat," she said, "if you wish it—"

"You'll do no such thing!" Millie cried.

The squabble that followed did not end in victory for Wat. It was Millie's contention that they were not bound to receive every "freak" that he might "pick up"; and Mrs. Tyler—who, in social matters, was usually glad to remain in the quiet background of the family—put herself forward inadequately in Wat's behalf. She succumbed to her husband's decision that she "had better leave it to the girls"; he ended the dispute indifferently by leaving the table; and Wat realized, with desperation, that he had failed in his diplomatic attempt to engage the family interest for Miss Janes by introducing mention of her and her virtues into the table talk.

2

He went back up-stairs to his bedroom and locked himself in with his chagrin and his sentimental secret. It was a secret that showed in a sort of gloomy wistfulness as he stood gazing out the glass door that opened, from one angle of his room, upon a little balcony—an ornamental balcony whose turret top adorned a corner of the Tyler roof with an aristocratically useless excrescence. You will notice it in the picture of "Sir Watson Tyler's Boyhood Home" in *The Canadian Magazine's* article about him. From the door of this balcony, looking over the autumn maples of the street, through a gap between the opposite houses, Wat could see the chimney of the Janes house.

It was a remarkable pile of bricks, that chimney. All around it were houses that existed only as neighbors to that one supreme house. And around those were still others, less and less important, containing the undistinguished mass of lives that made up the city of Coulton in which she lived. The heart of interest in Coulton had once been his own home—as, for example, when he came back to it from college for his holidays. Now, when he returned in the evenings from his father's office he found himself on the circumference of a circle of which Miss Janes's home was the vital center. He saw his own room merely as a window looking toward hers. And this amazing displacement had been achieved so imperceptibly that he had only just become acutely conscious of it himself.

His mother and his sisters had spent the summer on the clay-lipped lake shore that gave the name of "Surfholm" to the Tyler cottage in the society news of *The Coulton Advertiser;* and Wat and his father had remained in town, from Mondays to Saturdays, to attend to the real-estate and investment business that supplied the Tyler income. (They also owned the Coulton horse-car line, but it supplied no income for them.) On a memorable Tuesday evening Wat had "stopped in" at the Janeses' on his way down-town with his friend Webb, to let Webb return to Miss Janes some music that he had borrowed. And, by a determining accident of fate, as they approached the lamplit veranda of the Janes cottage, Alicia Janes was sitting behind the vine-hung lattice, reading a magazine, while her mother played the piano.

Observe: There was no veranda on the Tyler "residence"; no one ever sat outdoors there; and no one ever played anything but dance-music on the Tyler piano. Alicia Janes looked romantic under the yellow light, in the odor of flowers, with the background of green leaves about her. Her mother had more than a local reputation as a teacher of music, and the melody that poured out of the open French windows of the parlor was elo-

quent, impassioned, uplifting. The introductions
were made in a low voice, so as not to disturb the
music, and it was in silence that Alicia put out a
frank hand to Wat and welcomed him with the
strong grasp of a violinist's fingers.

Wat's ordinary tongue-tied diffidence went unnoticed under these circumstances. He was able
to sit down without saying anything confused or
banal. The powerful music, professionally interpreted, filled him with stately emotions, to which
he moved and sat with an effect of personal dignity
and repose.

These may seem to be details of small importance.
But life has a way of concealing its ominous beginnings and of being striking only when its conclusions
are already foregone. So death is more dramatic,
but less significant, than the unperceived incep-
tion of the fatal incidents that end in death. And
in the seemingly trivial circumstances of Wat's
introduction to the Janes veranda there were hidden the germs of vital alterations for him—alterations that were to affect the life of the whole community of Coulton, and, if the King's birthday list
is to be believed, were to be important even to the
British Empire.

Alicia Janes was dressed in a belted black gown,
like an art student, with a starched Eton collar
and cuffs. Instead of the elaborate coiffure of the
day's style she wore her dark hair simply parted
and coiled low on her neck in a Rossetti mode. Her

long olive face would have been homely if it had not been for her eyes. They welcomed Wat with the touching smile of a sensitive independence, and he did not notice that her lips were thin and her teeth prominent. In dress and manner she was unlike any of the young women whom he had met in the circle of his sisters' friends; if she had been like them, the memory of past embarrassments would probably have inhibited every expression of his mind. Her surroundings were different from any to which he had been accustomed; and, as a simple consequence, he was quite unlike himself in his accustomed surroundings. Perhaps it was the music most of all that helped him. It carried him as a good orchestra might carry an awkward dancer, uplifted into a sudden confident grace.

When she asked him some commonplace questions in an undertone he replied naturally, forgetting himself. He listened to the music and he looked at her, seriously thrilled. When Webb asked her if she wouldn't play the violin, and she replied that she always played badly before strangers, Wat begged her in a voice of genuine anxiety not to consider him a stranger. She said, "I'll play for you the next time you come." And he was so grateful for the implied invitation to come again that his "Thank you" was sincere beyond eloquence. He even met her mother without embarrassment, although Mrs. Janes was an enigmatic-looking, dark woman with a formidable manner.

She became more friendly when she understood that he was the son of the Tylers of Queen's Avenue, and he felt that he was accepted as a person of some importance, like herself. That was pleasant.

After a half-hour on the veranda he went on down-town with Webb, as calm outwardly as if he had parted from old friends, and so deeply happy in the prospect of seeing her again that he was quite unaware of what had happened to him. The following afternoon he telephoned to her eagerly. And he was back with her that night for hours in the lamplight, among the vines—without Webb—talking, smiling, and listening with profound delight while she played the violin to her mother's piano.

And there was an incredible difference between Wat on the veranda and Wat at home. Under his own roof he was a large-headed, heavy-shouldered, apparently slow-witted, shy youth, who read in his room, exercised alone in a gymnasium which he had put in his attic during a college vacation, wrote long letters to former classmates in other cities, and, going out to the post-box, mooned ponderously around the streets till all hours. He had never anything much to say. Although he never met any one if he could avoid it, and suffered horribly in a drawing-room, he was—like most shy men—particular to the point of effeminacy about his appearance. He bathed and shaved and brushed his hair and fussed over his clothes absurdly, morning and night. He was, in fact, in many ways ridiculous.

19 [279]

On the Janes veranda he was nothing of the sort. As the son of the owner of the Coulton street-car line and the Tyler real estate, he was a young man of social importance in a home where the mother earned a living by teaching music and the daughter had only the prospect of doing the same. He was a man of the practical world, whose opinions were authoritative. He was well dressed and rather distinguished-looking, with what has since been called "a brooding forehead." He was fond of reading, and he had the solid knowledge of a slow student who assimilated what he read. Alicia deferred to him with an inspiring trust in his wisdom and his experience. She deferred even to his judgment in music—for which, it transpired, he had an acute ear and a fresh appreciation. She played to him as eagerly as a painter might show his sketches to a wealthy enthusiast who was by way of becoming a collector. Their evenings together were full of interest, of promise, of talk and laughter, of serious converse and melodic emotion.

There was in those days, in Coulton, no place of summer amusement to which a young pair could make an excuse of going in order to be together, so that Wat was never called on to make a public parade of his devotion. The best that he could do was to take Alicia to her church. But it was not *his* church. He was not known there. Mrs. Janes was the church organist; Alicia often added the music of her violin; and she sat always in the

choir. Wat, in a back pew down-stairs, was incon-
spicuous and not coupled with her. It was for
these reasons that his interest in Miss Janes was
not at once generally known. That was entirely
accidental.

But it was not an accident that he did not make
it known to his family. At first he foresaw and
dreaded only the amusement of his sisters. Wat
"girling"! What next! And then he shrank from
the effect on Alicia Janes of getting the family
point of view on him. It was almost as if he had
been romanticizing about himself and knew that
his family would tell her the truth. And finally,
as guilty as if he were leading a double life, he confronted the problem that haunts all double lives—
the problem of either keeping them apart or of
uniting them in any harmony. As long as his
family had been at "Surfholm" it had not been
necessary that they should recognize Miss Janes,
but, now that they were back in town, every day
that they ignored her was an insult to her and an
accusation of him.

He had to tell them. He had to put into words
the beautiful secret of his feeling for her. "That
freak!" He had to introduce Alicia to his home and
to the shame of his belittlement in his home, and
let his contemptuous sisters disillusion her about
him.

A horrible situation! Believe me or not, of a
career so distinguished as Sir Watson's this was the

most crucial point, the most agonized moment. It is not even hinted at in the official accounts of his career, yet never in his life afterward was he to be so racked with emotion, so terrified by the real danger of losing everything in the world that could make the world worth living in. And never afterward was he forced to choose a course that meant so much not only to himself, but to the world in which he lived.

3

That is why I have chosen this autumn Sunday of 1892 as the most notable day to scrutinize and chronicle in a character-study of Sir Watson Tyler. I should like to commemorate every moment of it, but, as the memoir-writers say—when their material is running short—space forbids. You will have to imagine him trying to dress in order to take Miss Janes to church: struggling through a perspiring ecstasy of irresolution in the choice of a necktie, straining into a Sunday coat that made him look round-shouldered because of the bulging muscularity of his back, cursing his tailor, hating his hands because they hung red and bloated below his cuffs, hating his face, his moon face, his round eyes, his pudding of a forehead, and all those bodily characteristics that were to mark him, to his later biographers, as a born leader among men, "physically as well as mentally dominant."

He never went to church, to his family's knowledge, so he had to wait until they had gone in order to avoid inconvenient questions. They were always late. He watched them, behind the curtains of his window, till they rounded the circular driveway and reached the street. Five minutes later he was cutting across the lawn, scowling under a high hat that always pinched his forehead, on his way to the Janeses'.

He did not arrive there. He decided that he was too late. He decided he could not arrive there without having first made up his mind what to do. And he turned aside to wander through the residential streets of Coulton, pursued by the taunts of the church-bells. He came to the weed-grown vacant lots and the withered fields of market-gardeners in a northern suburb that was yet to be nicknamed "Tylertown." He ended beside Smith's Falls, where the Coulton River drops twenty feet over a ridge into the Coulton Valley; and he sat down on a rock, in his high hat, on the site of the present power-house—his power-house—that has put the light and heat of industrial life into the whole community. He resolved to see his mother privately, tell her the truth, get her to help him with his father, and let his sisters do their worst.

But it was not easy to see Mrs. Tyler privately in her home on Sunday. They had a long and solemn noon dinner that was part of the ritual of the day, and after dinner she always sat with her husband and her daughters in the sitting-room up-stairs, indulging her domestic soul in the peace of a family reunion that seemed only possible to the Tylers on Sunday afternoon when they were gorged like a household of pythons. Wat retired to his bedroom. Every twenty minutes he wandered down-stairs, passed the door of the sitting-room slowly, and returned up the back stairs by stealth. They heard him pacing the floor overhead. Millie listened to him thoughtfully. The younger sister, Ollie, was trying to write letters on note-paper of robin's-egg blue, and she blamed him for all the difficulties of composition; it was so distracting to have him paddling around like that. Finally, when his mother heard him creaking down the stairs for the fourth time, she called out: "Wat! What *is* the matter with you? If you're restless, why don't you go for a walk?"

He answered, hastily, "I'm going," and continued down to the lower hall. Millie waited to hear the front door shut behind him. She had just remembered what he said at breakfast about Jack Webb taking him to see the Janes girl. She went at once to the library to telephone.

And she came flying back with the news that while they had been away Wat had been spending almost every evening with Lizzie Janes; that he had been going to see her since their return; that Jack Webb thought they were engaged. "And the first thing *we* know," she said, "he'll be married to her."

Mr. Tyler tilted one eyebrow. He thought he understood that there were things that were not *in* Wat.

"Well, what's the matter with him, then?" Millie demanded. "Why has he been hiding it, and sneaking off to see her and never saying a word about it, if he isn't ashamed of it and afraid to tell us? They've roped him in. That's what *I* think. Lizzie Janes is a regular old maid now. If she isn't engaged to Wat, she intends to be. No one else would ever marry her. I bet they've been working Wat for all they're worth. They're as *poor*—"

Her father continued incredulous.

"Well," she cried, "Jack Webb says Wat's been going to church with her twice a Sunday."

Wat's indolent aversion to church-going being well known, this was the most damning piece of evidence she could have produced against him.

Mrs. Tyler pleaded, "She can't be a *bad* girl if she goes to church twice a—"

"What difference does that make?" Millie demanded. "It doesn't make it any better for *us*, does it?"

"I'll speak to Wat," Mrs. Tyler promised, feebly.

"It's no use speaking to Wat! *He* has nothing to do with it. Any one can turn Wat around a little finger."

"Do you know her?" Mr. Tyler asked.

"I used to know her—before she went to—when

she was at school here. She used to wear thick stockings, and woolen mitts."

Ollie added, as the final word of condemnation, "Home-made!"

Mr. Tyler may have felt that he did not appreciate the merit of these facts. He made a judicial noise in his throat and said nothing.

"She's older than any of us—than Wat, too."

"Well," he said, reaching for his newspaper, "I suppose Wat 'll do what he likes. He's not likely to do anything remarkable one way or the other."

"He's not going to marry Lizzie Janes," Millie declared. "Not if *I* can help it."

"Millie," her mother scolded, "you've no right interfering in Wat's affairs. He's older than you are—"

"It isn't only Wat's affair," she cried. "She isn't only going to marry Wat. We're thrown in with the bargain. I guess we have something to say."

"Tom!" Mrs. Tyler protested. "If you let her—"

"Well," he ruled, "Wat hasn't even taken the trouble to ask us what we thought about it. I don't feel called on to help him. It means more to the girls than it does to us, in any case. They'll have to put up with her for the rest of her life."

"I guess *not!*" Millie said, confidently.

"Now, Millie!" her mother threatened. "If you—"

"If you want Lizzie Janes and her mother in this family," Millie said, "*I* don't. I guess it won't be hard to let Wat and them know it, either. And if *you* won't," she ended, defiantly, as she turned away, "*I will!*"

She went out and Ollie followed. Mrs. Tyler dropped back in her chair, gazing speechlessly at her husband. He caught her eye as he turned a page of his paper. "All right, now," he said. "Wait till Wat comes."

They waited. Millie did not. She distrusted her mother's partiality for Wat, and she distrusted her father's distaste for interfering in any household troubles. She trusted herself only, assured that if Wat's ridiculous misalliance was to be prevented it must be prevented by her; and she felt that it could be easily prevented, because it *was* ridiculous, because Wat was ridiculous, because Lizzie Janes was absurd. What was Wat's secrecy in the affair but a confession that he was ashamed of it? What was Lizzie Janes's sly silence but an evidence that she had hoped to hook Wat before his family knew what was going on?

What indeed? She asked it of Ollie, and Ollie asked it of her. They had locked themselves in Millie's bedroom to consult together—Ollie sitting, tailor-wise, cross-legged on the bed, and Millie gesticulating up and down the room—in one of those angry councils of war against their elders in which they were accustomed to face the cynical facts of life with a frankness that would have amazed mankind.

4

And Wat, meantime, arrived at the door of the Janes house because it was impossible for him *not* to arrive there. Alicia greeted him with her usual unchanging, gentle smile. He began to explain why he had not come that morning to take her to church; that his family—

"There's some one here," she said, unheeding. "Some one who wants to meet you. My brother!" And touching him lightly on the shoulder, she turned him toward the parlor and ushered him in to meet his future in the shape of Howard Janes.

Janes was then a tall, gaunt, feverish-eyed, dark enthusiast, of an extraordinary mental and physical restlessness—a man who should have been a visionary, but had become an electrical engineer. He had been working on the project to develop electrical power at Niagara Falls, and in ten minutes he was describing to Wat the whole theory and progress of the work, past, present, and future. "In ten years," he said, "Niagara power will be shot all through this district for a hundred miles around, and here's Coulton asleep, with one of the best power projects in Canada right under its nose. Where? Smith's Falls. And here *you* are, with a dead town, a dead street-car line, a lot of dead real estate, and the power to make the whole thing a gold-mine running to waste over that hill. Why, man, if it was an oil-field you'd be developing it like mad. Because it's electricity no one seems to see it. And in ten years it will be too late."

He talked to Wat as if Wat owned the car line, the real estate, the town itself, and when Wat glanced at Alicia she was *looking* at him as if he owned them. The power of that look was irresistible—hypnotic. He began to listen as if he owned the car lines and the real estate, to think as if he owned them, to ask questions, and finally to reply as if he owned them. Very grave, with his eyes narrowed, silent, he became a transportation magnate considering a development scheme proposed by an industrial promoter.

They were interrupted by the telephone in the hall. Alicia answered it. "It's for you," she said to Wat, looking at him significantly. "Your sister."

He went to the 'phone, puzzled. It was Millie's voice. "You're to come home at once," she said.

Wat asked, "What's the matter?"

"You know what's the matter," she snapped, "as well as I do. You're wanted home here at once." And while the meaning of that was slowly reaching him, through the preoccupied brain of the railroad magnate, she added, "I don't wonder you were ashamed to tell us!" and slapped up the receiver.

He stood a moment at the 'phone, pale. And in that moment history was made. He went back to Alicia, face front, head up. She looked at him expectantly. "They want me to bring you to see them," he said.

It was what she had expected, he supposed. Mark it as the beginning of his great career. What she expected! There's the point. That's the secret, as I see it, of the making of Sir Watson Tyler.

After a moment's hesitation she went to put on her hat. He said to her brother: "Can you wait till we get back? We'll be only a few minutes. I want to go into this thing with you in detail." And when he was on the street with her he explained, merely: "I want you to meet mother. I don't suppose we'll see dad. He's always so busy he doesn't pay much attention to what goes on at home."

"I don't think I've ever seen any of your family," she said, "except your sisters." She was thinking of them as she used to see them in their school-days, in short dresses, giggling, and chewing candy in the street-cars.

"They're very young," Wat warned her, "and they've been spoiled. You mustn't mind if Millie— She's been allowed to do pretty much as she likes. Our life at home isn't like yours, you know. I think our house is too big. We seem to be—sort of separated in our rooms." '

Strange! He appeared apologetic. She did not

understand why—unless it was that he was fearful of her criticism of his family. She knew that they were not socially distinguished, except by newspaper notice; but she thought she had no reverence for social position. And he could hardly be apologizing for their income.

5

The house, as they approached it, was pretentious, but that was probably the architect's fault. It was modestly withdrawn behind its trees, its flower-beds, and its lawns. For a moment she saw herself, in her simple costume, coming to be passed upon by the eyes of an alien wealth. Wat was silent, occupied with his own thoughts. He rang absent-mindedly.

A maid opened a door on a hall that was architecturally stuffy and not furnished in the rich simplicity that Alicia had expected. And the sight of the drawing-room was a shock. It was overcrowded with pink-upholstered shell-shaped furniture that gave her a note of overdressed bad taste. The carpet was as richly gaudy as a hand-painted satin pincushion. The bric-à-brac, of a florid costliness, cluttered the mantelpieces and the table-tops like a tradesman's display. The pictures on the walls were the family photographs and steel engravings of an earlier home. It was a room of undigested dividends, and she thought that she began to see why Wat had been apologetic. To his credit he seemed uncomfortable in it. "I'll just tell them you're here," he said.

He left her there and went out to the stairs. Millie was coming down to see who had rung. "Well," she cried from a landing above him as he ascended resolutely, "will you tell us what you think you're doing with that Lizzie Janes?"

He caught her by the arm. He said in a voice that was new to her: "I've brought her to call on mother. Tell her she's here."

"You've brought her to—! I'll do nothing of the kind. You can just take her away again. *I* don't want her, and *they* don't want her." She had begun to raise her voice, with the evident intention of letting any one hear who would. "If she thinks she can—"

"That's enough!" He stopped her angrily, with his hand over her mouth. "You ought to be—"

She struggled with him, striking his hand away. "How *dare* you! If you think that Lizzie Janes—"

He was afraid that Alicia might hear it. He grabbed her up roughly and began to carry her upstairs, fighting with him, furious at the indignity—for he had caught her where he could, with no respect for her body or her clothes. No one, in years, had dared to lay hands on her, no matter what she did; the sanctity of her fastidious young person was an inviolable right to her; and Wat's assault upon it was brutal to her, degrading, atrocious.

She became hysterical, in a clawed and tousled passion of shame and resentment. He carried her to her room, tossed her on to her bed, and left her, face down on her pillows, sobbing, outraged. She could have killed him—or herself.

He straightened his necktie and strode into the sitting-room.

"Why, Wat!" his mother cried. "What's the matter?"

"Miss Janes," he said, "is down-stairs. I've brought her to call on you."

She rose, staring. His father looked at him, surprised, over the top of his paper. "Well," he demanded, "what's all this about Miss Janes, anyway?"

Wat gave him back his look defiantly. "She's the finest girl I've ever met. And I'm going to marry her, if I can."

"Oh," Mr. Tyler said, and returned to his news.

Ollie rushed out to find her sister.

Wat turned his amazing countenance on his mother.

"Yes, Wat," she replied to it—and went with him obediently.

6

Of the interview that followed in the drawing-room there were several conflicting reports made. Ollie slipped down quietly to hear the end of it—after a stupefying account from Millie of what had happened—but *her* report to Millie is negligible. From that night both the girls ceased to exist as factors in Wat's life; he saw them and heard them thereafter only absent-mindedly.

Mrs. Tyler's report was made in voluble excitement to her husband, who listened, frowning, over his cigar. "And, Tom, you wouldn't have known him," she said. "He wasn't like—like himself at all! It was so pretty. They're so in love with each other. She's such a sweet girl."

"Well," he grumbled, "I'll have nothing to do with it. It's in your department. If it was one of the girls it 'd be different. I suppose Wat 'll have to do his own marrying. He's old enough. I hope she'll make a man of him."

"'A man of him'! She! Why, she's as— No, indeed! You ought to see the way *she* defers to *him*. She's as proud of him! And he's as *different!*"

He was unconvinced. "I'm glad to hear it. You'd better go and look after Millie. She accuses him of assault and battery."

"It serves her right. I'll not go near her. And, Tom," she said, "he wants to talk to you about a plan he has for the railway—for using electric light to run it, or something like that."

"Huh! Who put that in his head?"

"Oh, he made it up himself. Her brother's an engineer, and they've been talking about it."

"I suppose!" he said. "She'll be working the whole Janes family in on us." He snorted. "I'm glad some one's put something into his head besides eating and sleeping."

"Now, Tom," she pleaded, "you've got to be fair to Wat!"

"All right, Mary," he relented. "Run along and see Millie. I've had enough for *one* Sunday."

As for Alicia Janes, it was late at night when *she* made her report to her mother in a subdued tremble of excitement. She had overheard something of Wat's scuffle with Millie on the stairway, but she did not speak of it except to say: "I'm afraid the girls are awful. The youngest, Ollie, is overdressed and silly—with the manners of a spoiled child of ten. It's her mother's fault. She's one of those helpless big women. Wat must have got his qualities from his father."

"Did you find out why they hadn't called?"

"No-o. But I can guess."

"Yes?"

"Well, it isn't a nice thing to say, but I really think Wat's rather—as if he were ashamed of them. And I don't wonder, mother! Their front room's furnished with that— Oh, and such bric-à-brac!" She paused. She hesitated. She blushed. "Wat asked me if I'd— You know he had never really *spoken* before, although I knew he—"

Her mother said, softly, "Yes?"

She looked down at the worn carpet. "And I

really felt so sorry for him— The family's awful, I know, but he's so— I said I would."

7

She had said she would. And Wat, long after midnight, lying on his back in bed, staring up at the darkness, felt as if he were afloat on a current that was carrying him away from his old life with more than the power of Niagara. His mind was full of Howard Jaues's plans for harnessing Smith's Falls, of electrifying the street railway, of lighting Coulton with electricity and turning the vacant Tyler lots of the northern suburb into factory sites. He was thinking of incorporations, franchises, capitalizations, stocks, bonds, mortgages, and loans. He had been talking them over with Janes for hours on the veranda, at the supper-table, on the street. There had been no music. As Wat was leaving he had spoken to Alicia hastily in the hall—asking her to marry him, in fact—and she had said, "Oh, Wat!" clinging to his hands as he kissed her. He could still feel that tremulous, confiding grasp of her strong fingers as she surrendered her life to him, depending on him, proud of him, humble to him. He shivered. He was afraid.

And that was to be only the first of many such frightened midnights. A thousand times he was to ask himself: "What am I doing? Why have I gone into this business? It 'll kill me! It 'll worry me to death!" He had gone into it because Alicia had expected him to; but he did not know it. The maddest thing he ever did—

It was when the power scheme had been successfully floated, the street railway was putting out long radial lines along the country roads, and the gas company was willing to sell out to him in order to escape the inevitable clash of competition with his electric light. The banks suddenly began to make trouble about carrying him. He was in their debt for an appalling amount. He felt that he ought to prepare his wife for the worst. "Well, Wat," she said, reproachfully, when she understood him, "if the banks are going to bother you, I don't see why you don't get a bank of your own."

It was as if she thought he could buy a bank in a toy-shop. She expected it of him. Miracles! nothing but miracles! And it was the maddest thing he ever did, but he went after the moribund Farmers' Trust Company, got it with his father's assistance, reorganized it and put it on its feet, while he held up the weak-kneed power projects and Janes talked manufacturers into buying power sites. The Mechanics' Bank of Canada passed to him later, but by that time he was running, at "Tylertown," an automobile factory, a stone-crusher, a carborundum works, and the plant of Coulton's famous Eleco Breakfast Food, cooked by electricity, and the success of the whole city of Coulton was so involved with his fortunes that he simply could not be allowed to fail.

And here was the fact that made the whole thing possible: Janes had the vision and the daring necessary to attempt their undertakings, but he could not have carried them out; whereas Wat would never have gone beyond the original power-house; but with Janes talking to him and Alicia looking at him he moved ahead with a stolid, conservative caution and a painstaking care of detail that made every move as safe and deliberate as a glacial advance. He worked day and night, methodically, with a ceaseless application that would have worn out a less solid and lethargic man. It was as if, having eaten and slept—and nothing else—for twenty years, he could do as he pleased about food now, and never rest at all. He was wonderful. His mind digested everything, like his stomach, slowly, but without distress. His shyness, now deeply concealed, made him silent, unfathomable. He had no friends, because he confided in no one; he was too diffident to do it. Behind his inscrutable silence he studied and watched the men with whom he had to work, moving like a quiet engineer among the machinery which he had started, and the uproar of it. And the moment he decided that a man was wrong he took him out and dropped him clean, without feeling, without any friendly entanglement to deter him, silently.

He had to go into politics to protect his franchises, and he became the "Big Business Interests" behind the local campaign; but he never made a public appearance; he managed campaign funds, sat on executive committees, was consulted by the party leaders, and passed upon policies and candidates. *The Coulton Advertiser* annoyed him, and he bought it. His wife had gathered about her a number of music-lovers, and they formed a stringed orchestra that studied and played in the music-room of Wat's new home on the hill above "Tylertown." She expected him to be present, and he rarely failed. As a matter of fact, he seldom heard more than the first few bars of a composition, then, emotionalized, his brain excited, he sat planning, reviewing, advancing, and reconsidering his work. Music had that effect on him. It enlivened his lumbering mind. He became as addicted to it as if it were alcohol. .

He followed his wife into a plan for the formation of a symphony orchestra, which he endowed. When there was no proper building for it he put up Mozart Hall and gave it to the city. She wanted to hear Beethoven's Ninth Symphony, so the orchestra had to be supplemented with a choir. He endowed the Coulton Conservatory of Music when she objected that she could not get voices or musicians because there was no way in Coulton to educate or train them. And in doing these things he gave Coulton its fame as a musical center. (Lamplight on the veranda, and Mrs. Janes playing the piano behind the open French windows!)

It was the campaign against reciprocity that

put him in the Senate. He believed that reciprocity with the United States would ruin his factories. He headed the committee of Canadian manufacturers that raised the funds for the national campaign against the measure. The consequent defeat of the Liberal party put his friends in power. They rewarded him with a Senatorship. He was opposed to taking it, but his wife expected him to. He went into the Cabinet, as Minister without portfolio, a year later. It was inevitable. He was the financial head of the party; they had to have him at their government councils. When the war with Germany broke out he gave full pay to all of his employees that volunteered. He endowed a battery of machine-guns from Coulton. Every factory that he controlled he turned into a munition-works. He contributed lavishly to the Red Cross. And, of course, he was knighted.

It is an open secret that he will probably be made Lord Coulton when the readjustment of the colonial affairs of the Empire takes him to London. He will be influential there; he has the silent, conservative air of ponderous authority that England trusts. And Lady Tyler is a poised, gracious, and charming person who will be popular socially. She, of course, is of no importance to the Empire. She still looks at Wat worshipfully, without any suspicion that it was she who made him—not the slightest.

I do not know how much of the old Wat is left in him. His silence covers him. It is impossible to tell how greatly the quality and texture of his mind may have changed under the exercise and labor of his gigantic undertakings. I saw him when he was in New York to hear the Coulton orchestra and choir give the Ninth Symphony, to the applause of the most critical. ("The scion of a noble house," one of the papers called him.) And it certainly seemed impossible—although I swear I believe it is true—that the solid magnificences of the man and his achievements were all due to the fact that when he came back from the Janes telephone to confront the expectancy of Alicia Janes, on that Sunday night in 1892, he said, "They want me to bring you to see them," instead of saying, "They want me at home."

FROM THE LIFE

District-Attorney Wickson

DISTRICT-ATTORNEY WICKSON

WICKSON, Arthur John, lawyer; Mar.
19, 1867–Aug. 25, 1912; see Vol. VII
(1912-13).—*Who's Who.*

1

TO tell the truth, I did not at any time know
District-Attorney Wickson well enough to be
able now to do an intimate portrait-study of him
at first hand. But I know his town—having
"muckraked" it while he was in office. I know
many of the circumstances of his story, because
they were part of the material that came up in the
raking. And I know a number of his closest friends
and associates, from whom I have gathered the incidents of that day in his life which I wish to record
—the great and culminating day of his career.

The men whom I have relied upon for the details
of that day are "Jack" Arnett, sculptor of the
Wickson Memorial, McPhee Harris, president of
the Purity Defense League and the local Anti-
Saloon Association, and Tim Collins (or "Cole"
or "Colburn"), the detective who helped Wickson
in the investigations and prosecutions that made
the District Attorney a national figure. These
three men were the chief actors in the dramatic
crisis of Wickson's life and in those crucial incidents

which seem to me to express him most completely. Furthermore, McPhee Harris had been associated with him for years, and Jack Arnett was a boyhood friend who knew him better, probably, than any one except his mother.

I have met his mother, but I have never had sufficient reportorial ruthlessness to ask her about him.

2

Arnett has given me one anecdote of Wickson's early days that I should consider vital to an understanding of him. "Wickson," he says, "left home as a boy, and came to town because he had been beaten by his father." The father he described as a petty tyrant who ruled his poverty-stricken family and his starved farm with all the exacting imperiousness of incompetency aggravated by indigestion. Arthur Wickson was an only child. He went one morning to his mother in the kitchen and blurted out to her that he had to leave home, that he couldn't stand it any longer. "I remember," he told Arnett, "how she was washing dishes, and when I told her she didn't say anything. She didn't even look at me. She was working in front of a window, and she just raised her eyes from the dishpan and stood looking out of that window as if there were bars across it. I had the feeling that a convict must have when he tells his cellmate he has a chance to escape and can't take *him* along.

"She asked me what I was going to do, and I told her I was going to be a lawyer. I don't know where I got that ambition. She dried her hands on her apron without a word, and went up-stairs to her room, and when she came down she had two dollars that she'd saved—I don't know how. God! When I think of those hands and those two dollars!

"I didn't want to take them. She made me. I promised her I'd pay them back, and I've been trying to ever since, but I couldn't do it with a million.

"Funny thing. She kissed me sort of timidly, and there was a look in her eyes as if I had some resemblance to *him* that frightened her. You know what I mean. It made me hate him so that when I walked off down the road and he shouted at me from the field I didn't even answer him. He was plowing. It was chilly, and the steam was rising from the horses as they stood there at the end of a furrow. I remember yet that he and the horses looked small—like little figures in lead—and I felt that he was a stranger—that I didn't know who he was. Can you explain that?"

3

I consider that incident illuminating because it really explains why Wickson became a reformer. Undoubtedly he transferred to the governing power of society the feeling that he had against his father, the governing power of his youth. He did it, of course, unconsciously, sympathizing with the victims of social injustice as he had sympathized with his mother and himself. And that, I believe, is the reason why he "never thought" of his father again.

Moreover, it was probably his early revolt against paternal injustice that inspired him with the ambition to be a lawyer so that he might be able to defend himself and others against wrongs, and help to administer justice equitably.

I advance the theory because I have found a similar transference in many other reformers.

4

In any case he arrived in the city that afternoon in the rain and set about finding work. It was about four o'clock, according to all accounts, when he came into the office of McPhee Harris and asked if they needed an office-boy. No one pretends to know what attracted him to that particular door, but I venture to suggest that it was because of the word "Defense" in the sign, "Purity Defense League." Harris was then counsel for the League. He remembers being instantly struck by the boy's air of self-reliance. "He was dripping wet," Harris says, "his hair was in his eyes, and his clothes were pathetic. But he stood up there and confronted me like a young David. He had wonderful eyes—always. I couldn't have turned him away."

Harris employed him, and, finding that he had no place to sleep, Harris sent him with a note to the Y. M. C. A. building, where they put him in a room with another of Harris's protégés. And this second protégé was Jack Arnett, the sculptor of the Wickson Memorial, then a young waif who had come into the hands of the Purity Defense League because he had been hanging around barrooms, making a living by drawing caricatures of celebrities in the sawdust on barroom floors. Harris was supporting him and paying his tuition in the local art-school.

"I remember," Arnett says, "that before Wickson went to bed that night he sat down and wrote a letter to his mother and sent her back one of her own dollars on account."

5

Wickson proved to have a brain as hardy as his body. He worked and studied methodically, thoroughly, and without the effort of a frown. He became chief clerk of McPhee Harris's office by virtue of a mechanical efficiency that was the first expression of his basic integrity of mind. On that efficiency Harris came more and more to rely. Wickson shared in Harris's prosecutions of the venders of "picture post-cards," the proprietors of "nickelodeons," and the managers of "variety shows" who offended against the League's standards of public purity. Arnett, having an artist's views of nudity, often quarreled with Wickson about these prosecutions.

"He wasn't morbid, as McPhee Harris *was*," Arnett says. "He did it to protect young people from contamination. Harris did it because he was rotten himself—that's my idea, anyway—and his inward struggle with himself made him a crazy fanatic. He could see something nasty in any— in any naked innocence."

As McPhee Harris's junior partner, Wickson himself conducted some of the Purity Defense League's later cases against saloon-keepers and the owners of "dives." And when Harris became president of the local "Drys" Wickson succeeded him as attorney for the League, and so came to prosecute the "white-slave" cases that first made him notorious. His election to the office of District Attorney followed unexpectedly. He was carried into power on a reform wave that was blown up by a violent agitation against the "red-light district."

It was as District Attorney that his real career began—and his real difficulties. Both culminated together on the day whose incidents I wish to give. McPhee Harris has his own account of those incidents. Jack Arnett has another. And I have coaxed a third out of the detective, Tim Collins. Putting the three together, it is easy to reconstruct a dramatic story of the day.

6

It began in an interview with McPhee Harris, who came smiling into the District Attorney's

office soon after Wickson arrived there for his
morning's work. "Just a moment, Arthur," he
apologized for taking Wickson's time, and Wickson
shook hands with him without replying.

McPhee Harris has a smile that at its most
perfunctory moments is something more than
polite. It is the smile of austerity made benovolent
by the conscientious sympathy of a professing Christian. His chin, clean-shaven between gray side-
whiskers, repeats the bony conformation of his
narrow skull, which is bald between two bushes
of gray hair. He is one of the few men left in
America who still wear on all occasions the tall
silk hat.

He said to Wickson, "I had a visit last night
from friend Toole." And Toole being a corrupt
machine politician, the "friend" was said sarcastically, of course.

Wickson leaned forward on his table-desk intently.

"We have put the fear of God into them," Harris
assured him. "They are prepared to nominate a
ticket of good men."

Wickson waited, watching him, silent. (Harris
remembers that silence well—as a justification.)

"We are to name them," he went on, "practically
all. They reserve a few of the minor offices—as, for
instance, the sheriff and the county clerk and
recorder."

"If they nominate those three officers," Wickson

said, in his high, unpleasant voice, "they'll have control of the local machinery of elections."

"Perhaps so," Harris conceded, amiably. "It's difficult to get everything at once. They'll accept our nominee for the Supreme Court."

"Because they control the rest of the bench," said Wickson.

"Still," Harris pointed out, "we must begin somewhere—and one is a beginning. We're also to have the coroner, two of the county commissioners, some of the members of the Legislature, some Senators, and some of the state officers. The details aren't decided. It's for us to decide—largely. They're very conciliatory."

Wickson asked, at last, "And who nominates the district attorney?"

Harris replied, "We do."

But he replied with a look that was somewhat too steady—with a look that was rather self-consciously defiant.

The District Attorney had come to know McPhee Harris as "a man of indecisive character and small mind, strengthened and enlarged by the sense of a divine power relying on him as its instrument." There was in Harris's eyes, now, the glint of that resolute instrumentality. Wickson's scrutiny probed and questioned him.

"They don't think," Harris admitted, "that we can re-elect *you*. They believe you've made too many enemies."

That was "the nigger in the woodpile," as Wickson would have said. And having uncovered it, he nodded and rose.

He began to walk thoughtfully up and down his office, ignoring McPhee Harris, as if, having discovered "what was up," he had turned to concentrate on *that* instead of the familiar face behind which the secret had been concealed.

7

Wickson had been carried into office, as I have said, by an agitation against the red-light district. And as long as he had devoted his office to a crusade against vice he had been backed by the Purity League, by McPhee Harris, by the Federation of Women's Clubs, by the church-goers and all the good people of the town. But he had found vice protected by both the political organizations, and when he attacked *them* he found them protected by the rich men of the community who owned the public-utility monopolies that had been voted to them by the politicians. He had made enemies not only in the dive district, but among the best citizens "on the Hill." He had been accused of "attacking vested interests" and of "stirring up class hatreds." He had offended some of the most generous contributors to the funds of the Purity Defense League. He had offended McPhee Harris.

Hence the silence with which he had listened to Harris and the suspicion with which he had scrutinized him. Hence, also, Harris's righteously defiant look and the complacency of his announcement, "They don't think that we can re-elect *you*." He was the meek bearer of the bowstring.

The condemned man took a few turns up and down the room, paused before a window, turned suddenly, and said: "When you look out that window and see the upper town—up there on the Hill—you see it as the abode of decency and virtue and everything that's godly. And you see it warred on by the vice of the lower town—where everything is sin. Don't you?"

Harris did not answer. He laid aside his hat on the table and crossed his arms, settling himself to hear an argument and reply to it as soon as he had heard it all.

"When I look out that window," the District Attorney continued, "I see the upper town as the abode chiefly of the men who keep the lower wards living in the dirt and the evil conditions that breed sin. I see the lower town working in conditions of pollution to pay the money that makes the Hill rich—decent—respectable. That's the difference between us. And there doesn't seem to be any way of reconciling it."

His office was on the sixth floor of the Settle Building. He could look down on the roofs of half the city in the morning sunlight. "It isn't vice that I want to fight any more," he said. "It's the conditions that make vice."

"And yet," Harris retorted, "you admit, I suppose, that there may be such a thing as 'honest poverty'?"

Wickson wheeled on him. "I'll go farther. I'll admit that there may be such a thing as honest wealth."

Harris spread his hands. "I don't wish to think," he said, "that you've lost your faith in the spiritualities. I don't wish to believe that you've become wholly a materialist. God has manifested Himself in your work." And Harris could say these things without any trace of cant, in a voice full of conviction. "You've been a great power for good, but in struggling against the evils of this world I think you're forgetting to rely on the saving grace that can alone work the miracle of regeneration in the soul of evil."

"I know." Wickson sighed. "I know. You're sincere. You believe it. There's no use in arguing."

"There is nothing to argue," Harris said, pontifically. "It is *so*."

Wickson ran his hand through his hair—a rough shock of hair that had grown sparse in a dry tangle. He sat down again at his desk. "Well," he said, "they don't think I can be re-elected, eh? They tell you 'the boys' won't vote for me—the rank and file. I've made too many enemies. Some of our own friends don't like my remarks about the connection between street-railway franchises and protected vice. Bill Toole—and it comes, I suppose, from old Bradford himself—Bill Toole offers to compromise on a good ticket if I'm dropped."

"No!" Harris cried. "No! That's not true."

"Not in so many words. Of course not! But if you insisted on having me on the ticket it would come to that. Isn't that so? Isn't it?"

"I don't believe you could possibly be re-elected."

"We didn't believe, in the first place, that I could be *elected*. Yet we made the fight."

"There's no necessity of running any such risk. We're to have the nomination for the office. We'll pick a good man."

Wickson took up some papers on his desk. "If it were only a question of the office," he said, "I'd be glad to get out. But there's more than that. There's— However, it's useless for us to talk. You'll have to excuse me. I'm busy." He unfolded a sheet of typewriting and pushed the button for his stenographer.

As McPhee Harris reached for his silk hat he looked down on ingratitude coldly. "I expected as much," he said. "Good morning."

Wickson did not reply. He allowed Harris to go out of his life as he had passed his father in the field, plowing.

His stenographer answered the bell, and without raising his eyes he muttered, "Get me Collins on the 'phone."

The clerk replied, "He's been waiting here to see you."

Wickson tossed aside the sheet eagerly. "Send him in."

8

There was nothing personal in the furnishings of Wickson's room—an official desk-table, some bare chairs, some framed photographs of men and buildings on the walls, and beyond that not even a bookcase. There was nothing characteristic about his "ready-made" clothes that hung on him as if their one purpose was to impede his impatient movements. And in his interview with McPhee Harris he had been impersonal, withdrawn, and as colorless as his surroundings.

But now, to receive the detective, there came a relaxing in the muscles of his mouth and a meditative widening of the eyes. He pushed his papers back from him. He began to beat a tattoo on his desk blotter, looking aside out of the window and allowing his mind to rove with his eyes. It was evident that the detective gave him a sense of security.

Collins entered, hat in hand, closed the door behind him, and crossed to a chair with a peculiar noiseless placidity. He was plump, clean-shaven, commonplace, with mild and rather vacant brown eyes, broad-shouldered, short, and slow. He might have been the proprietor of a commercial travelers' hotel. He did not look genial enough to be a saloon-keeper, yet he had the sort of figure that you would

associate with barroom tables or the chairs of hotel
lobbies. He had the bronze button of a fraternal
order on his lapel and a masonic trinket on his
watch-chain. There was nothing whatever about
him to suggest the detective of popular tradition.

Yet he had been brought from Washington by
the Purity League with enough scalps on his official
belt to give him a reputation in those circles where
fame can have no notoriety. He was rated by Wickson as "the only real detective I ever knew." And
he had performed miracles for the District Attorney.

He turned his chair to face the door and sat down
squarely with his hands spread on his knees. He
said: "They tell me Madge was down at Headquarters the day before yesterday. She's keeping
Cooney. He's out again. They're using her to
frame it up with him to bump you off."

That is to say, he told Wickson that at Police
Headquarters they were arranging to have the
District Attorney murdered by an ex-policeman
named Cooney whom Wickson had prosecuted
and sent to prison.

Wickson raised one eyebrow at him, smiling
wryly. "Tim," he said, "McPhee Harris has
slumped on me."

Collins repeated: "They're going to try to bump
you off. They've got Cooney worked up to it.
They're keeping him just drunk enough to do it.
He's going to shoot you. That's what he's hanging around the court-house for."

In the earlier days of their work together Wickson might have asked, "Are you sure?" or "How do you know?" But he had long since learned that Collins never spoke till he was sure and that the means by which he made sure were not open to inspection. He kept his sources of information secret from Wickson, even.

"When you challenged that juror yesterday," Collins said, "you noticed how pale Sotjie got? Well, he didn't turn pale because he lost the man. He turned pale because Cooney had come in behind *you*. He was afraid that Cooney was going to shoot. That's what gave me the tip—the way Sotjie's hands shook. I've given orders to our boys to keep Cooney outside the rail after this. Plummer will trail along with you."

The Sotjie of whom he spoke was the chief of police. He was under indictment on charges of corruption in office; Wickson was prosecuting him; his trial had begun; and the detective had discovered that, in order to escape prosecution by Wickson, the chief of police was conspiring with the ex-policeman, Cooney, to have Wickson shot.

Wickson considered for a moment the incredibility of such a plot. "The strangest part about it is," he said, "that these fellows are able to do these things just because no decent citizen would believe it possible. It's a funny situation. You can't go out and cry 'Help!' because, if you did, everybody would think you'd gone mad." He snorted a dry laugh. "Well, I don't see what I can do. He could come up behind me on the street at any time."

"No. I think not," Collins held.

"Why not?"

"It never happens that way. They always seem to wait for you somewhere that they know you'll come—and work themselves up to it."

Wickson tipped back in his swivel-chair and clasped his hands behind his head. "I'm done, anyway, Tim," he said. "Our own people have gone back on me. They don't believe they can re-elect me. And I can't win without their support. . . . I don't seem to be able to make them understand what the game is in this town. I can't make them believe it—any more than we could make them believe that Sotjie was putting up Cooney to shoot me." He swung a fist down on the table. "My God! If we could only make them see these things."

Collins shook his nead with slow finality.

"We can't, of course," Wickson agreed. "We can't reach them. We can't make them believe it. I wouldn't have believed it myself when I first came in here—hardly. And sometimes I wake up at night, now, and wonder if I haven't been dreaming it."

Collins nodded solemnly, looking at his feet.

Wickson began to pace up and down the room again. "Besides," he asked, with an air of relieving his mind of something that had long been burdening it, "what's the use of prosecuting this man Sotjie? He's not to blame. The town has to have a crooked chief of police, and they'll always get some one who'll do what Sotjie did. And if we could reach old Bradford and the 'higher-ups' what would be the use of prosecuting them? As long as these public utilities are lying around loose, waiting for some one to steal them, they'll be stolen. It's a whole community that's been to blame. You can't prosecute a whole community. And prosecuting a man like Sotjie is like prosecuting a man for having typhoid fever—when he got it drinking from a city tap!"

Collins looked worried.

"Of course, I have to prosecute. Just as you have to get evidence. That's what I'm paid for. That's what I'm here for. And if they shoot me for it Bradford and the rest will be the first to sign a testimonial to my good character—so that they sha'n't be suspected of any lack of public spirit." He laughed rather despairingly. "It's funny, isn't it?" He sat down. "God! I'm tired of it!" he said.

The "Bradford" to whom he referred was the great William D. Bradford, the financial "boss" of the town, owner of the street railway, the gas company, the most successful newspaper, one of the banks, and two of the trust companies.

Collins mused behind a mask of mild vacuity.

He had not been so much listening to Wickson's argument as considering the state of mind that spoke in the words. He indicated his conclusion when he replied, "I'll put Plummer on your door."

If he had spoken out that conclusion he would have said, "You probably don't much care whether you get shot or not, just at present, but it's my business to see that you're protected."

Wickson did not understand—and did not try to. "Tim," he asked, "what do you think about things—the way they are in this town? What the devil can we do?"

The detective rubbed his palms on his thick knees. "I guess," he said, "the trouble with me is I don't get time to think—about things—taking them in the large. I'm too busy trying to dope out what the other fellows are thinking."

"Well, then, what do you suppose they're thinking now?"

"They're thinking they've got to stop you from trying this case against Sotjie—if they can. If you go ahead you'll mark them with the evidence you've got so that they'll never be able to touch you for fear of making the town too hot to hold them. And if you go ahead they'll maybe lose the election. If they're going to stop you they've got to stop you now. I don't think they want to kill you, but they want you in the hospital till after elections. That's dead sure. You've got to be careful."

It was Collins's opinion that the District Attorney somewhat lacked the instinct of self-preservation. He admitted that Wickson could not have done his peculiar work for the community if he had had that instinct very highly developed. And consequently he accepted as natural Wickson's lack of attention to the warning that he must be "careful."

Wickson had glanced at his desk calendar, at the mention of elections—as if to figure out how many weeks remained—had turned the yesterday's leaf to arrive at the day's date, and had found a note in his own handwriting. He reached at once to his desk-telephone. "Send Arnett in," he directed, "as soon as he comes. Yes." . . .

"He's leaving for New York this afternoon," he explained to the detective. "I promised him a letter." He began to scratch squares and crosses on his blotter with a dry pen. "Do you think Bradford or any of the big ones know about Cooney?"

"Not if they can keep from knowing it. That's the sort of thing they make it their business not to know."

"Come in!" Wickson called to a knock at the door. And, "Hello, Jack!" he greeted the sculptor. "I nearly forgot about you. What time does your train go?"

"It doesn't go," Arnett said, taking the outstretched hand. "I'm staying to do a portrait bust of old Bradford."

"Bradford!"

"On an order that Harris got me."

"Bradford!" Wickson turned to enjoy the joke with Collins, but the detective had already gone—inconspicuously—and the door had closed behind him.

9

Arnett sat down at once, on his shoulder-blades, in the loose-jointed attitude of a tall man whose work kept him on his feet. He felt in his pocket for his inevitable pipe and hooked it into the corner of his mouth. "I sold him my 'Nymph,' too," he said.

He was as unconsciously individual in his appearance as the detective had been consciously indeterminate—a lank, black-haired, strong-handed man in clothes that showed the dust and plaster of his sculptor studio in spite of brushing. His eyes were wrinkled from a puckered scrutiny; he watched Wickson (and took no note of his background) with a professional interest in the human spirit as it expressed itself in the flesh. He had not seen Wickson for months. Their careers had separated them.

"A bust of Bradford!" Wickson laughed. "That's great! Do you ever do tombstones?"

Arnett sucked his cold pipe humorously. "Are you going to bury some one?"

"No. They're going to bury me."

"What for?"

"For trying to can Sotjie. They have a man out to shoot me."

Arnett took his pipe from his teeth as if to put aside his jocular air with it. "What's up? Do you mean it?"

Wickson nodded, smiling.

"Who's doing it?"

"Well—Sotjie, first of all. And then—the men who have helped to make Sotjie what he is, including Bradford. And then—all of us who have allowed conditions to become what they are in this town. You, for instance. You never vote, do you?"

"Murder? You mean murder?"

"No. The man 'll be drunk. It's a fellow I sent up three years ago, and he has that grievance. It 'll only be manslaughter."

Arnett stared at him. "Are you growing fanciful?"

"You'd think so, wouldn't you?"

"Oh, pshaw, Wick! I don't believe it."

Wickson laughed. "I knew you wouldn't. That's why I told you." He began to gather up the papers from his desk. "The devil of it is I don't want to prosecute Sotjie—I don't feel that he's been to blame—but conditions make it necessary. And I don't suppose he wants to shoot me—if he could avoid it. It's a gay life. Will you walk over to the court with me?"

Arnett rose silently, dropped his pipe into his

pocket, and looked a long time at the lining of his hat before he put it on. "Why don't you have him arrested?"

Wickson patted him on the shoulder and turned him to the door. "We can't do that until he shoots me."

"If you know he's going to shoot you, you can prove it."

"You think so?" He turned the knob. "There are a good many things in this business that a man knows and can't prove."

With the opening of the door the activities of the outer office interrupted them and silenced Arnett. He followed or waited for Wickson as the District Attorney excused himself to a visitor, gave instructions to an assistant, bent to hear a hurried report in confidence, or stopped to "jolly" a newspaper man. When they reached the elevator Collins's young detective, Plummer, was with them. He stood aside, at the ground floor, and followed them out to the street, carefully unalert, with the comprehensive glances of an apparently idle eye.

"But I don't get this thing at all," Arnett complained, as they turned up the street.

Wickson took his elbow. "I'm in the position of a policeman in a thieves' quarter—where the political boss of the quarter protects them—in return for their help in elections. See? Only in this case the whole town is the quarter, and Bradford is the political boss, and he hasn't been able to keep me from bothering the thieves, and so the thieves are going to 'get' me."

"Oh, come off," Arnett broke in. "Bradford isn't that bad."

"Surely not. I'm putting it very crudely, of course. I'm willing to believe that Bradford doesn't see it that way at all. He probably feels himself as much the victim of conditions as I do. He'll tell you that the thieves run the town—that he has to operate the street railway—and that he couldn't operate it unless he stood in with them. See? He'll tell you that the fault is with the citizens who won't be bothered with politics—who leave the thieves to take that trouble. But you'll notice that when I try to rouse those citizens to make them take an interest, I get notice from Bradford, through Bill Toole to McPhee Harris, that I can't be renominated."

The street was busy with trolley-cars, wagons, hurrying people, and the displays and activities of trade—the business of a life from which Arnett's mind was as much withdrawn as any artist's. Usually he walked through it unseeingly, hurrying to escape it. He looked at it now as the public life in which Wickson played a leading part, and blinked at it, feeling himself asked for advice about it, and bewildered to find that he could not see below its shifting surface. He shook his head.

"I don't know. I don't know what to make of it," he complained.

"If it were only the case of the policeman and the thieves," Wickson said, at the court-house steps, "it might be a good thing to let them shoot. If it would attract attention to the conditions— But I don't want them simply to 'mangle' me."

Arnett caught him by the sleeve, alarmed by the very matter-of-factness of his tone. "My God! Wick! You're not going to do anything so foolish?"

Wickson smiled slowly at him in a sort of amused appraisal of his horror. "It isn't what I'm going to do that counts. It's up to them. I have to go ahead with my job. However, I don't believe they'll dare. . . . You run along now and get to work on your bust. Come in and tell me how it goes, will you? I hope you're not going to do the old boy in the nude, like your 'Nymph.'"

Arnett laughed, nervously relieved by the jocularity. "I believe Harris got me the order so I'd have something to do with clothes on. He thinks I do the other because it sells—such being the depravity of the artistic rich!"

"Well, good-by," Wickson said. "Be good."

"And you be careful."

Wickson waved his hand and turned up the steps. Arnett brushed against the nonchalant Plummer as he hurried off.

And half-way down the block the sculptor remembered that he had seen this same man in the elevator—that he had seen him pass into the court-house, look around the corridor and come out.

And now he was following Wickson into the court-house again!

He hastened back with a frightened suspicion that in Plummer he had seen the assassin.

10

He lost himself at once in the corridors of the ground floor of the court-house, where the doors were marked, "County Commissioners," "Local Imp.," "Sheriff," on the yellowed frosting of their glasses; and when he demanded breathlessly of a passing clerk, "Where 'll I find the District Attorney —Wickson?" the official replied, curtly, "Settle Building," and went on about his business.

It was from the Settle Building that Arnett and Wickson had just walked to the court-house.

He blundered upon the elevator shaft and had to wait endlessly for the cage to descend to him. The elevator man replied to his confused explanations, "Second floor. First door to your right," and held him despairing in the cage until three other passengers came one by one at their leisure. He had the feeling of a man in a nightmare shouting for help to people who passed him either deaf or horribly indifferent. And it was as if he had wakened to the comforting realities when he came to the open door of the court-room and looked over the heads of the spectators on their benches and saw Wickson talking at the counsels' table with a young lawyer in spectacles. His suspected assassin,

Plummer, was nowhere to be seen. The whole thing had evidently been a ridiculous false alarm, and Arnett felt suddenly very foolish.

The judge had not yet entered from his chambers. There were only three jurors in the jury-box— for the others were still to be chosen from the panel. A buzz of low-voiced conversation hung over the groups of lawyers, court officers, and privileged spectators within the rail; and those in the public seats coughed and scuffled their feet, uneasily expectant. In the light of high windows the room was shabbily ugly, with walls painted a sort of greasy robin's-egg blue and its cheap furnishings worn by the contact of innumerable bodies—as repellent as a prison, as sordid as the tragedies that had soiled it, as if the beautiful ideals of justice had left it to be a place only for the craftiness of statutory law.

Arnett sat down in a back seat, intimidated by the crowd of strangers, shy of his intrusion upon the business of the court, and vaguely depressed by the commonplace and sordid aspect of the reality before him. He was an idealist in art.

He sat watching Wickson. The detective, Collins, was also watching Wickson, but with a very different sort of eye.

The District Attorney was consulting with an assistant over a jury-list of typewritten names, each name of which was followed by a few brief notes that represented Collins's work of investigation; and this investigation had been made, with Collins's usual ingenious audacity, by a man who had pretended to be working for the city directory. Collins was proud of the job. He noticed that Wickson looked at it without interest, absent-mindedly.

He was again aware of the same thing in Wickson's manner that had worried him during his interview with the District Attorney when they had spoken about Cooney and the police plot. Collins might not have been able to say what it was that worried him, any more than Arnett could; yet it had worried Arnett, too, though it had expressed itself to *him* in Wickson's air of genial superiority to the sculptor. And there can be no doubt that it was this dimly felt emotion in Wickson, detached and dangerous, that moved him to involve himself now in the final catastrophe of the day.

While Wickson was standing inside the rail Cooney, the ex-policeman, slunk into the courtroom and loitered there, leaning against the rear wall—a disheveled, unshaven, blowsy derelict of a man, horrible, but pathetic. Plummer had followed him in, and Plummer went at once to notify Collins. He tapped Collins on the shoulder from behind, and Collins turned his head away from Wickson while Plummer whispered in his ear.

At that moment Wickson himself saw Cooney, and saw him with pity, obviously, and with a desire to aid him. He said a word of excuse to his assistant for leaving the jury-list, passed the rail, and came down the court-room aisle toward the ex-policeman. He came toward Arnett also, and the sculptor half rose from his seat before he realized that Wickson was not aware of him. There was a look of solemn friendliness and sympathy in the District Attorney's face as he went by—a look that ignored Arnett and yet moved him to turn and watch.

Wickson put his hand on Cooney's shoulder. "I'm glad to see you out again, Cooney," he said. "I've been mighty sorry for what happened. I had to do it. We all have to do things sometimes that we don't want to do. But if I can help you in any way now, I want to know it."

Cooney scowled up at him out of bloodshot and befuddled eyes, dropped the puffed lids sulkily, and muttered something unintelligible.

"I've never felt it was your fault," Wickson went on. "I know what it is to be a policeman in this town. I know what the conditions are. If you think of any way that I can help you to make a fresh start, come and see me, will you?"

Cooney looked up again, and there was the beginning of a maudlin self-pity in his bleary gaze.

"I don't want to fight vice any more," Wickson said—with his absurd seriousness that never saw itself incongruous in any circumstances. "I want to fight the conditions that make vice."

But by this time Collins had seen what had happened, and had seen, too, the danger of it. "Look out!" he warned Plummer.

He started to make his way down a side aisle so as to reach Cooney from the flank. Plummer, less experienced, started hastily down the center aisle in full view of Cooney, and Cooney, looking over Wickson's shoulder, saw the detective coming.

Instantly into that drunken brain there must have flashed a suspicion that Wickson was trying to hold him with a show of friendliness until Plummer could seize and search him. He cursed out an oath, and threw his hand back to his hip pocket. Plummer saw the movement and plucked out his own revolver. Arnett immediately sprang from his seat and threw himself on the detective, still mistaking him for an assassin. At the same moment Cooney's revolver exploded in Wickson's face and Collins shot at Cooney.

The ex-policeman leaped as if he had been speared in the side, and fell, screaming. The District Attorney staggered back with his hands to his face. Collins caught him. "Are you hurt?"

Wickson relaxed with a tired sigh that slowly shuddered down to a choking catch in the throat where the blood strangled it.

11

At the mass-meeting of indignant citizens who gathered to pass resolutions upon this "irremediable loss to the community" a subscription was started to pay for a "suitable memorial" of the tragedy; and the list of subscribers, as published in the morning paper, began magnificently with the names of William D. Bradford and McPhee Harris. It was Bradford, as president of the Wickson Memorial Committee, who formally handed over the completed monument to the Mayor at its unveiling; and he stood, proudly modest, on the wooden platform, before the transfixed figure of Wickson turned to bronze, while the Mayor felicitated himself and the city upon "the possession in our midst of a citizen whose public spirit puts him always in the forefront of every public movement to—to beautify, to—to elevate—to raise the tone of our public life both by his private benefactions and his activity as a citizen of the public life of our city."

Wickson's white-haired mother, a little deaf, on the back row of the platform seats, heard the burst of applause, thought the Mayor was speaking of her son, and wiped a flattered tear from her cheek.

The bronze face of her son, above them all, remained exaltedly impassive. Arnett had done him from his early photographs, before worry and illness had hardened the lines of his face. He stood on his granite pedestal, sacrificially erect, with one arm doubled across the small of his back to grasp the other at the elbow in a characteristic attitude that made him look as if he were waiting to be shot, with his arms pinioned, his chin held high, confronting eternity. At the foot of his pedestal a bronze "Grief" crouched, weeping in her hair.

It was McPhee Harris who started the public protest against the semi-nudity of this crouching figure. Fortunately the protest failed of effect. Arnett's "Grief" is now rather more widely known than Wickson himself. It will probably be famous to a posterity that will have no very accurate knowledge of the event which the memorial was erected to commemorate.

THE END

IMPORTANT BOOKS

THE OFFENDER
Harper's Modern Science Series
By BURDETTE G. LEWIS
New York State Commissioner of Correction

This book on prison reform is for the general reader as well as for the judge, the lawyer, the student. It enumerates all the latest theories on the subject and the experiments which have tested them, and makes practical suggestions for dealing with the various phases of the many-sided problem of the offender.

SAFETY
By W. H. TOLMAN AND LEONARD B. KENDALL

Methods for preventing occupational and other accidents and disease. This volume is the result of years of study on the new industrialism from the point of view of safeguarding the human factors. It is based on the best American and European practice.

Fully Illustrated

PRINCIPLES
OF SCIENTIFIC MANAGEMENT
By FREDERICK W. TAYLOR

The author is the originator of the system of Scientific Management, and for nearly thirty years was at work on the principles which have made such changes in this and other countries.

SHOP MANAGEMENT By FREDERICK W. TAYLOR

A practical exposition of the theories discussed in the foregoing.

APPLIED CITY GOVERNMENT
By HERMAN G. JAMES

The author is associate professor of government and director of the bureau of municipal research and reference at the University of Texas. The subtitle of this book is " The Principles and Practice of City Charter-Making."

HARPER & BROTHERS
NEW YORK ESTABLISHED 1817 **LONDON**

BOOKS BY
ZANE GREY

———

THE U. P. TRAIL

THE DESERT OF WHEAT

WILDFIRE

THE HERITAGE OF THE DESERT

RIDERS OF THE PURPLE SAGE

DESERT GOLD

THE LIGHT OF WESTERN STARS

THE LONE STAR RANGER

THE RAINBOW TRAIL

THE BORDER LEGION

KEN WARD IN THE JUNGLE

THE YOUNG LION HUNTER

THE YOUNG FORESTER

THE YOUNG PITCHER

———

HARPER & BROTHERS

NEW YORK　[ESTABLISHED 1817]　LONDON

NOVELS OF
THOMAS HARDY

The New Thin-Paper Edition of the greatest
living English novelist is issued in two bind-
ings: Red Limp-Leather and Red Flexible
Cloth, 12mo. Frontispiece in each volume.

HARPER & BROTHERS
NEW YORK   ESTABLISHED 1817   LONDON

BOOKS BY
SIR GILBERT PARKER.

—

THE WORLD FOR SALE

THE MONEY MASTER

THE JUDGMENT HOUSE

THE RIGHT OF WAY

THE LADDER OF SWORDS

THE WEAVERS

THE BATTLE OF THE STRONG

WHEN VALMOND CAME TO PONTIAC

THE LANE THAT HAD NO TURNING

NORTHERN LIGHTS

PIERRE AND HIS PEOPLE

AN ADVENTURER OF THE NORTH

A ROMANY OF THE SNOWS

*CUMNER'S SON, AND OTHER
SOUTH SEA FOLK*

—

HARPER & BROTHERS

NEW YORK   ESTABLISHED 1817   LONDON

Lightning Source UK Ltd.
Milton Keynes UK
UKHW041623040119
334726UK00010B/786/P